VANTAGE POINT

A GRAY GHOST NOVEL—BOOK 4

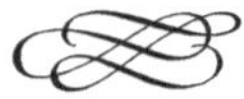

AMY MCKINLEY

FOREWORD

Dear Readers,

A few of you have asked for Hawk's story next—so here he is! Hawk broke my heart, and Stella made me laugh. They are a good balance for one another. I'm so excited to share Hawk's journey and sincerely hope you enjoy reading it as much as I did writing it.

The quiet ones are often a puzzle and can have such hidden, and sometimes painful, layers. However, when the right person enters their lives, they can calm those stormy waters, and kick-start the healing process. Until there is a threat, and the sea churns once more. With that in mind, there is a chapter that may be too graphic in nature when the guys engage in a desperate and time-sensitive interrogation. I wanted to warn you so that you can skip chapter twenty-eight if it's upsetting. The next chapter sums it up enough so that you won't miss anything in the story or plot.

I wanted to take a moment to welcome back the seasoned readers of this series; I'm thrilled you're back for more. If this is your first book in the Gray Ghost series, welcome to the Gray Ghost team! *Vantage Point* can be read as a standalone. Some prefer to start from the beginning, and so as not to risk any spoilers; I'd recommend that as well. Either way, I hope you like the team as much as I do. And once you've finished, I'd love to hear from you.

Enjoy!

Amy

CHAPTER 1

HAWK

FATE WAS A VENGEFUL BITCH WHO DIDN'T LIKE TO BE DENIED.

Head tilted, I aligned my dominant eye with the rifle's sight, keeping both open to provide a full picture of the scene before me. With a few adjustments to the scope, I accounted for the mild wind and climate. The low roof ledge before me stabilized and supported the weight of my weapon, eliminating the risk of horizontal sway—not that I anticipated the need for accuracy in this scouting exercise, but old habits died hard.

In position, I waited. Across from my three-story San Francisco apartment building, I locked onto the top floor unit next door. Through the unadorned windows, I saw two people inside. I wanted—no, needed—to see what was happening and if he was a threat.

My goal wasn't to pull the trigger, to wound, or to kill. Not yet, anyway. It was a stakeout to gather additional intel. I knew my next move would become clear soon, and if necessary, I would take action.

The sun dipped low on the horizon, and heavy clouds kept the moon and stars from casting their glow. The neighborhood was an improvement from where I'd grown up. California evenings were pleasant, not too cold or hot. I held still, lying flat and taking slow even breaths. Watching. Waiting.

I'd planted a bug. I made a slight adjustment, and the volume increased in my earpiece. The conversation between the man and woman hadn't escalated. So far, nothing new had been revealed.

I'd tried to stay out of my neighbor's business and to ignore the yelling from the place next door, but I couldn't. Ugly, shrill tones of desperation had dripped from the man as he demanded money. Through the wall between our units, his intent was crystal clear, and when I heard his words, an avalanche of unwanted memories from my past bombarded me.

One in particular was the reason why I found myself with my rifle pointed at the man in her apartment—I needed a visual of the situation. And just like that, too many of the feelings from when I was young broke through the box I tried to keep them stuffed into.

The ones who had raised me weren't good people. Part of me knew that wasn't what mattered. Mom had done what little she could for me in a horrible situation. Her effort didn't equal what I needed, what any kid would have wanted. My life had been all I knew, and I didn't think I had options even in my last moments living with them.

Different scenarios of what could've happened played through my mind. I swallowed back bile as the sounds of my mom's screams broke free from unwanted memories that I thought I'd locked away. I could have snuck out, gone to the neighbors' house, or waited for the police to come. It weighed on me, and it always would. I swore that day that I would do everything I could to help another person in a similar situation.

But no longer was I five years old or even eleven, helpless in the face of neglect and abuse. My life was my own. I'd shaped my destiny.

A flash of red passed by one of the three windows, yanking me back to reality. There was something about my neighbor that kept me close. In my mind, I called her Red, mainly due to the color of her wavy shoulder-length hair. If it hadn't been for Red, I would have been back in Maine with the guys. But I'd stayed in hopes of meeting her.

I wasn't sure why I thought I had a chance with her. There was someone in her life already, a blond man I'd seen a time or two in the hallway. His intent concerned me.

Red cared about the man she frequently fought with. I could hear it in her voice and in the words she chose, even though she was as loud as he was. The arguing had increased in duration and intensity, his visits to her place more frequent. Red's words lacked the edge present in his. I'd heard enough over the past few days to realize things were coming to a head. It was time to act.

I peered through my rifle's scope, tracking them as they shouted at one another, visible more often than not in the three windows that faced west.

If nothing else, I was watching to see if he was physically abusive, and I vowed to pull her out fast if he was. It didn't matter that we didn't know one another or that her problems weren't mine. In a sense, they were. I'd lived a portion of the destructive loop they argued about, which was why my past kept getting triggered.

A soft buzz vibrated in my ear before I pressed a button on my phone to answer the incoming call. It was Jack, our unofficial leader of the Gray Ghost team. With my Bluetooth in place, I didn't need to move more than my finger to connect the call.

However, it would affect my accuracy if I needed to fire a shot. Any movement shifted the reticle I looked through. I could handle steadying my sight if the need arose. It was more a recon stakeout than anything else—I hoped.

After a quick hello, I set in motion the direction I wanted

our conversation to go based on my current position. "What do you know about the woman in the apartment next to ours?"

There was a pause. "The one with the red hair who recently moved in?"

"Yep." *Got her.* Red walked by the window again and leaned against the frame, her hair cascading around a face that had stopped me in my tracks the first time I saw her. She was stunning, with oceanic eyes, more blue than green, high cheekbones, and a full, kissable mouth. Whenever I'd caught her in the hallway, even in those fleeting moments, tension—the good kind—had crackled in the air.

"Not sure. I've only passed her once in the hall." Jack chuckled. "Is that why you stayed?"

"Maybe."

I could see the door that led out of her place as she walked toward it, motioning for the guy to leave. *What the hell is going on there?*

"What are you doing?" The skepticism in Jack's voice carried loud and clear through my earbud.

"Nothing. There's been a lot of yelling going on in her apartment. I'm checking it out."

"By 'checking it out,' do you mean you're watching her through the scope of your rifle?"

I paused. "No comment."

She opened the door, but the blond guy ignored the hint to leave. When he turned away from her, I got a clear view of him: maybe six feet tall judging by where her head reached his chin, with light hair, short on the sides and longer on top. He was the one I'd seen around before. Each time he'd visited, arguments inevitably followed. "Look, I've got to go. The boyfriend or husband is back."

"You bugged the place, didn't you?" Jack's tone was flat.

"What the hell would you expect?" Her window had been open one day, and I climbed over to her balcony and slipped a tiny mic inside. "Ask the others if they know anything about her."

"Yeah… I'm on it."

I disconnected before Jack could say anything further. He would have done the same damn thing, although he probably wouldn't scope out the situation through the sight of a sniper's rifle.

Red and the blond weren't arguing like before. Even so, I wanted a clear picture of their physical reactions.

I repositioned my scope so I could see her better. Their voices trickled into my ear. I tensed as he scooped her into what looked like a stiff hug then stepped away. His hand slipped into his pocket. When he pulled it out, he held something.

"What's that?" Her inquisitive voice teased my ear. I narrowed my eye, trying to see what he held, but she'd turned, and the object wasn't visible.

The guy flashed her a grin then stepped back, putting distance between them. "I thought you'd like it, because it's jewelry, and you know…" He motioned to a table I couldn't quite see. I only caught the far edge of it from this range.

She turned the object over as she examined it from another angle. "The etchings are pretty. They look familiar."

"That's because they're edelweiss flowers. It's not worth much, but I saw it and thought of you. I knew they'd remind you of our family."

She smiled, and my gut tightened, not liking the look she directed to the blond. "I love it, Max. Thank you."

Now he has a name.

She slipped the item on one finger after the other. *A ring.* Finally, she unclasped a long necklace that hung around her neck and added the ring there. *At least it's not on her finger.*

I couldn't figure out why I cared. The woman had me turned all around. When I passed her in the hallway, I struggled every time with wanting to talk to her. Her vanilla and cinnamon scent drove me wild. It filled the hall and wrapped around me as I brushed by her. Our brief passing greetings did nothing to satisfy the obsession I'd developed for her.

No other woman had interested me as she had. My attraction for her was instant, immediate, and unfamiliar in its intensity.

I wanted to know what caused Red to chew on her plump bottom lip and why she rubbed at her heart on occasion with a faraway look in her eyes. I wanted to know *her*, and that thought alone was a foreign one. She drew me in, and for once in my life, I didn't want to resist.

I didn't allow myself to get close to people. It was easier to associate only with the guys I'd grown up with. They were more family to me than my blood ever was.

A brisk wind blew, and I held still with my sight trained on them. Not a lot was happening, though. My mind drifted. *What the hell am I doing?* I was lucky, and I knew it. Adding a woman into the mix would complicate things. I wasn't equipped to deal with the turmoil, and I never had been. That's why I always kept things casual. No strings. No dates.

But Red, she was different. And whoever this guy was, there was no ring on her finger. I'd checked. *What about the one he just gave her?* I frowned, though it hadn't seemed to indicate a commitment.

I pushed the thoughts away and paid closer attention, wanting to learn what their connection was, what was going on with them, and if she was in any real danger. Max had his back to Red, and he shrugged as he sifted through something I couldn't see beneath the window. His shoulders rounded. "Sometimes, I need to make sure you remember you love me, despite how much of a mess I am."

I could work with that if I could get her to see what a tool the guy was. Boyfriend or not, he needed to go, hence my camping out on the roof across from our building so I could check things out. It was about her safety, but finding out if she was single or going to be was good too.

The guy picked something up and paused to scrutinize the object. It looked like jewelry. Red stomped over and grabbed it from his hand. "Stop. I don't have any precious gems. Nothing here is worth anything. You've already stolen what was." She threw her arms up. Her voice rose, and she leaned in. "Did you think I'd get more? That I'd have money to buy more?"

The guy picked up a bracelet. *Is she a designer?* She jerked it from his hand, their voices increasing in volume in my ear. They bickered, and I shamelessly listened for anything of value. They both had tempers, and the more worked up she got, the more I wished I could see the flash of her oceanic eyes as they sparkled in fury.

There was a theme here, one I knew all too well, and the hair along the back of my neck stood on edge. He wanted money, needed it. He had even stolen from her, taken things to sell. What they fought about heightened my concern with each argument, each word screamed at the other. I knew this trope well, and it inevitably ended badly.

The tool was half begging and half yelling again. Things were escalating. "You have to help me, Stel."

Is her name Stel?

"It's always something. What are you caught up in now?" She crossed her arms over her chest and glared. It was an intimidating sight.

The guy lost the aggression in his stance as he slumped against the wall. His next words chilled me to the bone. "I can't keep you safe. It's only a matter of time before they find you and use you against me."

CHAPTER 2

HAWK

A day had passed, and the warning Max had issued to Red circled in my head. I sat in the main room of the apartment while rain pelted the windows. I knew from experience that what they fought about could cause insurmountable problems. Memories from my youth stabbed through my consciousness with unwanted brutality.

So many times, I had cowered in my childhood room, hoping my parents wouldn't remember I was home—not that they wanted me there in the first place—while they had screamed at one another. A cold sweat broke out along my skin as I recalled the way the blond guy had yelled at Red. In his voice, I'd heard similarities to the man I'd thought was my father.

Rain beat against the glass panes closest to me with renewed fury, and with the direction of my thoughts, it brought an unwelcome memory.

Mom had been crying. I had pushed farther back into the corner of my room, as far from the door as I could get, near the single window, which was unlocked. *Will I be able to move fast enough? Should I go now?*

A shiver had raced over me. I drew my knees tight to my

chest and wrapped my arms around my legs. It was raining and would be cold. I didn't want to spend the night outside. My heart thundered in my ears, a steady countdown to my fate.

Something crashed beyond my door. Not thunder. Maybe the table. The man who wasn't my dad had thrown it before. They were fighting about me again. The words seared into my soul with a dark stain. I would never be able to remove the mark, no matter how good I tried to be. *I must be broken.* The truth was, I wasn't good enough for them and never would be.

They didn't like me and didn't want me. No one did.

"You spent more money on that goddamn kid?" he yelled, and I clung to the new shoes Mom had gotten me at the resale shop.

"He starts first grade soon," she dared to reply, and I flinched. It was better to stay silent. I'd learned that the hard way. "If I send him without shoes, they'll make him go home."

"I don't care. You won't spend any of my hard-earned money on that little bastard."

She cried out, and I rose on shaky legs and inched toward the window. I heard the sound and knew what it meant. He'd hit her. I wanted to help, but it never went well. He only got madder at both of us.

"Blue fucking eyes, Eve!" he screamed.

From the thump, I could picture her on the ground. He would start kicking soon. "Those aren't mine. No one has blue eyes in my family. Not yours either."

I pushed the window open. I was already wearing most of the clothes I owned, along with the shoes that weren't new, though they were to me. My palms rested on the windowsill as I waited for the next noise so I could sneak out. If he heard me, it would be so much worse. I wouldn't be going to school then. I would have been lucky if I survived. He hit so hard.

Their yelling got louder. Another crash, and I scurried through, careful to push the window closed behind me so that only a crack remained. I could fit my fingers in there to open it if he passed out. I didn't dare go back until then.

If he caught sight of me, he would only get angrier. I'd learned that more than once. The bruises on my back weren't visible any longer, but they would forever be as indelible as tattoos beneath my skin.

Rain splashed against my skin. It was dark but not too bad. Pressed against the side of our house, I crept toward the back until I found the small broken board by the steps. There was enough room for me to fit inside, underneath the stairs. It was dry enough. The spiders and other bugs were a safer bet than staying in the house. I curled on my side with my head on my bent arm. The shivers that racked my body were more from fear than the chill in the air.

Out there, the yelling was muffled. I tried not to think of what I would find in the morning. *Will she still be alive?*

I jerked as a shiver crawled up my spine, violently expelling me from that night. A few deep breaths and the warm, dry room snapped me back into reality. God, I hated thinking about those days.

My mom and her husband fought about so many things, and money was the root cause. If it wasn't about that, they would fight about me.

I wouldn't let Red live in fear the way I had. Unlike me, she had someone to protect her.

***

STELLA

MY FINGERS CURLED AROUND MY KEYS, AND I DRAGGED THEM off the counter along with my purse. I had ten minutes to get to work, which was fifteen minutes away on a good day without traffic. It was Max's fault. I was still reeling from his visit yesterday. The things he'd said…

I yanked open the door to my apartment, shut and locked it, then turned and slammed into what felt like a brick wall. "Umph." *What?*

I bounced off whatever I'd hit, my hair flying into my face as I lost my balance. Before I crashed to the ground, a firm hand wrapped around my arm and steadied me.

Shoving my hair out of my face, I blinked up at what I'd crashed into. My sight cleared, bringing the well-defined chest that my face had smashed into better focus. A gray T-shirt stretched across his chest, accentuating his pecs. Fear licked up my spine. *No, no, no… Is he one of the thugs sent to shake me down for Max's debt?*

Tilting my head back, I released a held breath in relief as recognition filtered through my panicked brain. It was my neighbor, the one I'd noticed more than once thanks to his chiseled face, broad shoulders, and tapered waist. I swayed toward him in appreciation of his drool-worthy looks. Heat climbed my cheeks.

"Sorry about that, Red. You okay?"

Red? Is he serious? Who was I kidding, I'd be fine with that overused nickname rolling off his tongue. His voice was deep, smooth, and made me shiver. Little electric pings continued to race along my arm where he'd touched me.

His brows rose.

Oh right, he'd asked me a question. My cheeks heated further at being caught ogling him. "Yes. I wasn't watching where I was going. I'm so sorry. Work, you know?" I pointed to the fitted black T-shirt with *Edmund's Café* printed across my chest in white script.

A grin curved his mouth as his gaze flicked down. *Oh God!* I took a step back. I'd pointed to my boobs. I had to say something. *Distract!* "Red? You nicknamed me?" I'd much rather he called me by my given name. *What would that sound like leaving those lips I keep glancing at?*

He chuckled, and warmth spread through me again.

Dammit. I have to leave, not stand here and fangirl over the hot neighbor.

"I don't know your name." He gestured at my hair. "I've been calling you Red in my head since I saw you at the mailboxes."

I'd seen him too. "Oh, well, my name is Stella."

The corners of his lips twitched, and I narrowed my eyes, not in the mood for a joke like my ex-boyfriend used to dramatically yell—it'd been one of the reasons I eventually dumped him. He was an idiot, and shouting "Stella" like that hadn't been remotely close to that scene in *A Streetcar Named Desire* where Stanley yells "Stellaaa!"

I shifted from foot to foot, conscious of the minutes ticking by. I opened my mouth to mutter a hasty goodbye, but he beat me to it.

"It's nice to put a name with your face. I'm Hawk."

Interesting. "Great to meet you too, but I've got to run." *Too bad I can't stay to find out the meaning behind his name.* "Late for work." I desperately needed that stupid waitressing job. I couldn't wait to dish to Val, a fellow waitress, about finally talking to my hot neighbor. She'd been harassing me to pull up my big girl panties and ask him out. I would have, but he was sort of intimidating, in a way that blew my mind.

I snapped back to the moment as the amusement melted from his face, and I almost took a step back. His features pulled taut—he was so intense. The look had an immediate effect on me.

"I know this is none of my business, Stella, but I overheard a few arguments you and your boyfriend have had."

No. This is not happening. I tucked my chin, letting my hair curtain around my face. *Damn you, Max. Way to ruin my chances with the hot neighbor.* "I'm sorry for disturbing you. My brother aggravates me." I pointed to my hair. "It's true what they say about redheads. Quick temper."

He didn't respond right away or laugh as I'd expected. I

peeked through the bright strands of my hair. *Wait. Is he relieved?* His previously furrowed brows had smoothed back to their natural position. I probably imagined it because I could use some attention from a guy who looked like him.

"It wasn't your anger that I'd noticed. I was concerned you were in trouble." He paused. "Are you? Because if you are in a bad situation, I can help."

Oh wow, how embarrassing. I was mortified. Those fights between my brother and me had been *very* loud. I bit my bottom lip. The air around us electrified. My body reacted and grew tense. Something was off.

I tilted my head, taking in more details. *Oh, whoa.* There was a stillness about him that went hand in hand with barely leashed danger. I'd pegged him as a loner. He kept to himself. He hadn't said more than one "hi" to me in passing. Come to think of it, I rarely saw him. The others in the building, I'd seen too much of, which caused a bit of an awkward situation when my brother ignited my temper.

"No, I promise. I'm totally fine. Normal sibling stuff, really. Do I want to slap my brother upside his idiotic head and knock him into tomorrow? Yeah. But that's the extent of it." I arranged my lips into what I hoped looked like a reassuring smile.

Truthfully, there was something different about how Max had been acting, and I wasn't entirely sure I was in the clear. His parting words the night before played again in my mind. "Out of curiosity, why would you help me if I was in trouble? I mean, unless you had a winning lottery ticket you wanted to give me? That, I'd be on board with." I winked at him, expecting a smile in return, but it didn't happen.

Silence filled the space between us, and I waited, fighting the urge to fidget. I was late. There was no getting around it. My boss was going to flip, whether I was ten minutes tardy or twenty.

"Your brother sounded pretty frantic. Desperate people

don't always do the smartest things. And"—he shrugged—"I'm in security. I thought I would offer to help."

Huh. Makes sense with the muscles and high-and-tight haircut he has going on there. What I needed was money. "Thanks. That's very sweet, but I'm fine. Just a family dispute."

He nodded, and I stepped around him with a small wave. "Got to get to work, but it was nice meeting you."

"It was." He rubbed the back of his neck. "The offer stands if anything changes. No charge, of course."

Noted. I would keep that in mind, since he wasn't going to ask me for money I didn't have. "I appreciate it, but I don't need any help." *At least I hope I don't.*

CHAPTER 3

STELLA

*I*f I'd had any idea what the night would've held, I would have called off work. Chatting with the hot neighbor would have been a much better use of my time.

I hurried down the sidewalk. The amber glow of street-lights pooled on the walkway. My shift at Edmund's Café went exactly as I'd thought it would, at least sort of. One of the other waitresses was sick, so we were short-staffed.

My boss screamed at me then tossed me my apron, and everything except the state of my feet went back to business. Waitressing was tough, even at twenty-seven. Each step delivered a volley of pain. In my hurry to leave my apartment earlier, I'd grabbed my old flats, the ones that lacked all semblance of support. The shoes were ancient and falling apart.

My shift ended relatively early for the streets to be empty, so I weaved around a bevy of late-night partiers. They wore varying expressions, from boredom to drunken revelry.

Two overly large men appeared through a break in the crowd. Their hard gazes drilled into me. My spine snapped straight, and my steps faltered. I broke eye contact with them, just in case.

Those guys couldn't have been related to what was going on with my brother. No way. Max better not have involved me in his situation. I worried my lower lip. *Could he have?*

Those two did not fit with the crowd.

My heart pounded inside my chest, and Max's words ran through my mind again: "I can't keep you safe. It's only a matter of time before they find you and use you against me."

I picked up my pace, wishing I had a hat or something to throw over my hair. There were way too many blocks to go until I reached my apartment. With the scary men, the fact that my entire body ached, and the lateness of the hour, I decided to splurge and hailed a cab.

As soon as one stopped at the curb, I climbed in and slumped against the vinyl seat, ducking down. We pulled away. I took a chance and peeked out the rear window. The men hadn't followed or even turned around. My entire body sagged in relief. It was a coincidence, that was all. I relaxed and pushed the incident from my mind, well, as much as I could in the back of a cab.

It took no time at all until I was dragging myself out of the car and up the stairs of the brownstone where I lived. I unwound my hair from the messy bun I'd worn while waitressing, eager to strip off my dirty clothes and fall face-first into bed.

I climbed the last few stairs with my shoes in hand, shoved the door open, and turned the corner for the short walk to my apartment. The dim light in the hallway did little to chase the shadows away, which was why it took me a second to notice the crumpled silhouette against my door. Not for anything would I have expected to find what greeted me.

"Oh no!" My shoes fell from my fingers as I rushed to where Max was slumped. His jaw was red and crusted with dried blood at the corner of his lip. His left eye was swollen shut. I dropped to my knees beside him and gently shook his shoulder.

Tears fell unchecked down my cheeks. "Max, wake up."

His right eyelid opened wide. He pushed me back as he stumbled to his feet. "Open the door, Stel. Hurry."

I picked myself up and would have shot him a severe frown if the circumstances had been different. Adrenaline pumped through my body, and my hands shook as I tried to fit my key into the lock. On the third try, I finally got it in, turned it, and flung the door open. Max limped in behind me then slammed and locked the door.

I flinched. *Bet my hot neighbor heard that.*

I flipped on the lights then whirled around. "Are you okay?" I couldn't help it. Dread pooled heavily in my gut. It wasn't good. Maybe those two guys I'd seen on my way home weren't a coincidence. "What the hell happened?"

Max limped to the cabinet where I kept the whiskey. I'd recently changed its location, as he'd polished off my last bottle. I didn't realize he knew where I'd put it. I couldn't even be mad about it. He looked like he needed it. So did I.

After retrieving a bag of frozen peas from the freezer, I handed it to him for his eye. He ignored it. Instead, the bag sat on the counter between us.

"You want to know what happened?" At my nod, he yelled, "*They* happened! I already told you, Stel. I need money. Like yesterday."

That put a stop to the river that ran from the corners of my eyes. *This again. Shit.* I waited while he downed his drink without stopping. I needed one myself. I set a glass down next to him so he could fill mine too. Once I had a good two fingers of whiskey, I waved his heavy hand away and took a sip. The amber liquid burned a satisfying path down my tight throat.

"Who are you involved with this time?" I didn't want to know. I really didn't. But with how panicked he was and the beating he'd taken, there was no choice. One of us had to face reality. "Who are you into?"

He drained his glass, set it down with a loud thwack, and

spun to face me. His good eye flashed a combination of fear and determination. "You're better off not knowing." He held up a hand at my ready protest. "I'm begging you, *help* me."

"I'm trying!" My voice rose, and I raked my hair from my face. *What the hell am I going to do with him?* I had nothing— nothing of value, anyway. If I did, I would gladly have given it to him. "You're aware I'm a waitress. I don't exactly have a bankroll stashed away from the minimum wage and tips I make."

With a snap of his fingers, he said, "Oma," as if that singular name was the solution to all our problems.

I didn't get it, and my eyebrows furrowed. "What about her?" Our grandma, our one stable relative, had died several years ago. I missed her.

"She whispered incessantly about a treasure to you. Family heirlooms. I heard her more than once, telling you about it when we were growing up." He pointed an accusing finger at me. "You know where it is."

"You're crazy." I shook my head in denial. Sure, she was always going on about some treasure and something about it being close to her heart, but that was just the ramblings of an old woman whose husband, the love of her life, had passed away. "There's no treasure, and you know it."

With a limp, Max went to my table. He stood there for a minute, perusing the contents strewn across the cheap plastic tabletop where I sat when time allowed to make jewelry I one day dreamed of selling. The tools and supplies were bought with the last of the money I'd gotten from the insurance company after our parents' death.

In one swoop, he upended the table, scattering spools of sterling silver, beads, and tools in a clanging mess across the wooden floor. I cried out, heartbroken at the wreck he'd made of my work, of my hopes and dreams.

A loud pounding thudded at the door, and we both turned as one.

"Red." Hawk's muffled voice sounded through the door.

Max raised his arm, fear swimming in his eye as he whisper-shouted, "Don't open it."

I swung it open.

Hawk stood there, his blue eyes blazing with fury. In an impressive display of muscle and height, he filled the doorway and glared at Max. *Oh, hell.* My embarrassment was complete as my hot neighbor witnessed my train wreck of a life.

I looked where Hawk did, at my brother standing amidst all my jewelry in a scattered mess on the floor. Max was beaten and bruised, looking like hell, and my table was on its side. It was bad.

My idiot brother barked out, "Who the hell are you?"

Christ. "He's my neighbor." I flung my hands up at Max. *What was I supposed to do? Really? Not answer the door after he'd made so much noise?*

"Is everything okay?" Hawk's deep voice rumbled, and I caught myself from almost swaying toward him.

That snagged my brother's attention. I wanted to groan. "I'm fine. I don't need help… yet." Because really, I wasn't entirely sure what Max had involved me in. I flashed the hot neighbor a smile. "I promise I'll let you know if anything changes." I glared over my shoulder. "And Max was just leaving."

Hawk stepped to the side and waited until Max took the hint and brushed past both of us. But of course, Max had to open his mouth and humiliate me further. "This the new boyfriend?"

Kill me now. "No. There's no one. The hell, Max?" Yeah, I didn't have to add the "no one" in there, but it was for the hot neighbor's benefit, not my brother's. I saw the gleam in my brother's eye and didn't like it one bit. Sure, I'd like to date Hawk, but that wasn't going to happen with the disaster that was my life. And I knew where Max was going. Hawk had offered help, and that's what had interested Max, not my relationship status.

It wasn't until my brother left that Hawk said goodnight, reiterating that if there was anything I needed, I should let him know. Oh, I needed all right, but not what he was referring to. At least, I didn't think I should take him up on his offer to help, although the image of my brother slumped against my door reminded me that maybe nothing was okay.

Hawk had waited for me to lock the door. I knew it because I stood there with my heart pounding until he left.

When it was quiet once more, and I was sure Max wasn't going to come back, I went to my bathroom to get ready for bed. The night had been exhausting. I wanted to fall asleep and wake up to a new day.

I sighed in relief at the silence. There was no one in my apartment and no windows in my tiny bathroom. Even so, I shut and locked the door before I took my brush out of my drawer. I needed to see it, to reassure myself that it was safe. It wasn't worth anything, really, but it was priceless in sentimental value.

I peeled the rubber grip back until the line where the base connected to the brush's handle was visible. I held onto the brush and unscrewed the end to reveal a hollow core. Grasping the small scarlet ribbon, I gently pulled the cloth bundle free. After untying it, I unrolled the hand-embroidered material, my grandfather's handkerchief, and uncovered the pretty silver locket my grandma had given me before she'd died. She'd worn it every day of her life.

Turning the antique locket over, I made the decision to entertain the idea that the family treasure Oma had spoken of was real. If finding those heirlooms could help my brother in any way, I had to try.

CHAPTER 4

HAWK

Something wasn't right with Stella's brother. I hadn't liked the look of him when he and I had stared each other down in her apartment. He'd been roughed up. The trouble he was in must have escalated. I recognized the progression and what would no doubt happen next. The real question was how long it would be until he brought that kind of danger to Stella's door.

I pulled my phone from my pocket and hit the number to dial Chris, another of my surrogate brothers and part of our Gray Ghost team. It rang twice before he answered.

"Hey, what's up?"

"I need you to run a check on someone for me."

Fast clicks carried through the line as Chris typed on his laptop. "A typical background check, or go deep?"

"Deep." I needed to know what and who Max was involved with. I was almost positive he owed money to someone and that this wasn't an issue of him needing money for drugs. He looked straight, not strung out. Nothing about his behavior, aside from the yelling, pointed to a drug problem. It didn't mean he didn't have a drug addiction—I just wasn't seeing it.

It had to be a loan shark. Just thinking of the type of people in that line of work sent ice shooting through my veins.

"What's the name?" Chris asked.

He didn't mess around with a bunch of nosey questions, and I admired that about him. He wanted the scope of the job and the information he needed to do it, and he would handle it. He'd always been like that. And since I kept to myself so much, mindless chatter tended to make my skin crawl. Except around Stella, which was odd. I could listen to her voice all day without the need to escape ever entering my mind.

"Better run two. They're brother and sister, Max and Stella Klein." Once, when she'd gotten her mail, I'd caught her last name as I brushed by on the way to my place. Her thumb had covered her first name.

Someone yelled in the background, rising over the sound of Chris's typing.

"Was that Liam?"

"Yep. Jack and I are at Liam and Liv's place."

I sat up straighter. "What's going down?" They hadn't notified me about any new missions, but that didn't mean one wasn't happening. It could be that they hadn't gotten a chance to spread the word to the rest of us.

Chris chuckled under his breath. "Mari dragged me over today, determined to help Liv with her shooting."

Chris's wife had a legendary temper and a deadly accurate throwing arm. When she was angry, we confiscated the knives. "What did Liv do?" Liam's wife, Liv, was an artist and incapable of killing anyone. Her nurturing personality was unfamiliar but something that we were all drawn to. Probably because most of us hadn't experienced anything like that while growing up.

The chair Chris was sitting on squeaked loud enough for me to hear. I could picture him leaning back, hands clasped behind his head. "Nothing," he said.

"Really?" I found that hard to believe.

"Fine. She'd disappeared into her studio for a few days, and I think Mari just missed her."

"So she's bullying Liv into shooting?"

Chris snorted. "Yeah, something like that."

"Who're you talking to?" Jack's voice grew louder the closer he got to Chris.

I didn't need to get into it with him. Not right now.

Scuffling sounded through the receiver, then Jack's voice filled my ear. "What's going on over there? Any more issues with the neighbor?"

"I found out it's her brother, not a boyfriend."

Silence. I could practically see Jack's mind turning, and I scrubbed my face. The urge to get off the phone escalated.

"Really. So she's not in trouble? Just fighting with her brother?"

I stood up and paced from one end of the small bedroom to the other. "I think there's more to it. He's desperate and begging her for money."

"I see."

Jack would understand that problem. So would Mike. They were the only two I'd ever confided in about what I grew up around. It wasn't necessary to tell the rest of the guys. Their lives were equally as challenging. There were seven of us who'd grown up together and later formed the Gray Ghost team. Three more from our time as SEALs brought our group to an even ten.

Jack would know that Red's brother hitting her up for money was a big problem for me, one I couldn't walk away from in good conscience. "The brother was at her place a few hours ago with a black eye and swollen jaw."

"What do you need right now?"

"Nothing yet. I've got Chris doing a full background check to see what comes up with the brother and who he's connected to. Stella's clean. If we can find out what we're dealing with ahead of time…"

"Right, we'll be more prepared." Jack cleared his throat. "I'll fill Chris in on the girl. We can head out early so you're not managing this potential shit storm alone."

"It's not quite at that point. She won't admit there's a problem." I leaned against the windowsill and scanned the street. Nothing. "I could be blowing this out of proportion."

"Doubtful," Jack clipped out. "We'll wait for something to come in from Chris's search then head to you."

"And if it's nothing?" I couldn't help it. In this, unlike most things, I questioned my ability to read the situation correctly.

"Then we'll spend some time together with the guys. Possibly the old crew in California once again."

I grimaced. "Better circumstances this go-round."

"That's for sure."

"Thanks, Jack. I'll be talking to you soon." I hoped it wouldn't be because of what I thought was headed Stella's way.

<hr>

STELLA

I REACHED AROUND MY WAIST AND SECURED MY WAITRESSING apron. I'd arrived on time and just before the dinner crowd was upon us. The clinking of silverware and glasses rose above the din from the chef and line cooks.

If I didn't work there, I would have loved to eat in the café on a regular basis, or at least as much as my budget allowed. It was clean and inviting, with warm wood tones and sought-after food that was both healthy and satisfying.

I caught sight of Mathew, my boss, as I rushed to start my shift in our outdoor section. He was handsome in a teddy-bear sort of way.

When I'd first started, he'd flirted with me relentlessly until I had to put a hard stop to it. Dating the boss rarely worked out, and I needed the job. To smooth hard feelings, I started calling him Bossman. It appeased his ego, and honestly, I couldn't care less so long as it kept him off my back. It was also a reminder to myself to keep our relationship strictly professional. He was truly a nice guy, and I could see myself being worn down and going out with him.

And if our dating didn't pan out, I'd be out of a job. It wasn't worth it.

The title stuck, and a few of the other waitresses started calling him that too. Each time, I swear his ego swelled just a little more, and my worry about succumbing to his prior advancements all but evaporated. I grinned at the image of his puffed-out chest and peacock strut. Whatever, the title had worked and cooled his crush on me, allowing a mutually beneficial and professional relationship, as it should've been from the start.

Notepad in hand, I hustled to the patio only to come face-to-face with my boss, who looked irate again. In an attempt to defuse whatever had set him off, I widened my smile. "On time and ready to go."

He grunted and blocked my way when I tried to sidestep him. "Not today."

I faltered in my next attempt to shift to the side. "What?"

"I don't know what kind of trouble you're in, Stella, but you need to get it sorted. Two men, the kind we don't want in our restaurant, showed up an hour ago asking for you. This sends a terrible message to the type of clientele we cater to. I may have to reevaluate your connection here."

"Who showed up looking for me?" It couldn't have been Hawk—he would draw attention of the female kind. Just thinking that caused me to clench my teeth, and I wondered if he meant my brother and his bruised face.

"Thugs. Hired muscle. Having them ask about you, one of our waitresses, will drive customers away. A four-top left, and

I'm not kidding when I tell you their expressions were fearful. Not even a free meal could persuade them to stay."

I flinched. Bossman despised free anything. Whoever showed up must have been pretty scary for him to resort to that.

He plucked my notepad from my hand and flung an arm out, index finger pointing to the rear door. "You need to leave and get your affairs sorted before you come back to work."

I wanted to be angry but couldn't be. It sucked, but it was a sound business decision on his part. At least he hadn't outright fired me. I gave him a sharp nod before returning my apron to its place and quickly heading out the back door before anyone could question what had happened.

Dammit, Max. I needed to make him tell me what was going on, since it was directly affecting me. I needed to know what to expect. I had bills to pay, and my fridge was empty. At least I had ramen noodles. I would have to survive on those.

God, I wish I could get him the help he so badly needs. I'd done my research about gambling addiction and even had a place picked out. He refused to go. Short of an overdose or jail time, I couldn't force him.

Head down, I rounded the restaurant until I was back on the sidewalk and headed home. So many things tumbled through my mind. *How am I going to make rent, buy groceries, or pay my freaking bills?* The most pressing problem was what the hell Max had gotten mixed up in, because it involved me.

I loved my brother more than anything, but he had an addictive personality. Even growing up, he'd had problems with obsessive behaviors, so much so that Oma stopped talking to him about the alleged treasure. She kept her reminiscing about family heirlooms to me, but was quiet about it around him. If only it was real, maybe it could solve our problems.

I knew it couldn't be, though. It had to have been a dream or something simple that to Oma was a treasure of the heart. It was most likely the locket, its only value sentimental due to the pictures of her and Opa mounted inside the delicate frame.

Now and then I glanced up. I was nervous and distracted. I had to keep checking to make sure I was on the right path to catch my ride. The thought of the thugs being close before transportation arrived sent a constant volley of goosebumps along my arms.

I loved riding the trolley, and it dropped me close to my apartment. Completely open, it boasted seats within, along with room for people to stand on the outer edges of the car, hanging on to the evenly distributed poles. It was old-timey and classic, a fun way to get home rather than an expensive and not always clean cab. I liked walking too, but I just couldn't—with the way my mind was spinning, I would probably have ended up in some shady neighborhood due to wrong turns my confused brain didn't realize I was taking.

Up ahead, I spotted the trolley. With a glance at my watch, I frowned. It would pull away any minute. I ran but was jerked to a halt by a hard tug on my jacket. I glanced over my shoulder and had to tilt my head up and up some more. My mouth fell open. *Shit.* I totally understood what Bossman was talking about.

Thick, meaty fingers had a wad of my jean jacket. His wide, square jaw was set with menace, and his thin lips pressed together in an uncompromising manner. I flinched away from his dead eyes, loosened my arms, and sprinted ahead.

The jacket slipped from my relaxed arms, and I broke free while the coat remained in the thug's outstretched hand. Refusing to look back, I ran with everything I had just as the trolley pulled from the curb.

"Get back here, bitch!"

Terror grew wings on my shoes. My arms pumped, and I lengthened my stride. I turned the corner seconds after the trolley did. No way could I look behind me, in case the guy was near. The trolley picked up speed, and so did I. *So close.* I could taste freedom and didn't dare look to see how far behind he was.

I could hear the pounding of heavy feet behind me. There had to be two of them—Bossman said "men."

With a last-ditch effort, I leapt for the back of the trolley. My fingertips curled around one of the poles, and I hauled myself onboard to the gasps of several fellow riders. Someone grabbed my arm and steadied me as I found my footing and moved behind the pole, facing out.

My chest ached as I sucked in air. Sweat beaded along my hairline and on my upper lip from fear or exertion, probably both. I ignored the few who rode with me asking if I was all right. I wasn't, not by a long shot. But I was momentarily safe.

For how long? The question echoed on repeat in my mind.

Whatever Max had gotten into wasn't something I could fix. I knew that. As my breathing began to regulate, so did my mind, and I found the answer I'd been searching for.

When the trolley stopped close enough to my apartment, I hopped off and then ran. There was a slight chance those thugs didn't know where I lived. I was no fool, though—they could be waiting for me. *Or they could have followed my battered brother here.* I had to get in before any other hired muscle spotted me, if they weren't already there.

I ignored the ache in my chest and arms as I sprinted. A few more feet, and I would be inside. My gaze shifted left and right. Everything looked okay. God, I hoped I was safe and a stray bullet wouldn't end up buried in my chest.

Unable to slow my speed enough, I slammed into the front door with a thud. I jammed my hand into my pocket. When my shaky fingers curled around my keys, I jerked them out and unlocked the door as fast as possible then headed for the stairs. The elevator wasn't an option, as it was as slow as molasses on a cold winter's day. I took the stairs two at a time until I was afraid I would fall. Legs burning, I pushed open the door to my floor. When I exited the stairwell, I tripped and sprawled across the dirty hall carpeting. On shaky legs, I stood again and stumbled, not to my apartment but to his.

I pounded on Hawk's door while looking over my shoulder. It opened, and I almost fell into his arms. In some weird way, I wanted to. He exuded an unshakable competence, a barely checked power. His hands grasped my shoulders, and my trembling slowly subsided.

"What's wrong?"

I met his steely gaze with desperation. It was time. I knew that. "I need your help."

CHAPTER 5

HAWK

The ring from my cell phone was quiet as I double-checked that Red was still in the bathroom. I'd gotten her to calm down, but I suspected she was in there crying. After I'd made sure her apartment was empty, I ushered her inside and waited while she got cleaned up. Then we would clear out of there.

I surveyed the street below. We had to be quick, couldn't take too much time. I scanned the area while leaning against the windowsill, partially hidden behind curtains that I'd moved to block the view. I continued to do so until she emerged from the bathroom and I could get her to pack.

When my phone rang, I answered the call, hoping Chris had some news for me.

"You were right. The brother has a serious gambling problem. He switched loan sharks after paying off a large debt, but we don't know who the new moneylender is yet. I've got some feelers out to find out who he's into this time."

"Does he owe money elsewhere?"

"As far as I can tell, no. But it's possible he borrowed from the new loan shark to get the old debt off his back."

I knew that game well after watching my mom's husband for all those years. It never worked out.

Chris read the standard background check information about Max at a fast pace: parents were deceased, had one sister, was working as a stock market runner on the pit floor. While all that was good, I wanted the name of the person or company he was in debt to. Because he was in deep, whether or not Chris had found a record of debt owed anywhere.

"I've known a few traders." Apparently, Jack was on the call too. "The ones I've interacted with had a pretty heavy party life. Drugs may also be in play here."

That would make a bad situation even worse. Great. "Let me know as soon as you find out anything."

"Goes without saying." Chris tapped away at his keyboard, no doubt hacking into every available place to reveal what we needed to know. "We're coming out there. It's not a matter of if. It's a matter of when."

The tension I didn't realize I'd been carrying between my shoulders eased. "Yeah, Jack said something similar. I think we're good right now. Not much to do."

"Let us know the moment you suspect things are going south or if you find out information that's worse than what I've already told you. We'll hop on a plane immediately."

A smile played at the corners of my mouth, despite how much I fought it. I had no idea what I'd done in my screwed up youth to warrant these guys' support. Jack had been the one I'd mainly gone to, and if he wasn't there, then Mike.

It was like that for the rest of the guys in our crew too. We looked up to Jack. He was a natural leader. Back in the days when we lived in the warehouse, he had assumed that role, even with the shit he'd faced on a daily basis with his girlfriend and her messed up brother.

"Who all's there?"

I could hear the squeak of the chair as Chris leaned back. "Most of us. Jack. Mike is heading out here later today.

Keegan and Hayden too. Just not Trev. He's wrapped up in a job."

"On his own?"

"Pretty much. Right now it looks like a glorified babysitting job, but you know nothing has ever been easy for us."

"Isn't that the truth."

"Right, so I suspect some shit will hit the fan eventually. But for now, we need to concentrate on what's going on with your end of things."

While I liked the thought of our core crew getting back together to face whatever we learned about the loan-shark network, our group had expanded. It felt a little weird not having everyone in on that one. I suspected it would explode sooner rather than later. "What's up with Liam, Connor, and Matt?"

"They're working a small job for Rich and left early this morning." Rich Stevens was our CIA contact. "All of us weren't needed, so they're handling it. It'll be done in a couple of days, a week tops. They'll jump at the chance to get their hands in whatever you've got going on, assuming the problem is still there when they return."

"Yeah, I know they will." It was personal for me because of the gambling trigger. Whenever any of us had an issue that was a result of our past bullshit, we all rallied together, paid mission or not. I heard the running water from the bathroom shut off. "I've gotta go. Keep me posted."

"Always," Chris said.

Usually, I could handle whatever came my way, and Red's situation had seemed relatively easy. It was the palpable anxiety I read off her brother that brought my past a little too close to the surface. The memories I worked hard to keep buried didn't want to stay that way.

The door to the bathroom opened, and Stella walked out. Her eyes were rimmed in red, making the blue even more vibrant than usual. She'd pulled her wavy hair on top of her head in a messy bun. The urge to protect her was compelling. "Pack up what you need for the next week or two. Include anything you don't want to risk having stolen or broken."

Panic warred across her features, conflicting with the defeated slump of her shoulders. I felt a momentary pang of regret, but it had to be this way, at least until I figured out whom we were up against. Leaving her alone to face whatever may come would have been like tightening a noose around her neck.

Family didn't always do what was best for one another.

I should know. I lived that way most of my childhood. There was nothing worse than going to sleep, thinking I would be safe and that I would make it through the night unharmed, then finding that notion to be false. As I stood in Red's apartment, one such night sliced its way through my mind. I was a few years older than I'd been that night my mom had gotten me the pair of shoes, but I was still no match for him. It'd been quiet when I'd fallen asleep—he was out for the night, so there was no constant fighting. Or so we'd thought.

I awoke with a jerk to a hand clamped tightly around my ankle, dragging me from under the open sleeping bag on the floor. Panic shot through me in a violent burst of lightning. I slammed my hands down, trying to gain purchase and stop what was happening. My eyes were wide, and the soft light from the living room illuminated Mom's husband, Lenny.

I'd stopped calling him Dad a long time before.

I sucked in air, willing myself to take in my surroundings, to be alert, and not to let mind-numbing fear take hold. Everything would be over then. If I fought the fear, I stood a chance.

"Where is it?"

What? My brain raced to figure out what he was accusing me of. I caught the doorway and clamped my hand on it, using the leverage to tear my ankle from his grip. "I don't know what you're talkin' about!" I scrambled to my feet, ready and watching.

For an older guy, he was damn fast.

Alcohol-laced breath hit me in the face as I stood inches from him. We were matched in height by then, just not width. He still had that on me. And muscle. *Not for long, old man.* I would keep growing, getting stronger. He would only get older.

His fist connected with my shoulder too quickly for me to avoid. Grunting, I absorbed the blow. I had to learn to be faster. I'd seen it coming, barely, but I hadn't moved in time. A dull ache throbbed there, but I blocked the pain. "What're you talkin' about?"

"My money, *boy*." He bared his teeth, and hatred flashed in his eyes. "Where is it?"

His fist shot out. I weaved left. Knuckles grazed the side of my face. Again, I wasn't fast enough. A former boxer, Lenny knew how to hit. Things could have been different if I'd looked like him, if I were his, or if he'd taught me how to fight. But he hadn't and wouldn't.

I heard a small gasp. It was Mom, but she said nothing. There was no cry for him to stop.

Mom watched from the hallway, her face a pale oval in the dim light. I recognized the way her lips pressed together and her body smashed up against the wall. It was her tell. She'd taken the money. It didn't matter. She would never have my back. To her, it was easier if I took the fall.

I hated them. What I couldn't understand was why it still hurt so goddamned much.

———

Stella

Hawk flexed his muscles as he dropped several duffel bags on the floor near a small closet. I nervously glanced around his apartment. Through an open bedroom door, there was a king-sized bed. I hoped there were other bedrooms. Of course, I hadn't walked through the two other doors that were shut on the other side of the living room. His place was much larger than mine.

"This isn't necessary. I can check in to a hotel."

He crossed his arms and settled the heavy weight of his gaze on me.

"We may need to do that, but right now I'd rather be close by."

"Because of the cameras?" While I'd packed, he'd stuck several tiny little cameras in a few places around my apartment. I'd never seen anything like them. They were small and round, about the size of a dime and either black or clear to match their surroundings, and they blended in seamlessly wherever he installed them.

"The cameras are there for us to monitor anyone breaking into your apartment, which we can do from elsewhere. I thought it best to stay close for now, in case your brother comes back."

Oh wow, I was a horrible sister. "Yes, I want to be near if he comes looking for me. But what's the point of staying here, in your place?"

"So that no one attacks you while you're alone in your apartment. I have a camera on the building's entrance too. We'll know if your brother is by himself or not…"

I stole a glance at Hawk. I didn't know how to do what I was supposed to do. If he hadn't introduced himself and offered his help… *God, Max, what have you gotten yourself into this time?*

CHAPTER 6

*H*iding out in my neighbor's apartment while monitoring my own via video feed was so out of my league. But after the scare on my way home from work, I'd agreed to stay with him.

I looked around Hawk's spacious living quarters, which were done in a dark color scheme of gray and blue with tan couches that boasted pillows and a soft throw. There were a few scattered pictures of Hawk with other people. I made a mental note to take a closer look later.

Across from me, Hawk sat in front of a laptop. Various images from the cameras he'd installed filled the screen. The ones in my place, the hallway, and the entrance to the building were displayed.

My thumb smoothed over the polished wood of a jewelry box that Oma had given me. It had been hers. *This holds part of my heart, Stella, as do you. Remember, always.* Her words whispered through my mind as I hugged the small antique treasure. It'd come with her when she'd fled with her family from Germany to America all those years ago.

I shook off my thoughts and glanced again to Hawk. I didn't like any of this. Not only that, but I'd involved my hot neighbor. This wasn't how I'd hoped to end up at his place. I nibbled on my lip nervously and wracked my brain for something to talk to him about.

"Do you expect someone to show up? Do you think they know where I live?"

Hawk turned and settled his gaze on me. God, he was intense. My spine straightened from the weight of his focus. He saturated the space with his stillness. It made me feel like prey, and it was unsettling but comforting at the same time. Or maybe I was crazy.

"In time, yes, based on what you told me happened at work with the men hanging around and how your boss sent you packing."

Ugh. I tasted blood and released my lower lip. I ran my tongue over it to catch any stray drops from my horrible nervous habit.

His gaze flicked to my lip then back up. "Is there anything else you're leaving out?"

"No." I pulled my legs under me and sat the jewelry box next to me. "They must have followed me when I left work. One of the men got a fistful of my jacket, but I got away."

"You didn't show up here with a jacket on. Where is it?"

I shook my head. "I slipped out of it to get away. They probably have it."

"Was there anything in the pockets?"

"No. I'm positive there wasn't." I usually hung up my jacket with the rest of the staff at the restaurant. I wouldn't have taken a chance by leaving anything of value in there. It was easier to keep my key and money in my pants pocket unless I brought a purse, which I always stored securely in the office.

"That may buy us a little time, but whoever is after your brother will find you eventually. What do you know about who he has dealings with?"

I shrugged. Max had been getting into trouble for a long

time, but he handled it—sort of. I'd learned the hard way by losing the few expensive possessions I had owned. Anything of value was fair game. He'd taken those things and sold them.

Oma had left her childhood jewelry box with me. I'd threatened him within an inch of his life, saying that if he ever took it, I would never forgive him. Even though he was a complete shit, we were family and loved one another, and there were some lines that even he wouldn't cross.

Oma knew what he was like—after all, she'd raised us. I remember her lovingly patting him on the cheek and telling him to get his priorities straight. But her mention of treasure that time or two had cemented in his head, and he'd asked her relentlessly about it for a while. After that, she'd referred to her hidden secret as "family heirlooms" only. I tended to believe that the locket she'd given me was it.

Even with Max screwing up throughout school and getting into trouble, once for an underground gambling circuit, she'd never turned him away. She'd always known what Max was mixed up with, but one thing she'd made sure we understood was the importance of family.

I should have kept closer tabs on who he dealt with. I knew better. But after a while, the shady men turned downright evil, and I wanted nothing to do with them.

There were a few things I did know about Max's situation, but… I worried my lip again and cringed. It was sore from where I'd bitten it before. I pulled out some lip balm and spread it over my lips as I checked out my hot neighbor. *What if I've invited more problems for Max and me? Has my crush on Hawk blinded me so that I've added to Max's problems?* "Are you a cop?"

A smile stretched across Hawk's face, and I sucked in a breath. He was stop-in-your-tracks handsome before, but when he smiled, he looked like a model.

"No. I promise. I'm in security."

"So what's with the haircut and the job? Are you an ex-cop?"

He chuckled, and my face heated.

"The hair's low maintenance, and I was in the military before. Now, I work mainly search and rescue."

"Oh, okay." *That's good, right?* He had skills. I had none. "Are you going to have my brother arrested? 'Cause if that's what the cameras are for, you can count me out of this." And I would tell Max too.

"Red, it's strictly for monitoring who comes and goes, to capture the images of any potential threat so we know exactly what we're up against. You're sure you don't know what kind of trouble your brother is in or who those guys were?"

Maybe. Can I trust him? I wanted to. I at least had to try. I didn't know what else to do or who to go to for help. "My brother has been in tight spots before with owing money he doesn't have. Then the loans come due." I got up and started pacing. "Mostly because of his gambling debts."

"What type of gambling does he do?"

I paused in my pacing when something in Hawk's demeanor drew me close. *Is he sad? Lost? Wait, that isn't right. Maybe wary?* "Um, he usually bets on fights. Sometimes, he'll go to the track." *Had he flinched when I said "fights," or did I imagine that?*

His features went back to a neutral expression so fast that I couldn't be sure. "Anything else? Casinos?"

I shook my head. I didn't think so. "He parties sometimes. Cocaine, I think. I haven't seen him strung out for a while. He could have the drug issue under control. The real problem is the gambling…"

"Do you know who he associates with, maybe who he owes money to?"

"No. He said it was better I didn't know anything."

A tic pulsed at the corner of Hawk's jaw, and my stomach clenched. Hawk's quiet concern rocketed mine. "What's wrong?"

The tension I'd previously read on his features melted away.

"Nothing yet. We'll figure this out." Movement on the screen caused Hawk to pause. His gaze flicked to the monitor. It was another one of the residents. No cause for alarm. "In the meantime, I need you to stick close to me. If you have to go anywhere, we'll go together. It's not worth the risk."

I tapped my fingernail against my thigh. Admitting I needed help was hard and not something I liked to do, but I was scared. He was offering to be a personal bodyguard of sorts, and it made me feel indebted to him. I didn't like that. "I should pay you."

Hawk grinned, and I had to stop myself from sucking in a loud breath. I had to get used to seeing him smile. He needed to do that more often.

"No, you shouldn't. Honestly, this is… It's something I've had some experience with before, and in good conscience, I can't let you handle it on your own."

That's all I was to him, a charity case. *Noted.* Heat infused my cheeks again. I had to keep a tight rein on my hormones. The attraction was one-sided and all on my end. I pulled the box back into my lap, sort of like a buffer.

"What's that?"

I smoothed my hand over the surface, missing my Oma terribly. "A gift from my grandmother. We called her Oma. It's the jewelry box that her mom gave to her when she was a little girl. It was one of the things that made it over here when she escaped with her parents from Germany."

"May I?"

He extended a hand toward me, and I clutched the box tighter. He waited. I was being stupid. I handed it to him.

He turned the box over, and I had a sudden, overwhelming urge to reread Oma's words. Family was everything. Max tested the limits of what we could endure. It didn't change the fact that he was my brother, and I would never turn my back on him. Oma and her parents hadn't turned their backs on her brother. He was taken from them through death instead.

Hawk's phone rang, and he handed the jewelry box back to me. My brush was in the small backpack I'd packed, where it would stay and where I would safely return the box after I read one of Oma's letters.

While he talked on the phone, I moved over to the opposite side of the room for some privacy. I should have waited to read her letter later, but with everything that had happened, I needed her. I got settled on the couch closest to the window and farthest from where Hawk was.

With care, I opened the envelope on top of the pile of three secured by a ribbon. I knew them by heart but desperately wanted to feel close to her again.

My Dearest Stella,

I see so much of myself in you, from your penchant to test the waters around you to your love of art. I wish I could show you the world I came from before my country was infested with hate and genocide. As you know, my family fled our war-torn home as soon as we were able, sick for what had happened to so many friends and loved ones. While most of us fit the profile to remain untouched, we couldn't stand by and support such madness. My family's views were known by many, which resulted in our family being placed under the watchful eye of Nazi supporters.

It has forever haunted me that my parents hadn't found a way to leave earlier. Or that my brother, Stefan, hadn't been able to reach the escape route they'd learned to plot before every endeavor. A large part of our personal tragedy could have been avoided. But I don't blame them or Stefan and his friends for forming a band fashioned after the Edelweiss Pirates, led by another brave group of rebellious teenagers. Their protests began with expression through song, clothes, and growing their hair long. Peaceful protests soon led to confrontation and violence.

At the time, the outlet was what he needed to rail against the injustice inflicted upon his fiancée and so many of our friends. Even through peaceful resistance of song, violence was sure to follow. One horrifying night, many of their group were caught and beaten, and it ended with their heads shaved. They were alive, and that's what we focused on while planning how to escape undetected.

When Stefan's continued resistance against the German Youth Group resulted in him and several of their band being beaten and publicly hung, we fled, wracked with grief and guilt that we hadn't left earlier and potentially saved my brother's life. I'll never forget the fear, the terror.

Through my very fortunate, long life, my heart has fractured in the face of tragedy, death, and love. I don't regret many things, only the loss back in Germany.

You, my sweet Stella, are another one who holds a portion of my heart. I am so very proud of you—always remember.

All my love,

Oma

I swiped at the tears tumbling from my eyelids. Her letters got to me every time. Reading them was as if she were next to me, repeating what she'd penned, word for word. Oma talked about Stefan to us, even though reliving those years was painful. It was how she kept his memory alive.

Lost in my world, I didn't notice that Hawk had paused in whatever he'd been doing. Not until he had crouched down in front of me, his beautiful eyes conveying concern.

Cupping my cheeks with his hands, he ran his thumbs under my eyes and brushed the tears away. "Are you okay?"

I sniffled. *Dammit.* I hated for anyone to see me cry. "I'm fine. It's my Oma's letters. I miss her so much."

He reached out and squeezed my knee, leaving little sparks of awareness where his hand had been even after he removed it. "I'm glad you have something to remember her by."

"I am too. It's something my brother doesn't see much value in whenever he checks the jewelry box for anything to sell. I guess he thinks I would hide cash in here too. That's where he's wrong, though. The letters are worth more to me than any amount of money. They should be to him too."

"But he never finds any in there. And he keeps checking?"

I nodded. "I don't have much. I mean, I'm a waitress. I'm not rolling in cash. He should know he's wasting his time."

"Why does he keep coming back to you for money? If he's already sold what you've given him, what does he expect to find?"

"Treasure."

His eyes widened. Disbelief shimmered in their blue depths.

"Oma used to talk about a treasure. It was probably a figment of her imagination. Or she was talking about what meant the most to her—us, her locket, this jewelry box, things like that. Honestly, there isn't anything I have that's worth the kind of money he's looking for. Maybe there once was, but I suspect whatever she was referring to was left behind when she and her family fled Germany."

"But your brother believes you may have what she considered valuable or know where it is?"

"Yes. Oma used to talk to me all the time about it, little hints here and there. Not my brother, though, not after that first couple of times."

A pained expression came over his face. "I'm sorry, Red."

My shoulders tensed. "Why?"

"If your brother believes a treasure exists and you have information about it, he could have shared that with the people he's indebted to. If he did, they wouldn't stop searching for you."

The blood drained from my face, and I knew if I hadn't already been sitting I would have fallen. Max was desperate, and I knew it.

Hawk started throwing the things I'd taken out of my bags back in. "We need to leave, now."

CHAPTER 7

HAWK

Stella hurried beside me, a bag over her shoulder along with her backpack. Two large duffels hung from my shoulders, and one held my rifle. After checking into a hotel not too far from where our building was, I ordered room service for us.

If things went to hell, I wasn't sure when we would be able to eat, and I'd skipped breakfast. And with the news of the treasure or family heirlooms, I guessed they would be relentless in their search for her. My stomach rumbled in protest, something I hated—it'd happened too often when I was a kid. Those weren't memories I needed to deal with just then.

"Ah, this place is pretty nice." Stella shifted from foot to foot. "I—"

"It's on me." I could tell she was worried about the cost. "Our company can handle the bill, and I would rather stay somewhere decent." I'd stayed in enough run-down places to last a lifetime. All the guys in my crew felt the same. Plus, Chris handled investments for all of us. Speaking of Chris, I needed to check in. "I've gotta make a call."

Stella nodded, the tension in her shoulders lessening as they dropped about half an inch. She sat on the couch, pulled her knees up, and clicked on the TV. Vulnerability shimmered briefly across her features before she locked it down. I admired that about her. Her looks were deceptive, so beautiful and soft, but from the few glimpses I'd had when talking to her, I knew there was steel underneath.

I'm doing the right thing. In part, I had to keep reminding myself that, especially because the family issues she was dealing with caused a constant jackhammer to fracture the lockbox where I preferred the memories of my family remain.

I tapped Jack's contact on my phone. As I waited for him to pick up, I went to one of the two bedrooms off the main room of our suite. I set my laptop on the dresser then powered it up. Once it was booted, I clicked on the link to the cameras. Three guys were in front of Stella's door. *Shit, we got out just in time.*

"Tell me you see this too," I said when Jack answered.

"Chris is uploading their pictures to face-recognition software right now. We're going to need to sweep our apartments for bugs or video surveillance."

Our private military corporation, Gray Ghost Securities, owned the place I was staying in next to Stella's. That would be a red flag. Once those guys got wind of the fact someone in security lived next door or Max told them about me, they would look for Stella there. They shouldn't be able to get any clues if they broke in. I needed to get that dealt with now and mentioned it to Jack. We had to maintain the advantage.

"I'm sending Keegan to handle it. Where are you now?"

I glanced out the window. I'd chosen the east side, claiming we wanted to be able to watch the sunrise when we woke tomorrow, a bullshit story that the blushing receptionist seemed all too eager to buy into. That wasn't the real reason. "We're at the hotel a few blocks away. I have a partial view of our building."

"I'm heading out now. We'll be there as soon as we can. I think Mike and Chris are coming too. We'll text you when we're in the air."

Good. "Let me know when Chris gets a hit from facial recognition."

"Will do."

I headed back into the main room, and a knock sounded at the door. Stella's eyes widened, and I held up a finger for her to hold on. "It's probably room service," I whispered, motioning for her to go into the bedroom and stay out of sight. She frowned, but I went back to the issue at hand: who was at our door.

I doubted the men after her would've tracked us already, especially when they were spotted going through her apartment a few minutes ago. A second knock sounded with "room service!" announced through the door. My hand gripped the door handle, my other on my Glock. I looked through the peephole, which revealed a guy wearing a hotel uniform and his hands on the side of a cart, looking bored. There weren't any signs of stress on his face or in his posture.

Stella came back into the main room. I opened my mouth to tell her to hide when I noticed what she had on and almost laughed. Brilliant. She'd taken a towel from the bathroom and tightly wrapped it, turban style, around her head. Not a strand of her gorgeous hair showed through. Her eyebrows were red, but I doubted the guy would notice. She had her arms crossed over her chest, and I realized she had a stubborn streak. I guessed she didn't like taking orders.

I opened the door and grinned. "Sorry, man. My wife was just getting dressed."

I tipped him and ushered him out as fast as I could. With a turn and click, I locked the door, sliding the chain home for good measure. Stella already had the covers off the food. She whipped the towel from her head, and the corner of her mouth quirked up. "Wife?"

My mind warred against the word, what it meant, and what I was soon coming to realize I might want some day.

Marriage hadn't been a part of my plans, ever. Not even a steady girlfriend.

I shoved the confusing thoughts away. "If I'd said sister that could have been a red flag if the staff was compromised and questioned by one of the people after you. They'd be looking for a brother and sister, not a husband and wife." It was a long shot, but I was uncomfortable with the idea of her reading into what I'd said.

Her arms dropped to her sides. "Oh, I didn't think of that. Smart."

The fact was, my blood was tainted. I had no business wanting what I couldn't have. There was always the possibility that I was more like the people who'd raised me than I thought. It was my worst nightmare. I never wanted to have a kid and have him or her feel like I did growing up.

She returned to her spot on the couch in front of the TV while I retrieved the laptop. I set it up on a portion of the stand that held the TV then angled it toward where I planned to sit.

"We've got some time to relax. Might as well take advantage of it." I set the food on the coffee table.

I dropped onto the couch next to her and picked up one of the burgers. "What the hell are you watching?"

She blushed then fumbled for the remote. "It just came on. I wasn't paying attention."

I laughed—I couldn't help it. She'd been watching a sappy Hallmark romance movie. She flipped through the channels, stopping when she saw a rerun of HGTV's *Fixer Upper*. I leaned back, finishing the burger in a few bites while she nibbled on hers.

"I love this show," she said around a mouthful.

"Same. They crack me up." I liked how the couple bantered. It was another example of what I'd grown up without. For some reason, they gave me an odd sense of hope. Some of my surrogate brothers had that. Matt, Liam, Chris, and now Jack were happy, and that was enough for me. Their wives—Jo, Liv, Mari, and Hannah—were like sisters to me, and for that, I would forever be grateful.

It wasn't in the cards for me. I knew that.

"My grandparents loved one other like they do." Stella waved at the TV. "They were always building each other up, and their bickering was good-hearted."

They weren't alive anymore. I'd figured that much out. "What about your parents?" I hoped she'd had a happy childhood.

She shrugged then picked up a French fry slathered in ketchup. "They were always working. I'm not sure if they were much more than roommates before they died. But they loved Max and me and were there for us in most ways until they weren't."

"What do you mean?"

"They died, and my grandparents raised us until I went off to college. My grandparents passed away during my freshman and sophomore year."

"I'm sorry."

She finished off the fry. "It's okay. It was a long time ago. I miss them, but I'm happy I had the time with them that I did."

We ate the rest of the food and watched the end of the show. I glanced at the time. The guys would be arriving soon, probably close to midnight and only after they did a sweep on our place and Stella's.

She leaned over and swiped one of my sweet potato fries. The muscles on my thigh tensed from the press of her palm. Electricity shot through me.

She yanked her hand away. She must have felt the same attraction. I shifted in my seat as she gasped.

"Oh my God!" Her hand extended, and she pointed to the laptop.

Shit. I thought I'd angled it far enough from her view. She must have seen it when she leaned over.

"What do we do?" Her voice trembled. "I-I-I don't know how to deal with this. They're touching my stuff."

Her voice rose at the end. It was personal. I got it. I pulled her close and wrapped an arm around her. "We're not going to do anything—yet. You're safe. That's all that matters." Three men were in her apartment, and her stuff was everywhere. They were ransacking her bedroom. "You have what's important to you from your place."

I didn't tell her the entire truth. It wasn't okay.

CHAPTER 8

The afternoon passed quickly, as did the evening. As it grew dark, we decided to grab a few hours of sleep. Or one for me and several for her. I promised to wake her up when it was time to go. If we stayed off the radar, we could remain there for a couple of days. She headed to the bedroom farthest from the door. I set the alarm on my phone and stretched out on the couch, closing my eyes.

The bed would have been better, but I wasn't about to let anyone have even the slightest chance of slipping past me to her. Even as my breathing evened out and I started to drift off, a sense of dread played at the edges of my consciousness. There was a similarity I couldn't quite place about the way one of the guys moved or his shape. I wasn't entirely sure. But it was there, and my brain wanted to pull it from whatever memory it was filed away in.

Chris would have news about the men who'd been into Stella's place. For the time being, we had to wait at the hotel. We should have had more time, but I didn't think we had that luxury. Unfortunately, I knew it wouldn't last. With several deep breaths, I relaxed enough to sleep.

Sleep brought dreams, and those ushered in more of the

reasons why I couldn't have what some of my brothers had. I would never be good enough.

Suddenly, I was a twelve-year-old boy again. Through the threadbare T-shirt, the sun had warmed my back and splashed my shadow across the steps. I had taken that first step and had committed to whatever I would face inside.

I placed each footfall with care.

I paused before opening the front door. It was quiet. That didn't always equate to safe. There were times when silence was deceptive.

Please, no one be home. That was rarely the case. My hand shook as I touched the dented doorknob. In slow increments, I turned it before pushing the door open a crack. Any more, and it would squeak. My eyes narrowed, and my breath caught. A glimpse within was all I would need to know if I had to get the hell out of there. Otherwise, it would have been a minefield of a chance.

I squinted. Assessed. *Is anyone even home? Could I have gotten lucky, for once?*

I ticked off what I saw through the crack in the door, while possibilities and memories played through my head like a spliced movie.

The armchair Mom's husband occupied most of the time was empty. My mind raced. *Had I heard him tell Mom he would be out? Did the door slam behind him last night?* Those were the nights I slept easy. If I stayed out of Mom's sight, I wouldn't be harassed, and at least she never hit me.

I'd found out where he went on the nights when I could sleep without fear. He had a girlfriend he stayed with sometimes.

It was a fun evening when my mom learned that bit of information. They screamed their usual insults. I wished I could've changed who I'd come from. I didn't look like him. If I did, things could have been different.

He suffered our presence. That's what he'd said more than

once. Our good fortune, as he'd often lectured, depended on his. He'd been talking about gambling. His occupation. I hated it and knew I would never get involved in what he was addicted to. Over the years, we saw less and less of that good fortune.

After good nights at the track, he'd begun to stay with the girlfriend. More often than not, we got the other side of the coin. He came home when he'd had a shit night, which happened all the time.

I couldn't wait out on the steps any longer. When no sound came from within, I pushed the door wider, enough to squeeze through. Red-rimmed dark eyes in a sea of tangled hair met my gaze. Leaning back against a counter with a drink in hand, she glared at me with hatred as I stepped inside.

That she didn't like me was like a knife twisting in my gut on a daily basis. I thought she loved me, in her way, but I wasn't sure. But I was positive that she never liked me. I was a mistake.

With jerky movements, she set the glass on the counter with an irritated clink. Already in the house, I took a careful step and weighed my chances of a quiet night by her expression. Could have gone either way. I wasn't sure, and the risk was high, but I needed a few things. I'd left a school textbook at home with homework stuffed between the pages. Not only that, I wanted to switch out the clothes I stashed in my backpack for clean ones.

With my bag hanging over my shoulder, I kept one hand clamped around the strap. A teacher had taken pity on me. It wasn't new, but it didn't have holes in the bottom, and the zipper worked. My mom and her husband hadn't noticed it yet, but I knew they would. I had no idea what they would do. Take it from me, probably. Nothing was safe in that house.

Nothing was mine except my room, which was about the size of a closet and had a small window. I had no bed, just a sleeping bag on the floor and a clock I'd gotten from the second-hand store. I'd lifted it and somehow made it out of there without getting caught. I needed it to make sure I was on time for school. When I wasn't home, I tried to hide it under the sleeping bag as best I could.

I took another step and hunched my shoulders, dropped my head, and made a beeline for my room.

"Where do you think you're going?"

The high-pitched accusation locked my muscles. *Shit.* It wasn't going to be one of the times Mom pretended not to see me.

"Nowhere." I inched closer to the wall. My room was close. *Why can't she be passed out? Or watching one of her favorite shows on the TV we still had by some miracle?*

"I asked you a question." Her voice cracked like a whip.

I lifted my head, careful not to meet her eyes. When I did that, both she and her husband got angrier. "To my room to do homework."

She laughed, and that horrible, bitter sound cut through me. "You think that'll matter? That someday you'll make something of yourself? You'll never crawl out of here. Same as me. You'll always be nothing."

I flinched. She was probably right, but I could hope. *Someday, I will leave this place.*

"Don't be expecting dinner. And your father will be home soon. I don't want to see or hear you for the rest of the night."

He's not my father. I nodded and slipped into the only space that was sometimes mine. Aside from homework and hopefully sleep, I had nothing to do in there but think.

The door clicked quietly behind me, and I took care to step lightly and around any floorboards that squeaked. There were two spots. I avoided them like the blaring alarms they were.

My stomach growled, and I froze. Seconds ticked by. When no movement sounded by my door, I released the tension I'd been carrying. It was a never-ending cycle.

At school, I had access to food. And sometimes in the middle of the night or early morning, I could sneak into the kitchen at home and take something that wouldn't be noticed. That wasn't always possible. On occasion, there was bread and peanut butter. The fridge only had beer in it.

The emptiness in my stomach rarely eased since I kept growing. I was almost as tall as Mom now, but still no match for him. He towered over us. I was fast, but couldn't escape if he got even one hit in. I'd learned many times to stay quiet and out of sight.

The area we lived in wasn't much, and I wasn't the only one dressed in clothes that were too small and had holes. Some kids didn't have it great at home, either, but not too many were on their own like I was.

Sixth grade was different than the first few years in my school. Not everyone had enough food or two parents. I wasn't the only one who had it rough. I recognized hunger, loneliness, and pain in some of the others. We kept to ourselves, mostly. Some would start shit with the kids who had more.

I looked over my meager belongings, contemplating what I could wash out in the sink when they were asleep. My shoes were too small again. I'd have to go over to the church and see if they had anything in the donation boxes in my size. I'd gotten lucky and found a sweatshirt, but shoes were the hardest to come by. I wanted to keep growing. Maybe when I was big enough, I could stop him from hitting me.

Carefully, I lay down on my sleeping bag, the floor hard beneath me. It was quiet, and I wanted to get some rest.

I had light-brown skin like both my parents. My coloring still passed for Cuban, which they were. If that had been it, they might have wanted me. It wasn't. My eyes were what betrayed that my mom had cheated. No one in either of their families had blue eyes. To them, I was an abomination.

My eyes flew open, and I sat up and looked around, realizing I was still in the hotel room. Gun in hand, I stood, taking inventory. Nothing moved. The door was shut and the chain still in place. My instincts continued to flare. *What is different?*

I checked Stella's room. A sliver of moonlight fell across her. Her hair splayed across the pillow as she slept. A small flare of light flashed from the main room. I strode back, ready to confront the threat. I grimaced at missing that. What had woken me wasn't an intruder—it was a text lighting up the screen of my cell phone.

Jack texted. *Landed. Be there after our place is secured.*

They must have left later than they'd planned—maybe they'd waited for Hayden too. Jack would check out Stella's place and what was done to it, and Keegan would go straight to our apartment. Luckily, we all have an app installed on our phones that allowed Chris to connect the feed from any cameras we planted. Keegan wouldn't be taken unaware.

That wasn't entirely true, because Keegan usually spoiled for a fight. He was fury walking. If an enemy showed up, it would be their disadvantage.

I sat back on the couch, intending to go back to sleep when I heard a phone ring. Not mine. Not the hotel's landline either. *Stella.* In two strides, I was at the entryway to her room as she lifted the phone to her ear and uttered a sleepy hello.

A tic pulsed at my jaw. She wasn't supposed to be on her phone. It changed things. We weren't safe any longer.

Her eyes widened, and her mouth formed into a small o before she pulled the phone away from her mouth to whisper, "It's Max. He said they know about us. We need to leave."

CHAPTER 9

HAWK

A fierce wind slapped us in the face, plastering our clothes against us as we left the hotel. Dark clouds rolled overhead, and a few fat drops of rain fell, promising one hell of a storm. Bags secured over my shoulder, I grabbed Stella's hand and pulled her along. Her hair whipped around her head in a fiery mass of loose curls, which had to challenge her ability to see.

The weather matched my mood. I couldn't put my finger on what my problem was, whether I was being overly sensitive to the issues with her brother, or if it was about Stella powering up her phone.

Before we'd left, I'd texted Jack. Chris set up a hasty registration at another hotel, then Jack gave us those details. I recognized the name of the place. We tended to stay in better accommodations since our lives had changed so drastically. None of us wanted to live the way we used to.

"We're not going far, just a few blocks." I attempted to reassure her, but my irritation continued to spike. "You can't be on your phone. It needs to stay powered off and in the bag I gave you." The night before, I'd explained the significance of the soft phone sleeve. It was a Faraday case that would block all wireless signals and make her phone undetectable and untraceable.

"I'm sorry. I'm worried about my brother. What if he needs me? What if he's hurt?"

She would do it again is what she wasn't saying. I would too for any of the people who had become a family to me. "I'll get you a burner phone."

"Thank you."

I sucked in air and worked on not being mad. She didn't understand. Her life had been different than what I and the guys on my team lived. "You have to keep that one in the sleeve too. If they get your number from Max, you can be traced."

She nodded then worried her lip. "I don't like this. You're doing so much for me, and you don't even know me."

"This is our job. We're used to protecting people, and we've been doing that since even before we got into the military. I stayed here longer because I sensed something going on with you and your brother, and I'm glad I did."

Stella shivered and inched closer. I wrapped my arm around her despite the bags I was carrying. My hand curled around her hip. We weren't in the clear. My team was back at the apartment, sweeping all traces of us from the inside. When the money collectors broke in—there was no doubt in any of our minds that they would—they wouldn't find a thing.

In silence, Red and I hurried down several streets until the hotel came into view. I scoured the streets and buildings with her tucked close to my side. Lucky for me, she was tall. I often found it uncomfortable to walk with a woman against me, since I was just over six foot two. Red was close to the top of my shoulder. I didn't have to hunch to the side to wrap my arm around her waist.

She fit.

I ushered her in and pointed to the elevators. One of the guys had run over, checked us in, and handed me the keycard at the previous hotel after Stella had gone to sleep. That eliminated the need to go to the front desk.

We rode the elevator in silence to the top floor. The guys knew I would want easy access to the roof. I kept thinking that the hotel should be a safe place for us to wait out what would happen next, but that could change. Stella slid the keycard in and pushed open the door while I kept an eye on the hallway. Once inside, she seemed to deflate.

"You okay?" I dropped our bags to the floor before I grasped her shoulders.

"Yeah, it's just crazy." She wrung her hands. "I never thought I'd have to run from people my brother chose to get involved with. I'm so scared for him."

"It sucks. I'm sorry you're dealing with this, but I'm here to help you." I locked my gaze on hers. "You're not alone in this."

A sad smile curved her soft lips. "I know." She flattened her hand on my chest just as my cell vibrated in my pocket.

Not wanting to, but needing to get eyes back on her place, I dropped my hold on her, and her hand fell away. She turned to the windows as I pulled my cell out and answered it. I said hello then opened one of our bags and pulled out the laptop. Chris's voice was sharp in my ear as the computer booted up.

"We've got a hit on a few of the enemy." I could hear Chris's fingers flying over the keyboard as he filled me in.

"Anyone we know?" With the laptop powered up, I clicked on the app for the camera feed just as Stella walked into one of the adjoining rooms.

"Not yet. Two of the three guys were tagged in several pictures with Tridel. They're big as fuck, Hawk. They own several casinos in California."

Not what I wanted to hear. "We're going to have a hell of a fight on our hands, aren't we?"

"Looks that way."

"Who else is available to head out here?"

Chris cleared his throat, the click of the keys stopping. "I'm leaving now. Jack, Keegan, and Mike are already there. I'm going to see if Hayden is free. The rest of the guys are tied up with other jobs."

"Who will stay with Liv and Mari? You're not leaving them on their own, are you?"

I heard Stella snort in the other room, and I grinned. I got what she thought, but she had no idea what we'd gone up against. Liv's nightmare alone was enough for all of us to be extra wary about leaving them unprotected.

"Don't ever let Mari or Hannah hear you say that. Can you imagine?"

"Hey, I didn't say anything about Hannah. But yeah, they would crucify me. Jo too, since she's one of us." Jo and Matt were married and had adopted two kids. Even the kids were badasses, but that didn't stop my protective instincts from flaring at the thought of leaving any of those we called family vulnerable. "I still don't like it."

"I know, man. Hannah and Mari can hold down the fort. Jo and the kids will fly here too."

It was Liv who we all worried about. She could shoot, and in a pinch, she could defend herself, but she didn't have it in her to do what the rest of us did. It was endearing, really. Besides, she took care of us. She had a sort of ingrained intuition for when we were hurting the most but refused to tell anyone. That alone was worth all of our weight in gold.

I glanced at the screen. Movement in one of the apartment's windows caught my attention. "They're in."

"Yep. Looks like the same guys," Chris confirmed.

We stayed on the phone in silence for a few minutes, watching as three large men strategically tore apart Stella's apartment again. That sense of unease I'd had from the moment I heard her and her brother arguing tripled. "Send me what you've got on the Tridel Corp. I feel like there's something I'm missing."

"You got it." Tapping resumed on Chris's end. "I'm

heading out in a half hour. We'll all meet you at the hotel this afternoon."

I mumbled a reply and ended the call. Chris's email arrived, and I clicked it, revealing pages of documentation and pictures of the loan shark's operation.

"Hawk?"

The tension in her voice pulled me from what I'd been doing. She came up behind me and then pointed to the screen where the men were systematically trashing her place.

"They're in my place—again? Now, they're destroying my stuff." An edge of hysteria had crept into her strained voice.

I whirled around and stood tall, effectively blocking the screen from her view. I steadied her with my hands on her shoulders. Large blue eyes swimming in tears met mine. "But you're safe. It's just stuff. You got out what was important to you."

"I know, but…" A tremor ran through her body. "Nothing like this has ever happened before. I mean, why would they go after me?"

They want the treasure. "We'll figure it out. I promise." I slipped an arm around her shoulder and led her over to the couch. Sitting next to her, I flipped on the TV and surfed the channels until I found a show I knew the other guys' wives liked.

Lightning pierced the sky, and thunder crashed seconds later. The storm had rolled in fast. Hopefully, the heavy rain and winds would slow down the men after Red. I clicked on a weather app on my phone to see what we were in for. The live radar showed a red cell above us, moving quickly.

Stella settled next to me, pressed up against my side. I liked it. I wanted to offer her comfort. For once, I didn't mind someone in my space, leaning on me. Her vanilla-and-cinnamon scent teased the air, relaxing me.

The guys were a part of my world, and I would always be grateful—they were family, more than blood had ever been or shown me. Still, I kept to myself, and they'd always understood. With Stella, part of me didn't want to. I didn't want to let her go, even after the problem she and her brother were in was sorted. I was in uncharted territory.

With her leg against mine, I reopened the email on my phone. Chris had included details about Max, Stella's brother, and all the connections he'd been associated with—Tridel, the loan-shark organization he owed money to.

I'd heard the name before. Where and in relation to whom, I couldn't remember. It was on the cusp of a memory just out of reach. It would come. Part of me worried about what would follow when it did.

CHAPTER 10

HAWK

'd left Stella sleeping in our hotel room with a note on the counter, telling her where I would be in case she awoke before I returned. I worried, knowing the panic she could experience if she woke up alone in the room, especially given all the stuff she was trying to deal with. Not wanting to be gone long, I did a perimeter check. There hadn't been signs of anything to be concerned about. With care, I closed the stairwell door and turned to go to our room. The door opened, and Stella rushed out with coffee in hand.

"Oh." She halted, extending her arm with the drink. "I was bringing you coffee."

I took it from her and followed her inside. The warmth of the mug seeped into my chilled hand. The perfume of her hair trailed behind her. She smelled so good, and everything about her looked soft and inviting. I wanted to draw her close and breathe in her scent, but I couldn't. My feelings for her wouldn't help us stay focused on her problems.

"Thanks for the note."

I nodded, but my thoughts returned to what we would need at some point, backup. We didn't need it yet, but I had no doubt the men after her brother would come for us. My team had been at our apartment late last night, taking anything—all personal effects that would trace back to us—out. There had been some pictures and fingerprints, of course.

It wouldn't have been a lot, but Keegan didn't take any chances, and he had wiped the place clean. Not only that, but they would remain there for a day to see if anything happened to her apartment. An interrogation could go a long way.

Too bad the guys after Stella had trashed her place before my team had arrived.

She curled up on the couch, tucking her legs under her. "Since we've moved to another hotel, they'll lose interest soon and leave me alone, right? I mean"—she spread her hands out before her—"what could they possibly get from coming after me? I don't have anything of value."

But she did—her life.

I leaned against the kitchen peninsula in our suite. "They won't give up. It's not their way." The fragile hope that'd danced across her features crumbled with the slump of her shoulders. "I'm sorry, Stella. They would find a way to use you to get to your brother. Not only that, I'm pretty sure they're pursuing you so hard after learning about the treasure your grandmother left you."

"But she didn't leave me anything… Nothing of monetary value, anyway."

I hated doing this to her, but we needed to be fully prepared. If she didn't know the level of danger coming at her, she could make a mistake and put herself in danger without even knowing she had, such as when she accepted the call from Max. I was starting to hate her brother. "You said yourself that your brother didn't believe that. If he thought you might have something that could save him, it's possible he told the people after him to try to get them off his back and maybe buy some time." *So they wouldn't break or kill him.*

Her brows furrowed over those gorgeous eyes, amazingly blue with splashes of green. "Max wouldn't tell them about me. He may be difficult, but he's my brother, and I know he loves me. If he told them, it would put me in danger, and that's not something he would risk."

I wasn't so sure about that. The way he'd argued with her about money and how she'd said he'd already taken anything of value told me something very different.

She held up her hand to stop me from saying anything. "He used to take care of me. When I got teased in school, he would always defend me. It's not easy having red hair as a kid. And dating? Don't even get me started on how protective he was. That's my brother. He wouldn't throw me under the bus."

Maybe, but that was then. The man he had become was a different story. "From the little I know about your brother, it's obvious he has a problem. Not only that, but he's in a bad situation and desperate. While I'm sure he loves you and *wants* to protect you, he could've been in a tight spot. Your name might have slipped out in connection with whatever treasure he thinks you have."

"Maybe."

The pain in her voice had me crossing the room to sit next to her. "We'll figure this out." She pressed against my side, and I lifted my arm around her shoulder, pulling her close.

Stella leaned against me, seeking comfort. My heart rate picked up, and I struggled to keep my hands still. Everything about her drew me in and made me want things I never thought I deserved or could have. To prolong our contact, I asked her to tell me more about her life growing up with her brother.

Her hand settled on my thigh, and little electric zings shot from her touch. I played with the ends of her hair, unable to not touch her. I wanted to kiss her.

She hadn't given me a sign she was interested in me, so I couldn't touch her as I wanted. I would have been taking advantage of her. I shifted in my seat, and she cuddled even closer.

I needed to think of bullet wounds, doctor visits, football… Anything to take my mind off how amazing she felt pressed against me.

"Max was… Max." She gave a breathy laugh. "I never liked his friends, but mine sure did. He's two years older and hung with a crowd my friends were drawn to. You know, those boys who were always getting into trouble. The complete opposite of what we girls were."

I couldn't keep the smile from my mouth if I tried. *I bet she was cute when she was younger. Now, she's stunning.* "I can just picture you with braids and hanging out at your friends', studying."

She snorted a laugh. "I get the Pippi Longstocking image you're going for. Don't think you're the first one to use it. There's a reason I don't have long hair."

I tugged at one of her loose curls, which brushed her shoulders. "I like your hair."

She shrugged against me. "Thanks. I do now, but I didn't when I was growing up. As for the image you're visualizing, you're not far from the truth. I tried to stay out of trouble because Max was always in it, and I saw the hurt he caused to my parents and grandparents. Plus, I was way better than him with hiding when I'd done something wrong."

"Your grandparents lived with your family?" *What would it have been like to have had grandparents who may have cared and could have saved me?*

"They did. I never really thought much of it until my parents died. After that, my grandparents filled their roles. My brother took advantage. He acted out, easily influenced by others. And his friends were not the good sort."

"I know the kind." Dangerous kids were all we dealt with when we were growing up and trying to survive.

"Hm. Well, I didn't like the stress it caused my grandparents. He would get in trouble at school for smoking, ditching, or fighting. It only got worse after my grandfather passed away

Max's freshman year in college. That's when he got involved in gambling and heavier drugs."

"And your grandmother? How did she handle him?"

"She didn't. At that point, there was no way to manage him, and he moved out after he'd stolen my parents' china and sold it. My Oma hid what she valued most. I hated what he'd done to her."

"He still came around?"

"Yeah. She's old school in that way, and it's rubbed off. She used to tell me that no matter what, Max was family, blood. And we couldn't turn our back on him, but we could prevent him from pulling us down along with him." She toyed with a thread that'd come loose on the hem of my shirt. "She lost her brother when they were young. Family values were very important to her, and she instilled them in us as well."

"Or just in you? Your brother didn't understand what he had."

"I hear what you're saying, but that's where you're wrong. Max screwed up often, but he loved us and tried to keep us from any repercussions from his mistakes. He did things to help around the house, making sure everything was working and that any chores our grandmother had were done."

So on the surface, he took care of them, but if he needed something, their well-being was fair game. In regard to her brother, I suspected she wore blinders, at least partial ones. He was trouble and would bring her down whether he meant to or not.

I wouldn't let that happen.

Being in the same room with her was difficult. I wasn't sure how much longer I could hold out from touching her. Kissing her. I had no idea what she wanted, and with the shit storm that would happen, it wasn't fair for me to complicate things, so I had to put some space between us.

I left Stella in our room so I could do some surveillance. The peacefulness of being alone on the roof washed over me, transporting me to another time. I valued being invisible for entirely different reasons.

The wind raced, and menacing clouds rolled overhead. I made another pass around the roof's perimeter, determining nothing suspicious was nearby. At least not yet.

I wiped the beautiful marble counter after Hawk and I'd finished the deli sandwiches he'd run out for. Life in a hotel was different. As luxurious as the place was, I wasn't used to it. A wave of tiredness swept over me, a result of my full stomach. With all the recent events, I hadn't been eating much. He'd noticed. Those intense eyes of his had stayed on me while we ate our food until I finished the last bite of my BLT.

Something else sizzled in those sexy blue eyes, and it looked a lot like desire. I wished it had been. He'd taken the couch last night outside of the room I'd slept in. Lying beside me would have been so much better.

He stood beside me as I cleaned the table, and I touched his forearm, bringing his attention to me. There was something I wanted to do, and I was going for it if there was any excuse to touch him. That man packed a serious punch.

"Hawk, I want to see if there's anything to what my grandmother told me, if there is jewelry or money that she hid. Maybe it could help."

"Help your brother with the trouble he's in?"

I moved around the counter and sat across from him in the

sage-colored armchair. The room was gorgeous, but the colors weren't really to my liking, decorated in greens and cream. They'd tried some strange modern twist.

"Yes. Max told me he'd asked our grandfather about our grandmother's claim to hidden treasure. He wouldn't tell him anything."

"You know it isn't a good idea to give the people after him anything."

"I have to try. Will you help me with this?"

"Yes, but you can't give what you find to those types of people, to loan sharks. We'll deal with them another way."

We'll see about that. I pursed my lips. I could elicit his aid, and once I found what Oma had been talking about, I would use the heirlooms or whatever to save my brother. I would never forgive myself if something happened to Max. Decision made, I went and got the hairbrush and jewelry box. I had to trust Hawk, and it was time. I placed the jewelry box on the table between us but kept the brush in my hand.

I gestured for him to check out the small box. As he picked it up, turned it from side to side, then opened it, I worried the rubber grip at the end of my brush.

"From your grandmother?"

"Yes, it was hers when she was a little girl. My mom used it when she was young too." I cleared my throat from the emotion that clogged it. "Oma and my mom gave it to me when I was seven. That's when Oma's parents had given it to her."

He placed it back on the table, and I took a deep breath before handing him the letter. "My grandmother wrote this before she passed away."

As he opened the letter and read what she had written, the words played through my head, as they had so many times.

My Dear Stella,

This jewelry box is one of the happy memories I carry with me from my childhood home, where a slice of my heart will always remain. When I gave the box to you, I felt as if my mother was standing over my shoulder. It was a good day.

I'm so proud of you. We all are. You've grown into a beautiful woman. You too have another part of my heart.

Love always,

Your Oma

"She was always doing that, saying there were shattered pieces of her heart. I often wondered if she had any left for herself."

"It's nice that you have this to remember her by. I'm sorry, Stella, but I don't know if this is worth what you're hoping, and I don't think you should part with it."

"No. I won't sell it, but I can't help but wonder what she meant. She was always going on and on about our family heir-looms and how they were safe with the one who kept her love safe."

"So her child or her husband?"

"That's what I would have thought too, but my mom didn't know what Oma was talking about, and Grandpa was alive when she'd first told me. I asked, and he said he didn't have anything."

"I have something else from her, but I don't think that's it, either." I rolled back the rubber to reveal the false bottom of the brush. With a few turns, I had the end of it off and tugged on the ribbon inside. The wrapped cloth came out, and I unrolled it for Hawk on the table. "This is her locket."

"Nice hiding place." He grinned before carefully lifting the delicate locket.

I shrugged because there wasn't anything to say. He knew why I hid it. He'd heard the crashes and the fights when he'd lived next door to me.

"Do you mind?" he asked as he swapped the necklace for the jewelry box.

"No, of course not. I can't figure out what she meant or if

there are any other clues. That's why I wanted to share all this with you."

Hawk turned the small box over in his hands again. His fingers traced the edges until he finally opened the lid and did the same to the inside.

"Is the interior new?"

"What?" I leaned over to see why he'd think that. "Why would it be?"

He pointed to a strand sticking out from the seam in the back. "It doesn't look as aged as the rest of the box, and with the loose thread, I thought it could be."

"Oh, I don't know." Excitement pinged around in my stomach.

"Do you mind if I see?"

He met my gaze, and I grinned. "Not at all. Go ahead."

When he grasped the thread at the base of the box and gave a gentle tug, I leaned forward. *Could I have missed something so obvious?*

It unraveled with ease, and he pulled at the silk. With a soft whoosh, he separated and lifted the bottom piece out. It was a false bottom. The same silk fabric as the sides peeked from beneath a piece of folded paper. Our gazes collided as he handed the box back to me.

"Looks like another letter."

My hands shook as I opened the letter addressed to me.

My Darling Stella,

Today tested our patience and strength when your brother came home with alcohol on his breath and a bruise forming along his jaw. There is a part inside of Max that festers. He rebels against some-thing I'm not entirely sure of. I don't even know if he is aware of what drives him to do what he does.

I see a lot of my brother in Max. Their resemblance is uncanny. Stefan also had the same shade of blond hair, light eyes, tall and lanky build, and the heart of a poet. While Stefan embraced that side of himself, Max denies it and instead turns to destruction. Stefan channeled his pain and anger against an entity that needed opposing, maybe not by teenagers, but by many in a combined effort and force.

Creativity should not be denied. If it is, the soul suffers.

The family heirlooms I've told you about are for you to find. Follow the clues I've left for you, and when you locate them, use the legacy I've hidden behind however you see fit.

We were fortunate to escape with the few possessions from our past we could smuggle out. My mother hid the heirlooms within two of my dolls, then inside a small chest. You may remember the dolls. They sit empty atop my dresser as I write to you.

Know that I accept your decision surrounding the window to my past. You'll discover a part of our history, one we kept hidden for many years, someday. With the destructive path your brother is on, that day is not today.

I wish Stefan was alive to guide Max, to lift him up and show him we accept and love him, no matter what. Our job is to love Max, Stella, even though he will test your patience over the years.

Have faith, my dear child. There will be a day your brother will return to us.

Look to the locket, which holds pictures of your grandfather and me, and remember, not everything is visible from the surface.

All my love,

Oma

In the large bathroom with the spa-like rainwater shower and gorgeous travertine tile, I bent over the sink and splashed my tearstained face. The fluffy towel in my hand was soft as I dabbed the excess drops away, being extra careful around my already puffy eyes. God, I missed Oma.

There had to be a clue in the letter. *Why else would she have hidden it beneath the satin bottom of the jewelry box? What does it mean?* I'd looked at the locket every which way but couldn't find anything new. It was the same as always, an antique locket with two pictures inside, one of Oma and Opa when they were first married—they looked so in love—and one of my mom when she was a baby. She was so tiny and wore a cute little bonnet.

We'd taken the pictures out, but there was nothing behind them. That made the most sense with the last line in her letter. *What else could it have meant?*

Hawk had given me time to read the letter and deal with my emotions. He'd gone back to the roof, making me promise not to open the door for anyone, but no one would come. I hadn't told my brother where we were after I'd hung up with him the day before. I couldn't help it. I had to call to hear his voice, to make sure he was okay.

Especially after that letter from Oma.

Once I was sure Max was fine, I ripped into him, demanding to know how he could have told the people he was involved with about me. It was one of the most difficult conversations I'd had with him, aside from a few back in college where I had to hang up the phone because he was just too drunk to communicate. But it was college, and a lot of people indulged. Even I had a few legendary hangovers.

I couldn't make excuses for him any longer. I had stopped a long time ago. That didn't change the fact I would do anything in my power to protect him.

Dropping the towel on the counter, I wandered back to the main room of our suite. It was a lovely hotel, and I wished I could enjoy it instead of coping with the claustrophobic sensation of being trapped.

The sound of a cell phone ringing startled me. It took a minute to realize it was coming from my purse. *Oh no.* I'd forgotten to power it down and put it in that pocket thing Hawk had given me. I was just so worried about Max that I kept checking to see if he'd called. *How could I have done that?* Last time, we had to change hotels because Hawk thought we were compromised. I swiped a tired hand over my forehead then grabbed my phone.

After I peeked at the caller ID, my pulse went into overdrive. It was Max.

"Are you all right?"

"Of course I'm not all right," he whisper-shouted.

"Why are you trying to be quiet? Where are you?" An acute uneasiness skated across my suddenly chilled flesh.

"I need the ring. It was a mistake."

"What are you talking about?" *Is he drunk?* "The ring you gave me because it reminded you of family?" *Dammit, Max.* It was just like him to make a sweet gesture as he had and then take it away as if it had meant nothing. My hands started to shake from both anger and pain. *I'm trying, Oma, but he makes it so hard.*

A muffled sound came from his end, and the silence between us stretched. Minutes ticked by, but I couldn't bring myself to hang up. When the receiver cleared once more, I heard the clink of glasses. "Are you at a bar?"

"Stel," he slurred. "I gotta go. I'll grab the ring when I see you."

"Wait—"

The silence from the call disconnecting jolted me. *He doesn't know where I am. How will he find me?*

A door shut, and I gasped as I turned around with my phone raised like a weapon. "Oh, you scared me." I sagged against the couch, my back to the window, as Hawk walked into our suite.

He stopped, and the air crackled with expectant tension. "You were on the phone?"

"Yeah." I tilted my head, confused by the alarm that had momentarily crossed his features. Max had his phone, so no one would track us. We were still safe.

"With Max?"

I nodded. "Yes."

"Did you tell him where you're staying?"

I shook my head no. "But he said he needed the ring he gave me."

"What ring?"

"This one." I pulled the long necklace free from beneath my shirt. I'd kept it hidden away as we were running around, and I'd almost lost it once when the chain caught. The ring, a pretty little piece of jewelry, dangled between us. It was delicate and unique, even though it wasn't particularly expensive. "I don't know why. It's not worth anything."

Hawk frowned. "That looks familiar."

"Oh. Well, the etching is an infinity symbol, and the flowers that are between each sideways figure eight are edelweiss. Maybe you've seen the design somewhere before?"

He grunted a noncommittal response, and I rolled my eyes. "What I thought was odd was he gave it to me as a symbol to remind me that he loves me. So why does he want it back?"

My heart sank at the thought of wearing a ring my brother probably took. I would have wanted it back if it were mine, especially since the edelweiss flowers and the meaning behind them reminded me of Oma and Opa.

I met Hawk's gaze and caught the flash of alarm as he came to the same conclusion as me. "Maybe he stole it, and the owner knows?"

Glass shattered in a violent burst of deadly shards. My body tensed as Hawk lunged for me. *On no!*

CHAPTER 13

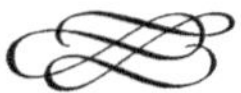

HAWK

*F*uck, *they found us*. A bullet had pierced the window of our hotel room.

I pushed off with my toes and lunged for Stella. In a blur of red curls, I tackled her to the ground. I wrapped my arms around her and twisted to the side to take the brunt of the fall.

On the floor, I lifted off her body, quickly scanning for signs of injury. A few minor cuts from the glass trickled blood down her neck and cheek. "Are you hurt?"

The wide, blue-eyed stare that greeted me offered nothing. Another visual scan revealed no punctures with blood blooming around them. "Stay down," I ordered.

Had to be the call to her brother.

I'd had no idea she'd removed it from the pouch. I should've conveyed the seriousness to her better or taken the damn phone away. I got that she was worried, but our situation proved how dangerous the people after her and her brother were.

My hand curled in a comforting grip around my sniper rifle, which I'd left on the coffee table. I hadn't disassembled it, and for that I was thankful. They knew what room we were in and could have seen us from the roof or a room in the hotel across the street from us.

With care, I moved around the room until I was on the side of the window that had a hole through it. Through a sliver between the wall and the curtain, I fit the rifle to my body and peered through the scope. Across from us, the four-story building mirrored the style of the one we were in, with its quaint charm and windows that opened. Some even had small balconies.

I scanned for an open window. *Found it.* One window was cracked, and a shadow formed in the room. Large men crossed the street and entered our building. There was no mistaking who they were. We were surrounded. I counted eight of them. The odds weren't that bad. I could easily take out two of them, but escape would be a better option. We needed more information about the company that was after Stella. Their actions didn't make sense. *Why would they risk shooting at her?*

I had to be the one they were shooting at. That, I could deal with.

I glanced at Stella. She had recovered enough. The glaze of terror was gone, and in its place was raw fear. I needed to give her something to do—that would help her pull out of her shock.

"Stay low and grab our stuff."

She rolled to her hands and knees and crawled into the bedroom. Our bags had remained packed in case we had to make a quick exit, unless she'd left something out. "Get the box, the necklace, the letters."

"Already packed," she whisper-yelled. Her face was pale.

I pulled my cell from my pocket and shot off a text to Jack with the number of people converging on us. They were close, and us sitting there wasn't smart. We had to get out, preferably without killing anyone.

I'd texted Jack the day before, after Stella had read her grandmother's letter. We agreed on where to go next. They would go ahead of us to the cabins on the lake. I sensed she needed time, not a group of guys packed into a car with her, when she was missing family.

In my head, I kept track of how much time we likely had until they arrived at our door. Not that it mattered. *We'll get away. I can handle this.*

Two duffel bags slid out from Stella's room before she crawled into mine. I only had a backpack with a few things and my rifle case, which fit into the pack. Once out of the room, Stella flattened herself to the wall next to me.

I could tell her heart was racing by the pulse hammering at her neck and her quick, shallow breaths. Dammit, I didn't want to have to leave our position, but it was the best way at the moment. I shifted so I sat next to her. I took my backpack, broke down my rifle, put it away, and exchanged my favorite gun for a 9mm.

She had too much stuff. I should never have let her bring it all, but I'd given in to the alarmed look she'd given me when I said to pack anything of value. The jewelry supplies added weight, but it was manageable enough. "Are your Oma's things in here?" I asked as I slid one of the duffels closer.

"Yes, in that one." A shaky finger pointed to the one farthest from us. Careful to keep my head away from the windowsill's sightline, I pulled the other bag over and put them on so the straps crisscrossed my chest. It was awkward, but we would be all right. "You'll have to carry my pack." It was lighter than the two duffels and wouldn't inhibit her movement.

She put the pack back on, and I tightened the straps so it was secure and fit to her body. Framing her face with my hands, I leaned close. "We're going to be okay." My thumb rubbed the softness of her cheek, easing a tiny bit of the stiffness in her posture. "Trust me?"

Steel infused her panic-filled eyes. "Yes."

"Good." I reluctantly dropped my hands. "We're going out

the door. There will be someone there. Stay behind me until I clear the hallway but be aware." I crawled under the windows, pulling the room-darkening drapes as I went. It wouldn't stop them from shooting, but it would give us a fighting chance, as the door was across from where they were firing.

A barrage of gunfire shot through the curtains, distributing random holes of pale light in the fabric. With a finger to my lips, I turned to her. *They're coming now. After, we will escape.*

When the shooting stopped, we moved to the wall closest to the door. I needed to be next to the frame to strike hard and fast.

Silence was thick as the dust settled. We waited. My pulse increased in tempo.

Bullets were fired in the hallway at our door's locking mechanism. Then a loud thud sounded as they kicked in the door. I didn't hesitate. At first sight, I cracked the butt of my gun against his temple. *First guy down.*

The second came in shooting. The burn of a bullet whizzed by my earlobe. No sounds came from behind me. Stella was a smaller target and pressed against the wall. I thought she was okay.

My hand thrust out, and I connected with the guy's wrist, throwing his aim off balance. I threw an elbow to the side of his head then a hard shot to his jaw, between his ear and chin. He dropped.

There would be more. We needed to move. I took Stella's hand and helped her to step over the unconscious men. The bags settled against my body, pulling at my shoulders. I ignored them. We'd carried heavier and more awkward packs and equipment when we were in the military. Our SEALs division got the job done every single time. *This will be no different.*

Stella made a choking sound as we rounded the first body, whose blood pooled in a slow leak from his temple to the floor beneath him. "They're alive." Well, I knew one was. I wasn't positive about the other. "Don't look. Eyes forward."

She slipped her finger through the belt loop of my jeans as I took a glance past our door. *Clear. For now.* Her body crowded mine as much as she was able with the bags. We left the room and hurried to the stairwell. "Keep a lookout behind us."

I felt her shift. Her finger tugged at my jeans as she tried to inch closer. Through a small crack in the stairwell door, I checked for movement. When none came, I pulled the door wider. The immediate area was clear. We entered with a quiet click of the heavy steel door behind us. I leaned over the rail enough to look for men and guns.

They weren't in the building yet, but I had no doubt more would be. If not, they would be waiting for us on the street. Two were in the building across from us, one in the room and one on the roof. Two had been at our door. Four were unaccounted for.

We traveled down the poorly lit stairwell as fast as was safe. What waited for us in the lobby would be at least four more guys, from what I'd seen earlier. If not inside, they would be near the doorway. We needed to leave through the back. It was undoubtedly guarded, but given the force in the front of the hotel and across the street, I figured the back wouldn't be as difficult to maneuver.

We left the stairwell without a problem and weaved through the halls to the back of the building where the service entrance was. I'd checked the layout on the map on the back of the door when we'd first arrived at our room.

With caution, I cracked the heavy steel door. No gunshots sounded, so I eased it further open. A bullet ricocheted off the door. Stella cried out. *Fuck.*

I leaned out with my gun raised and fired. It had come from up high. There had to be a sniper. A shadow hovered by a ventilation shaft on top of a roof kitty-corner to where we were. *Got you, motherfucker.* I squeezed off several rounds until he slumped forward.

The trill of sirens sounded in the distance. They were

closing in fast. We had to go.

I flicked my gaze over her. "You okay?" Blood trickled along her arm, staining her light-gray Henley. It didn't look bad. At her nod, I popped the clip and shoved another one home. She would be okay—she had to be. I told myself that to keep the fuck calm.

We burst from the doorway and raced along the alley. I'd parked a block away from the last hotel, hoping the car would blend in. We headed there now.

Keeping to the shadows from the setting sun, we went from building to building until we neared the SUV. Even in the dim light, her hair was a beacon. We made it to the car, and I hit the unlock button on the key fob. All our vehicles had been modified so there would be no sound when locked or unlocked. There were too many situations we knew we would inevitably run into, especially given our backgrounds and line of work.

I helped Stella in, threw the duffels in the back seat, then rounded to my side, gun at the ready. Once inside, I grabbed my pack and yanked out a T-shirt and hat. "Turn toward me." When she did, I tied the shirt around the wound on her arm then put the hat on her head, tucking her hair in as best as I could. It would have to do.

The engine turned over. I took a moment and cupped her cheek. She leaned into my hand and kissed my palm. My heart pounded. *Maybe she does want more? Or maybe she needs comfort.*

I pulled onto the street, heading away from the hotel. We steered clear of most of the guys waiting for us, but something nagged in the back of my mind. I thought I'd recognized one of them. The shape of him, the hulking muscles that were more stacked than lean, and the trail of cigarette smoke as he'd leaned against the building across the street just before he joined the rest as they closed in on the front of the hotel.

We had a few hours until we arrived at our destination. As the miles flew by, the uneasy feeling that I knew him from somewhere stayed with me.

CHAPTER 14

HAWK

*D*arkness blanketed the seven log cabin houses spaced along the edge of a lake. I pulled into the driveway of the middle one on the east side. Large pine trees offered coverage. The lake was seated beneath one of Kirkwood's majestic mountains, which provided additional security.

I parked in the gravel driveway, grabbed the bags, then helped Stella down. All the lights were out in the cabin we were heading into. The guys and I knew the owners. The place was extremely secure. Cameras littered the area. Nothing happened there without our former SEALs commander knowing about it.

We walked up to the cottage, and I felt under the windowsill for the small depression that hid the key. Cool metal met my fingertips, and I coaxed the key from its clever hiding place.

After unlocking the door, I flicked on the light and ushered Stella inside. I shut the door and locked it then took off the bags and put them down. We had to take care of her wound right away. I didn't think it was terrible, but infection could set in, and I wanted to see if it required stitches.

I grasped her hand and tugged her along behind me. "We need to get you cleaned up."

"I'm okay. I don't think it's all that bad."

I spun her around to face me and took in how pale she was. Even if it was a scratch, what had happened shook her up. With care, I lifted her and set her on the bathroom counter to get a better view of her arm. From under the counter, I pulled out the first-aid kit we kept beneath the sink.

"How did you know that was there?"

I met her gaze, weighing what to tell her. I'd taken her to the cabin when I should have taken her elsewhere. We could have flown to Maine. In the cabin, it was just the two of us, alone. I wanted it that way.

When Jack and I had talked, I told him it was best to stay off the radar and beyond prying eyes, so we could figure out what we were going to do next. Even though I wanted to, I couldn't divulge secrets to Red that involved the team, not regarding our safe house or who owned the property. That information was only for family, something she wasn't. The organization her brother was mixed up with made her knowledge of anything pertinent dangerous.

She'd asked how I knew about the place. I couldn't tell her. She wouldn't know where we were. There were no addresses on the cabins, and we were far from the road. "Lucky guess."

She pursed her lips. "You expect me to believe that after you found a hidden key under the window ledge? Is this your place?"

"No." I grabbed the seam at the top of her sleeve and, with care, tore it off. "Let's clean up your injury." The material of her shirt stuck to her wound, and she flinched. Blood welled in the reopened gash. It couldn't be helped. I had to get the shirt off her.

I clenched my teeth. *Shouldn't have brought her here.* Panic bubbled in the pit of my stomach, and I grimaced.

"Hey." Stella brushed my hands away before she cupped

the side of my face. Her thumb traced over my cheekbone. "Why are you pulling away from me?"

God, I loved her touch. She was trying to look inside me, figure me out. I could tell because it was something I tried to do to her more and more. "I'm right here."

"Well, yeah but I'm not talking about physically." She laughed quietly. "Mentally, it's like you're a million miles away. What's wrong?"

My hand closed around hers, and I moved both down to her thigh. I couldn't think when she touched me. It was foreign and sent me into an avalanche of conflicting feelings. I'd admitted to myself that I liked her, but it couldn't go past that. I knew she would realize that I wasn't worth loving or even knowing. Her eyes sparkled with concern and with what I thought was trust. I didn't want to see it extinguished. I wasn't sure I would survive that.

"I'm sorry," she said. "I should never have dragged you into this. The last thing I want is for you to get hurt when this is my problem."

"No. It's not yours. It's your brother's."

She shook her head, and I was momentarily distracted by the need to run my hand through her soft curls. "That's where you're wrong. My brother is my responsibility. He's family. I'd do anything for him, even if it means I'm in danger. Saving him is the same as saving myself."

I frowned as I studied the steely conviction in her eyes and the determined set to her shoulders. She meant it. A part of me understood, as that was how it was between my brothers and me. They weren't blood, but sometimes that was better, at least it had been for most of us. Trev and Chris were the exceptions. They were related, but their parents had been horrible too. *What would it be like to have her feel that way about me? Love me no matter what?*

I wanted that, but to wish for it was foolish. I broke from her gaze and focused on the task at hand, her injury.

Blood seeped in a trickle from where I'd removed the hastily tied t-shirt I'd wrapped around her to slow the bleeding. It was only a flesh wound, but it had to be cleaned and dressed. "This'll sting." I held her arm out and poured antiseptic over the injury. Her quick intake of breath was the only indication that it was uncomfortable. After I patted the area around the injury dry, I applied a heavy dose of antibiotic cream then bandaged it up.

"It's not bad. A scratch."

She flashed me a shaky smile through misty eyes. "No stitches needed?"

"No. It'll be sore for a few days, but it should heal with a minimal scar." My gaze dropped, and I busied myself with cleaning up the garbage and throwing the bloody shirt into the trash until her hands cupped my face and she forced me to meet her gaze.

"Thank you."

Her lips brushed over mine, and desire exploded in my gut from the contact. One hand threaded through her hair, cradling her head, while my other wrapped around her waist and pulled her close.

She melted against me and breathed a small moan into my mouth as I coaxed her lips open. Only a tiny ounce of restraint leashed me from crushing her lips to mine. But it couldn't go further. Even so, I couldn't help stealing that small moment of heaven. She was so soft and sweet.

I slid my tongue along hers, deepening the kiss and losing myself for a few moments in her warmth. Her arms wound around my neck, and I shivered until she flinched. *Shit. Her injury.* I pulled back and gently disengaged her arms from around me, careful not to hurt her more. I wanted to apologize but couldn't get the words past my lips that still tasted of her.

Confusion spread across her expressive features, and I wanted to smooth the uncertainty away. She had offered a kiss as thanks, not for me to pounce on her. Tempering the urge to kiss her again, I helped her down from the counter. Then I led her toward the kitchen, which I knew would be fully stocked. "Come on. I'll show you around."

The place was small, but the amenities were top-of-the-line. The kitchen had granite counters and a large gas range, double ovens, and an oversized fridge.

"Wow. I never thought there would be a kitchen like this from the outside of the cabin."

That was the point. The cottages were supposed to appear rustic, bare bones. Inside needed to have enough beds to sleep a full team and feed them too. We tended to gather in one place for meals and briefings.

I indicated for her to take a seat, and I got to work rummaging through the fridge. God, I was hungry. "I can make a burger, or I think there's some sandwich meat in here if you'd rather have that."

Stella leaned back in her chair and watched me. "Burgers sound great."

I couldn't help it. I grinned back at her. It was annoying when a woman only wanted a salad, afraid to eat in front of others. She would fit right in with the rest of the women who'd become part of our growing family. *If only that were a possibility.*

I pulled out everything I needed to make the burgers, including bacon and cheese. I opened the cabinet that held the pots and pans and found the grill plate. Once that was heating up I dumped the ground beef in a bowl and mixed in an egg, seasoning, and a dash of cheddar.

Stella went to the fridge and grabbed a tomato and some lettuce. "You don't mind if I help, do you?"

"Not at all." I rather liked it. After I'd formed the patties and had them cooking on the grill plate, I got out two beers and handed one to her.

She leaned against the counter and took a long drink after plating the lettuce and sliced tomatoes. The cheese, buns, and dishes sat nearby. She'd even found a bag of chips.

My stomach growled again.

"So you know the owners of this place?"

"Don't read more into it than there is, Stella. It's just a place for us to regroup."

She pursed her plump lips, and I was momentarily distracted. Once the burgers were ready, I removed them from the heat and put them on the buns. We took our food to the table and added the burger fixings.

After she'd eaten half of hers, she set it down and nursed her beer. *Shit, here come the questions.* I didn't want to answer any. I didn't want her to get closer because it was never a good idea when it came to me. On the other hand, I didn't want her to be afraid, especially given what she'd already seen me do. There was no doubt she would need some reassurances where her safety was concerned.

"You told me you're a part of a security company or team? I can't remember exactly what you said. But what you did earlier, then this place… I'm impressed with your skills. Seriously, though, is there something I should know? You said you're not a cop, but are you FBI?"

That was funny, and I fought the grin. If she knew my family and me, she would know that wouldn't have been a route open to us. I finished off my last bite before answering her. "No. Not at all, I swear. I haven't been watching your brother and have no plans of turning him in."

"But—"

"I know where you're going with this, and I promise that's not what's going on. I am a part of a security team, but we mostly do rescues and recoveries. Helping you was just being in the right place at the right time."

"Oh, wow. Okay." Her face heated. Her expressive eyes darkened too.

In what? Awe? Desire? I wanted to know.

"I can accept what you're telling me, but you're doing an

awful lot for Max, who's a guy you don't even know, and me." Her eyes narrowed.

"What do you need to know to feel safe?"

White teeth flashed as she nibbled on her full bottom lip. "What do you intend to do with my brother when you find out exactly what he's done and who is after him? That *is* the plan, right?"

I rotated my beer a few times on the table, wondering how much to tell her. Deciding, I took the last pull from the bottle. "The men after your brother are organized. They're professionals to a degree. I don't know what your brother is involved in, but I have a bad feeling it's on a much larger scale than you're used to dealing with."

"I figured that after they tried to grab me when I left work and then went through my apartment. What am I going to do?"

"You'll stay with me, and I'll figure it out with my team. My goal is to keep you safe."

"I don't know why you're helping me, not really, but I'm grateful. But you do know that my job is also to save my brother."

I nodded even though I wasn't sure what to do about him. "No contacting him for now. I'll give you a burner phone that you can text him the number. It can't be traced. If he needs to reach you, he can do so that way."

Her shoulders drooped. "Right. Because they found us from my talking to him, didn't they?"

"If what you said is true about the family heirlooms, then you're valuable to your brother's connections. The potential for money or jewels changes things—it's beyond them using you to hurt Max."

"But that doesn't make sense. They were *shooting* at us."

"At me. If they'd been aiming at you, they would have hit you with that first shot. Your back was to the window. My guess is they were aiming for me, as the person who's helping you."

"I don't know how to process this. I've put you in danger." She pushed away from the table, stood, and started pacing. "If I hadn't involved you at all, then you wouldn't be in so much danger. They could have taken the jewelry box if it would help my brother."

"That wasn't what they were after though, was it?"

She stopped her restless movements and looked at me. "No."

"It doesn't matter if you find what your grandmother was talking about when you were a kid. It won't make everything go away. That's just how they work. Their harassment will only stop when they bleed you dry, and then only when you and your brother are dead." Max was an addict—drugs, gambling, or both. That's what they would use to continue to control and drain Max and Stella.

The fear swimming in her beautiful eyes was my undoing. As she shivered, I stood and pulled her close. When her arms wrapped around me, she clung to me, and I could almost feel the click in time when my fate was irrevocably sealed. I would help the woman even if it meant my death.

CHAPTER 15

HAWK

"Took you long enough." Jack's voice snapped through the line late the following day.

If I didn't know him so well, I would have thought he was an ass, but that was just him. He made snap decisions that often saved our lives. His rough exterior was that of a leader shouldering more than his burden. I owed Jack and Mike my life. I'd never forgotten what they'd done for me.

"It hasn't been that long," I defended.

"This is a vacation for him? Is that what he's telling you?" Mike yelled to be heard through Jack's phone. Mike didn't speak unnecessarily, and his words snapped my spine straight. I'd known him since I was a kid, lost and needing a place to live. He and Jack had saved me—they'd given me a roof over my head and a family that was stronger than any blood ties.

"Not a fucking vacation." I shoved away from the cabin's kitchen island to pace. Something was going down, and his accusation meant it had to be bigger than we'd thought. "What do you have so far? Tell me you've got something on those guys."

I could picture Jack running his hand through his short hair with each second that ticked by with no response. "It's not that we don't know anything. The problem is that we don't know enough, and without involving Rich…"

We don't need a CIA contact right now. "If we did involve Rich, that wouldn't be good for her brother. He'd be in more trouble than he is now." I grabbed the back of my neck with my free hand. Max was putting us in a bind.

"Exactly," Mike said. "I don't have a problem with that."

"I wouldn't either if it wasn't for Stella. She has strong family values."

Jack snorted. "Could they be misplaced?"

I leaned back against the counter and stared at the ceiling. The majority of my team came from hellish childhoods. Those experiences had taught us when we needed to cut our losses and run. It could have been that Red had never had to do that. "I don't know. I want to say screw him and let him hang. But I can't do that to her. She's adamant that she needs to protect Max."

"There's our answer, then."

"Is Chris there yet?"

"No. He'll be here today, though. When he gets here, we need to have a meeting, all of us. We have some news, but Mike and I want to go over it with you at the cabin."

Chills raced over my arms. That sounded ominous. I scrubbed my hand over my face. I would manage, like always. It would be interesting with Stella and the guys together. "Right. Let's deal with that after Chris gets here."

"Are you worried about the woman?"

The fear in her eyes ate at my soul, but her determination told me she could handle anything, especially a group like ours. At first, we might be overwhelming, but she would get over it. "I'm not concerned that she'll betray us. It's more that this is a lot for her to process."

"It was for Liv and Mari too."

"I wonder if it would help to have Liv, Mari, Hannah, or Jo talk to her."

"Who were you thinking? Jo might be hard to reach right now. The others should be available by Skype at least."

"There's this thing she's been talking about, and I think that's part of the reason the people after her brother are also targeting her. Seems he's told them about a treasure Stella knows how to find."

Jack snorted. "You mean like gold and shit? A pot at the end of the proverbial rainbow?"

It did sound pretty far-fetched. "No clue really, but I doubt it. Maybe family heirlooms or jewelry?"

"I know where you're going with this, and it's not happening or what she wants to happen, 'cause I know you wouldn't have driven on this side trip. This isn't the time to go on a treasure hunt then turn whatever we find over to the people her brother owes money to."

I couldn't stop the grin from spreading over my face. "It's like you know me."

"Damn straight, bro." Jack chuckled. "All right. We'll head over around dinner. You cooking?"

"Seems like it. No Liam, Connor, and Matt?"

"No. They're still tied up with another job. Trev too."

"Too bad about Trev. It would've been like the old gang on this one." There was comfort in familiarity.

"Get Hannah on the phone—or better yet, Skype. She can talk to Stella and make headway in a way we may not think of."

Jack was right. Hannah used to be a Russian sleeper agent, and she saw things we often didn't. "Good idea." When we hung up, I called Hannah and filled her in. She agreed and suggested Liv too, as she had a background in fine art, which might help her bond with the jewelry artist in Stella.

With Hannah and Liv helping, I had hope that we would

figure out the clues in the locket and the letter. Maybe we would even find the heirlooms Stella's Oma had talked about.

***

STELLA

I couldn't get that kiss out of my head. Hawk was on the phone while I found another shirt, one without blood. Again, my hand went to my swollen lips, and I admitted something that I'd known from the moment I laid eyes on him. I wanted him. There was something so enduring about Hawk. He held quiet reserve. He'd been so gentle with me, so protective. He'd dropped everything to help me.

I sensed a deep hurt that lived inside him. I recognized it because my brother harbored it too, albeit to a lesser degree.

But Hawk… He would be mine. I was tired of tiptoeing around the attraction that I suspected was as strong in him as it was in me. It was happening. As I made my decision, I swapped my shirt for a tighter one then applied a fresh coat of light-pink lipstick, just enough to add some color and hopefully draw his eyes to my lips again.

I would say I heard him approach, but that wasn't true. He moved like a freaking ghost, which was shocking for someone that tall and muscular. When he filled the doorway to the room where my stuff was, a slow smile spread across my face.

"I was just thinking of you." Heat crawled over my skin from my toes to my scalp in anticipation of what I wanted to do with him. I had to push through that shyness of his. Because honestly, I needed a break, a momentary relief from the constant worry and tension we were drowning in. And I'd been thinking of him since our first tentative "hi" in the hallway.

"You were?"

His gaze flitted from my eyes to my lips, and I knew he was thinking of the kiss we shared too. I moved a few steps closer and placed my hands on his biceps because why the hell not? They were incredible. His hands went to my hips, and he tugged me to him. I went willingly.

My lips parted when I saw the matching desire swirling in his eyes, dilating his pupils. He dipped his head slowly, giving me time to pull away. That wasn't happening, I wanted him badly.

When his lips brushed across mine, I melted. My arms wound around his neck as he took control of the kiss, coaxing my mouth open. The bite of his fingers urged my hips even closer. I moaned into his mouth as one of his hands slid up my back to bury his fingers at my nape. The gentle pull on my hair sent sparks of need from the roots all the way to my toes.

With subtle movements, he commanded my body. With another light tug of my hair, my neck was exposed. Then he left a trail of kisses until he nipped at the sensitive spot at the crook of my neck, and I shuddered.

I wanted more, and I whimpered, squirming against him. Slowly, he peeled my shirt off. His mouth followed each inch of skin revealed, and light burst behind my eyelids at his touch. My breath was coming faster, and my pulse pounded. The feel of his lips on my skin was driving me crazy. I needed more. I needed him.

I gripped his shoulders, his muscles rippling beneath my fingers. God, he was a work of art. I had to see him. I urged him to help me with his shirt. He grasped the back and pulled it over his head in a very sexy way. *Holy hell.* I'd known he was lean and ripped, but I had no idea. I feasted on him with sight alone. I salivated, wanting to lick him everywhere.

He was so tall, so intimidating in such a delicious way.

The button on my jeans was suddenly undone. *How did that happen?* Then he slowly pushed the denim down my legs. The next second, his chest pressed against mine and I squirmed, reveling in his hardness. My fingers automatically traced each groove and dip, my lips and tongue following. A jolt of power shot through me at his intake of breath. *I could do this all day long.*

"You're good with this, Red?"

Damn straight I am. "I want you," I said breathily. Talking was so overrated.

A wicked grin curved his sexy mouth. Apparently, that's all the confirmation he needed, and his hands traced the underside of my breasts.

"I've wanted you since I first saw you," he almost growled, "when you were bent over in front of the mailboxes to pick up a letter you'd dropped. I wanted to take you right there. When you stood and looked at me over your shoulder, I had to fight not to touch you." His teeth sank into the sensitive flesh at the base of my neck, and I cried out, heat rushing through my body. I clenched my thighs together, my core a tight ball of need. I wouldn't survive him. He was both tender and wild. I craved both.

"I remember." I moaned as his mouth traveled down between the valley of my breasts, his hands cupping and kneading. "I called you 'hot neighbor' for the longest time."

He snorted against my burning skin, his body shaking with laughter. "Damn, Red. That would have told me so much. You should have said it. I would have taken you hard and fast against the mailboxes."

Fabric tore as he whisked my panties off. His body was pressed tightly against mine. Nothing was between us anymore. My hands moved restlessly over him. I reached for his hard length that was bruising my thigh. I wanted to stroke him, take him in my mouth, and watch him lose control just as he was causing me to do.

Somehow, he moved us to the bed. I was losing track of my surroundings. He was becoming my world, the air I needed to breathe. Electric pings sizzled along my skin every time he touched me. I'd never felt anything like that strong and all-consuming connection.

I shifted so I could touch him, and my fingers skimmed along the side of his cock. His head whipped up, desire burning in his cobalt eyes. I sucked my lower lip between my teeth as my fingers curled around his thickness. Holy hell, he was long and large.

With a slow shake of his head, he grabbed my wrist and removed my greedy hand. I growled at him, and he laughed, easing some of the tension that had pulled his features tight.

"Later." His mouth descended on mine, and I lost time in the way his tongue explored my mouth. When he drew back, the glint in his eyes should have warned me. He flipped me over and lifted my hips. Ass in the air, he spread me wide. Vulnerable. A half groan, half growl sounded behind me. I shivered in anticipation.

With one hand on my hip, holding me in place, his other slid down my spine to rest on my lower back, applying a small amount of pressure until I arched more. My body quivered with need. He shifted, and the loss of his heat against my skin raised goosebumps along my body.

I almost fell in a heap when his tongue caressed me, his teeth nipping gently at my nub. *Oh, God. His mouth is magic.* The more he feasted, the wetter I got. Panting, I could feel myself plump beneath his lips, and then his tongue vied with his fingers as they plunged into me.

"Please." I peered around my shoulder at him and begged. He teased then slowed his touch, making me crazy. "So close."

He looked up, withholding that talented tongue of his. "Please what, Red?"

Impatience warred with desire as I lifted my head again and glared at him. The sight of him almost sent me over the edge alone—his lips were full and slick from tasting me, and his blue eyes smoldered against his tan skin. His size made me feel small and delicate. Broad shoulders, muscles bunching. So fucking sexy. "Make me come, Hawk." My voice was lower, hoarse, and so very wanton.

He flashed me a wicked grin, then his mouth descended again.

I don't know what the hell we were doing or how he learned that, but holy hell. Explosions rocked my body, and I screamed his name. When the last tremor quieted, my body went limp, sated. I would have fallen except for Hawk's grip shifting and wrapping around my waist.

I heard the tearing of a wrapper, and then he was pushing into me. Electric pulses shot through my body, and I gripped him as he slowly eased in. I felt stretched to the max, and I shifted so I could peer over my shoulder at him. His shoulders were tense, with corded muscles strained against tight skin. My panic at his size subsided when I noticed his restraint. I had nothing to worry about, and that kicked my desire to unchartered heights.

I pushed back, desperate for more. His hands held me in place, and I growled, "Hawk!"

He laughed. "Red, I don't think I'll ever get enough of you." With a final push, he was fully seated, hitting that magical spot. My body reacted—it detonated. I screamed his name as my body gripped his.

He flipped me onto my back, and my legs automatically wrapped around his waist. The brief levity was gone, and intense desire pulled his features taut. He drove into me, each thrust making me whimper with need. I arched against him.

My core shot sensation after sensation with each powerful thrust. I gripped his biceps, mesmerized by every inch of him. Beneath my fingers, his corded muscles flexed and bulged. When he slid a hand under my hips and lifted me higher, I cried out, my body convulsing around his again.

He whispered my name as he chased my orgasm, following with his own. I felt the pulse of heat as he emptied himself deep inside me.

Shaken, I took his weight as he covered me. He'd branded

me, and I knew I would never be the same again. I didn't want to be.

My fingers brushed through his short hair as he nuzzled my neck. I floated in a haze of sensations. Limp and relaxed, I began to drift, stirring only when he pulled out and I felt the loss of him filling me. I was in trouble. One time would never be enough.

He took care of the condom, and the bed dipped from his weight again as he gathered me in his arms. I curled against him, my head resting on his shoulder. He made me want so many things. I just needed to convince that part of him that I sensed was broken that we were good for each other. Because there was no way in hell I would let this man go.

I'm not sure how long we lay wrapped in each other's arms. I was content and didn't want to move. Maybe we napped—it felt as if we had. When his hand ran along my side, I moaned. I wanted round two even though my brain had rebooted and I could think again. We had urgent matters at hand, and I couldn't have a sex-a-thon just then, no matter how much I wanted to.

I'd never been so relaxed or content in my life. *That man should bottle whatever he did to me. Wait, no… I'm selfish, and that's for me only.* I narrowed my gaze at him, assessing how to keep him all to myself. A slow smile spread across my face. He liked me. I could tell. We would work through whatever it was that was eating him alive inside. Then maybe he would fully commit, because I was quickly on my way to being a goner already. It wouldn't take much for me to fall in love with him. I toed the line.

"I'd like to stay in bed with you the rest of the day, but we have work to do." His voice rumbled in his chest and teased my skin.

He was right. By mutual agreement, we both got up, washed, and dressed. It wasn't what I wanted at all, and I could tell by how he watched me that he didn't, either.

"Are you all right?"

His concern softened me even more. "I'm great." There was so much I wanted to say to him, but we'd have time for that eventually.

Hawk guided me to the couch and set a computer in front of me. He sat close by as he typed in a few commands. I used the time to study him. He was tall and lean, ripped with muscle that made my fingers curl, and had brown skin and dark hair. But his gorgeous cobalt eyes were confusing. I couldn't place his nationality.

Rude or not, I was curious and wanted to know. "What's your heritage? I don't mean to be intrusive. It's just that your eye color is throwing me, and I can't figure you out."

A wall slammed over his features, shuttering all emotion. He locked me out, and I went instantly cold. Every part of me stilled at the coiled power I sensed in his body. The muscles in his thigh tensed to rock against mine. The only outward indication he was upset was the pulse that throbbed at the base of his neck beneath his tight cotton shirt.

"Mostly Cuban, but let's just say a melting pot of genes."

"Well, whatever makes up your gene pool, you got the best of it." I meant it. He was sculpted to perfection, from his model-worthy face all the way down his panty-dropping athletic body.

He grunted and went back to pulling up an app on his laptop. I struggled to think of something to say to fill in the awkward silence. I must have hit a nerve, though I had no idea why, because he was stunning. I could have stared at him all day and never tired of his chiseled features and mesmerizing eyes. I was riveted by him.

"I'm German and Irish. Obviously." I grinned and pointed at my red hair. "Max looks more like my grandparents and mom, with his blond hair and blue eyes, and I take after my dad's Irish descent."

He typed in a username and password before turning to

me. "I'm going to have you talk to Hannah about what your grandmother told you in that last letter." He got up and went into the other room.

Ouch. Note to self: don't bring up his heritage, at least not until we can talk about what bothers him so much.

The screen stared back at me with the Skype application opened but no connection made. I clasped my hands together. "Why?" I asked when he came back in with my jewelry box and brush.

"Hannah has a knack of figuring things out that aren't obvious, like things that are hidden or puzzles. We're missing something, and she's our best bet."

I shrugged then scooted closer to him so we'd both fit on the screen. That's what I told myself, anyway. I was sticking to it. It wasn't because he made my pulse skyrocket and my body burn or anything like that.

"Hawk."

A gorgeous woman appeared on the screen, and I straightened my spine. *Were they together?*

"Hannah, this is Stella. I'm sure Jack has filled you in on her situation?"

"He has."

She swung her gaze to me, and I fumbled with the box in my lap. God, the woman was icy perfection. "Hi, Hannah. It's nice to meet you."

"Are you talking to the guys?" Another woman's voice sounded from somewhere not too far from Hannah.

Another beautiful woman peered at us as she nudged Hannah over. *Goddamn. What's in the water they drink?* Hannah had flawless skin, light-blue eyes, and platinum-blond hair, which only highlighted her exotic features, high cheekbones, and full lips. The other woman was dark to her light, with olive skin and mahogany hair that fell past her shoulders, framing a face of classic beauty. I felt like Ronald McDonald next to them.

Hawk squeezed my thigh, and for some reason that evened out the balance enough, so I didn't feel like a complete idiot.

"Is this Stella?" The other woman looked to Hawk, and at his nod, she flashed a blinding smile. "I'm Liv. It's so nice to finally put a face to the name I've heard so often."

Her warmth made up for Hannah's aloofness. We exchanged greetings, and I found out Liv, the classic beauty, was Liam's wife, and Hannah was with Jack. Hawk cut off the conversation that was getting off topic fast and told them what we needed.

I held up the jewelry box for their inspection, turning it completely around, showing them the top and bottom, and then opening the inside to reveal the hidden compartment Hawk found. After reading them the two letters from my grandmother, I showed them the locket.

"It's lovely," Liv murmured.

Hannah tapped at the keyboard on her end. "Turn it slowly."

I did as she asked, not sure what she was looking for.

"Open it please."

After I did, she asked to see the hinge again. Hannah leaned back and smiled at Liv. "See it?"

"I do." Liv's eyes sparkled. "It looks like a tiny screw would be there. It's very deceiving."

"There is a tiny pinhole at the base of the hinge. Hawk, do you have anything small enough to fit in there?"

Hawk took the locket from me to gauge the size before answering that he did. When he came back, he stuck a skinny needle into the hole, and a small click sounded.

I sucked in my breath. Tears blurred my eyes as the picture of my grandparents popped open to reveal a fortune-cookie-sized piece of paper folded into a tiny square. I took the message out then set the locket down so I could unfold the paper. In Oma's even printing, she'd written another note that read, *so many layers to our hearts. The one that kept mine safe rests with a piece of my past.*

Adrenaline crashed through me. Oma was always talking about her heart and who she'd given pieces to. I turned to Hawk, excitement filling my veins. "I think I know where it is."

CHAPTER 16

HAWK

The smell of lasagna and garlic bread permeated the cabin. Stella stood at the counter and prepped a large salad with romaine lettuce, cucumbers, pine nuts, and parmesan shavings before adding the dressing and tossing it all together.

I wanted more. We'd been talking for the past hour while we prepared the food. It was something all the guys had done at one point or another with Liv and Mari—Hannah and Jo, not so much. Cooking with Stella was different, though—it felt more intimate, if that was possible. If I thought about how close we seemed to be getting for too long, it confused me. Sex was one thing, but the level of comfort we were sharing was entirely new.

"I could get used to this place." Stella waved a hand around the kitchen. "It's so much nicer than my tiny studio apartment, and the lake is gorgeous."

"I like being out here too, and the location is perfect. The apartment isn't bad, either."

"I didn't mean the building isn't nice, 'cause it is. Obviously, as you have a place there, especially a bigger one than mine."

I grinned at the mild panic that swept across her features. "I'm not offended. This is a great cabin. I prefer it over the city. I've spent enough time living there to know it's not where I want to be."

"Then why were you there? I mean, you said you had a business, but couldn't you handle it remotely?"

"Some aspects, yes, but this was personal, so I wanted to come to California. I'd planned to leave with the rest of the guys then heard the fights between you and Max escalating. Like I said before, I was concerned, so I delayed my departure." I'd already told her this so saying it again didn't seem wrong. "And I'd hoped to take you out on a date."

"You did? I would have said yes, even though the timing with my brother's issues was shit." Her eyes sparkled right before she ducked her head. "I feel terrible that you heard us fighting and that's why you stayed. If you'd left, none of this would have touched you."

I tucked a piece of her hair behind her ear, using it as an excuse to touch her cheek before I dropped my hand. She had no reason to feel bad about me hearing her arguments with her brother. My life had been one threat after another since I was young. "Stop apologizing. Being in a difficult or dangerous situation and helping people is what I do on a regular basis. This is nothing compared to most of the jobs we go on."

"Well, thank you. Again. I'm glad I'm not alone in this. I wouldn't have known how to handle it." She nibbled on her lower lip as her gaze traveled over me. "I just wish I was here under different circumstances."

That was the understatement of the year, and I vowed that when everything calmed down, I would make that happen. I wanted more with her beyond the battle with her brother's loan sharks. One thing was certain: if we would even have a shot, her brother would have to get help for his addictions. "If you want, when all this is over, I can bring you back here, and we can go out on the water."

"Yes." Her smile was blinding. "I'd love that. Hey, do you have a boat?"

I wanted to share so much with her, but I couldn't talk about the intense stuff. It wouldn't have been smart. We barely knew each other, and the place was where my family sometimes vacationed when we weren't using it as a safe house. "I could get my hands on one, and some water skis too."

"I love waterskiing, and it's been so long since I've done that. Now would be too cold to ski though."

That sense of unease I'd been battling washed over me again. I needed to get the problem with her brother and the loan sharks sorted. Not only that, I had to find out what we were dealing with. Everything in me sensed there was more to our involvement than what appeared on the surface.

Waiting for the guys to get there was causing knots to form in my gut. Jack and Chris had been cagey about who was after her brother. We knew the organization's name. My stomach cramped. There was more to Max's problems than a run-of-the-mill loan-shark operation. That was the most obvious conclusion and what we'd all assumed from the beginning. It's also why I'd been having so many flashbacks. Those, I could have done without. But the two couldn't be connected, so I questioned why I was on edge.

"Everything okay?" Her brows furrowed.

"You sure you're all right with the guys coming here? There are a lot of us."

She grinned, and her natural warmth sparkled in her eyes. "Of course. I'm looking forward to getting to know the people on your team. From the little you've told me, it's clear they're important to you."

"They are. After dinner, we're planning on having a meeting."

"Oh. Should I not be here for that?"

"It'll be about the people after you and Max, so yes, you're included."

She froze. "Have you found anything out?"

"Information is still coming in. It's going slowly because of who we haven't involved."

"The police?"

"Sort of. Anyway, we'll learn more tonight and put a plan in place for how to manage the threat going forward."

Her lips pursed, and I practically saw her mind working in overdrive.

"How did you all end up in business together?"

Luck? Good fortune? "The guys that you'll meet later I've known since I was a kid. Our core group, and a few more from our military days, make up our team."

"You were in the service?"

"Navy SEALs."

"Oh, wow." She leaned toward me. "I'm impressed. So you all decided to go into the Navy together?"

"Yes. When we went into the military, we were split across two teams. The new guys in our group have become family too. It's sort of how it goes with SEALs teams. On missions, you have to know how each other thinks, anticipate what everyone will do, and execute like one unit. Off mission, we maintained the same camaraderie. Bonfires, dinners, anything and everything in between that kept us close, a family. It carries over to life after being active duty."

"Why did you get out of the military?"

It'd been a no-brainer once Mike brought up the idea. It was always all or nothing with our group. Sticking together had saved us, and the same bond only grew stronger as we got older. "Mike decided he wanted to start a security company that focused on rescue and recovery. We're contracted as private military." That wasn't the only business we'd started. Jack and Mike formed the one that had brought us to California on that last trip—we set up shelters for homeless teens. It was personal and something we'd all taken part in.

With the cabinet open and a stack of plates in her hand,

she paused. I took them from her, and she mumbled her thanks. "So if one of you wanted out, all of you followed, just like that? That's pretty impressive."

I shrugged. "It's how we are. You, your brother, parents, and grandparents were a close-knit family that you'd do anything for, right? It's the same for us." In a way. Most families didn't follow each other's every move or career choice. We tended to stick close together.

She nodded, clearly still weighing her situation. "But if you work with the government, then what you're doing for Max and me—"

"Not all our jobs are government or military contracted. We're helping you outside of our connections." *Sort of.* "That's why it's taking a little longer to get all the answers we need. You've expressed how important your brother is to you. If there's a way to help without getting him arrested, we'll go that route. It's how we're operating right now."

The timer dinged, and Stella opened the bottom oven. Mitts in hand, she pulled out the first lasagna. After I got the second out from the top oven, I put in the garlic bread. Stella slid her tray in too.

"I think we're about ready. When are they getting here?"

The door opened, and I grinned at her. "Now."

She squared her shoulders and moved with me to the door.

"You must be Stella." The pretty boy of our group entered first. Of course. "I'm Hayden."

Mike knocked him aside with a smirk. "If you forget his name, he'll answer to 'heartthrob.'"

"Ah, because he's so pretty?" Stella winked at him, and my worry about her being intimidated by us fled. She wrapped her free hand around my forearm, and my other concern about meeting the guys, particularly Hayden, dissolved.

Hayden's laugh filled the room. "I like her. She calls it like it is."

"Stop. It's going to his head, and we'll never get him to shut up. It'll be like high school all over again." Keegan rolled his eyes before narrowing them on Hayden's face. "We could take care of that with a few hits to his nose." Even when he teased, the ever-present aura of danger that clung to Keegan caused Stella's smile to waver.

I put my hand on her lower back, and she moved closer. "Ignore him." I pointed to each of the guys, skipping over Hayden and Keegan, and made quick introductions. "This is Jack, Mike, and Chris."

"It's nice to meet you all." She smiled and shook their hands. "So this is the original crew?"

Mike shot me a look. "Except for Trev, Chris's brother."

"Did you cook?" Jack asked Stella, changing the subject. "It smells amazing, and I know Hawk didn't do that. When it's his turn, we eat hamburgers or brats. Is that lasagna?"

She smiled, and the warmth in her eyes made me shift my hand around to her hip, tugging her closer. "Yes, and we made it together."

"If you don't keep her around, Hawk, I'm moving in." Mike rubbed his hands together as his stomach growled. Hayden elbowed him and moved to get ahead, passing Chris. Hayden, Mike, and Keegan volleyed to be first to the table. Not much had changed for us over the years.

Dinner was loud and one of the best I'd had since eating at Liam and Liv's. Nothing was left to put away. As usual, everyone chipped in to clear the table, and we set the pans to soak. Then we loaded the dishwasher and moved to the large family room.

The cabin looked small from the front. It wasn't. It was deep enough to accommodate all of us comfortably, from the wraparound couches and scattered chairs to the oversized dining table. There was sleeping for twenty if you counted the pullouts, bunks, and Murphy beds.

Stella settled on the couch next to me and leaned into my side. I lifted my arm, and she nestled against me. I stopped myself as I bent to brush a kiss across her forehead. After that afternoon, we were closer physically, but I wasn't sure what would happen, and the guys didn't need to catch wind of the change between us.

I scowled as each one of them smirked. I should have kissed her. Whatever. I rolled my eyes at them to get them to knock it off. I would enjoy being close to Red while I could. It wouldn't last once she got closer to me. I could finally admit to myself I wanted us to last and to become something more than a guy who was protecting her, more than some dude she was into for a little while. But no one except the guys had accepted everything about me.

I'd made my peace with the fact that I would never have what Jack, Liam, Matt, or Chris had. It was different for them. Chris and Trev's mom wanted them. Jack had good parents before they'd died. Hayden's grandmother loved him and did the best she could even though they lived in poverty. Mike and Keegan had never shared their stories with me, but I couldn't imagine their parents didn't want them. I'd assumed they were on their own after their guardians had died, like Jack.

They weren't like me.

I needed to stop fantasizing about what could have been and focus on enjoying Red while I could. Movement drew me from my thoughts, and I tensed as Chris pulled out his laptop.

"It'll take a few more hours until I can get the rest of the information I need to confirm how much Max owes them." He flipped the laptop around so we could see. A man's face filled the screen. He had a flat nose and squinty eyes. Dark, wavy hair curled at the collar of his white button-down, and a cigar dangled from his mouth.

"Do we know him?" Relief washed over me that it wasn't anyone I recognized. The nagging sense of familiarity with Stella and Max's situation had made me paranoid.

"Not that we can tell," Jack interjected. "It is a big organization, and Chris is working on finding all the connecting parts, all the players. We'll know for sure after you look through them."

Fuck. I pushed up from the couch and paced. "How big, and are they limited to the north side?"

"Huge, and no. Their reach spans across the entire San Francisco area," Chris answered. He hit a few keys, and a slideshow of pictures scrolled. I narrowed my eyes, hunting for the men burned into my psyche from the day before. A few photos were blurry, and I couldn't make out their features, but their builds looked different than what I remembered. They didn't matter.

There were more images. This was a major fucking organization, one that could house the three men I would never forget—who quite possibly would remember me too.

I stopped, my furious gaze clashing with Jack's. He held up a hand. "That doesn't mean we've had dealings with this particular organization. It just leaves open the possibility."

"What do you mean by 'dealings'?" Stella asked.

"That we've come into contact with any of them in one form or another while on missions or"—his gaze flicked to me —"when we were younger."

Son of a bitch. My skin crawled, and I couldn't stay in the room one more second. Everyone was staring at me and probably wondering what was going on in my mind. It was too much. I pushed off the couch. Red reached for my hand, but I drew it away before she could latch on. With quick steps, I stormed toward the kitchen.

Jack and Mike were the only ones who knew, who had been there after the night I'd left home. We knew almost everything about each other, except for that one thing. I'd kept it to myself and sworn Jack and Mike to secrecy. The other guys had their own problems. It had been a risk—it always was. Chris and Trev were dealing with hell from their dad, and Keegan was a live wire waiting to detonate. He always had been.

Rounding the corner, I threw my bottle into the recycling

with a splintering of glass. *Fuck.* The smell of the smoke, the screams—they were back. That night was playing over and over in my head.

This can't be happening. Jack said it wasn't absolute that the same guys from the night of the fire would be with this group, but it made sense. I would know for sure when Chris got to work on finding all the members.

I turned, and a flash of red curls filled my vision. Stella blocked my path, and I ran my hands over my face, trying to calm down.

She didn't say anything, just moved into my space. Her arms came around me in a hug, and she lay her head on my chest. *Dammit.* After several breaths, I relaxed into her and held her tightly, dropping my chin to the top of her head.

Her words were muffled and quiet, but they pierced my armor like none ever had before. "Listen up, hot neighbor."

This woman. I grinned, and some of the weight I carried lessened.

"Whatever it is, I'm here for you. I know we haven't known each other long, but I care. I'm not going anywhere. I'll help you deal with this, just like you've stuck by my side through my brother's complications."

If only she would. I wanted to believe her. Part of me was selfish enough to cling to what she said and say a resounding "fuck you" to the truth I knew, the one the people who raised me had drilled into my head every chance they got. *My mother didn't want me, so why would Red?*

I shoved the destructive thoughts away and let myself accept her comfort for as long as she would give it.

CHAPTER 17

HAWK

*H*ayden sat on the couch with Stella, and they laughed at a comedy playing on TV. It was good to see her happy. With Red distracted, I could focus on the images Chris continued to pull up and the connections he found and identified with the Tridel Corp. It turned out that they ran the books for the track near the neighborhood we used to live in during high school.

My gut was a mass of cramps as I waited for confirmation. Chris organized the names and put them in order of hierarchy. The group had four arms covering four different territories. The images of the top guys who ruled over our old section of town weren't clear enough for me to be sure. I added my nicknames to keep track of them. The head of the operation was David Malone, aka the Boss. The four territory heads were Stan Jones, Ben Anderson, Henry Garcia, and Landon Johnson, aka Lando.

"Jack said you might know some of these people." Chris spoke in a subdued voice so no one could overhear our conversation. Even so, I was pissed that Jack had shared my possible connection to the Tridel Corp. I had no right to be, though. I knew all about Chris and Trev's past, including the abuse and neglect they'd suffered. Still, I would have happily traded parents. Mine were true monsters.

"My mom's husband gambled." I pulled a chair up and sat by Chris. "There were a few guys who came to the house to collect. It was always the same ones."

"Probably not the heads of the territory, then."

"I wouldn't think so, unless they moved up in rank."

Chris nodded. Out of all the guys, Chris and I were the quietest. The difference was that Chris used to lose himself in technology, his escape from the world. I would isolate myself on rooftops or in hidden places where I could observe what I needed to without being seen.

"What's your gut tell you?"

Everything. "Nothing good."

"I'm almost done." Chris rubbed a hand across his eyes, blinked a few times, then went back at it on his laptop. "Mari asked about you."

Chris could multitask like the genius he was. "Did she?" Mari was his wife and a total badass. She and Hannah would go at it sometimes, and if Jo was there, that was amplified. It was fun to watch, so long as we weren't dragged into their discussions. They all got along, in spite of being stubborn and hot-tempered. Hannah's personality was icier, but she was lethal as hell. That was one woman never to piss off. Mari too, if there were knives around. We'd learned fast.

I couldn't even remember what had gotten her so mad one time in Liam and Liv's kitchen in Maine, but if looks could kill, Chris would have been dead. He'd leaned back against the counter, not saying a thing, a small grin playing around the corner of his mouth. She was spewing Spanish faster than I could translate, and then a knife went flying. It stuck in the cabinet to the left of his ear, maybe a centimeter away.

The fucker had burst out laughing. He hadn't even flinched. It wasn't until Liv rushed in and took one look at the knife sticking out of the wood that everything calmed down.

Mari apologized to Liv for the damage, and Chris tossed Mari over his shoulder and went back to their house. We didn't worry as much when Chris and Mari went at it, but Hannah and Mari were frightening. Hannah was a walking weapon, and if Mari's temper ignited, the possibility of an all-out bloodbath was real.

Laughter pulled me from my thoughts, and I glanced to where Stella and Hayden were still cracking up at the movie. She fit with us.

"I've got a few more pictures." Chris got my attention, and I peered at what he'd added to his diagram. "This seems like the last of it."

I barely heard what he'd said. I reached over him, and with a few taps, I highlighted three of the four pictures he'd added, making them larger to see every detail. The oversized, square jaw and deep-set eyes that stared back at me from the screen were the same that appeared in my darkest nightmares. The man held a secret I'd only shared with Jack and Mike.

"Fuck." I stood so quickly that my chair crashed to the wood floor behind me.

Stella was by my side and clutching my arm in a matter of seconds. "What's wrong?"

I couldn't answer her. My mouth refused to move, and the secret I'd held onto lodged painfully in my throat. Fire cracked and sizzled in my mind's eye. I blinked it away and met her gaze. Any chance with her would die when I inevitably told everyone what I had to say. I ignored her concern and pointed at the screen while all the guys crowded around me. I couldn't stall any longer.

"I know this organization well. Until now, I didn't have names to put to the operation or these three." I met Jack and Mike's gaze. "Life comes full fucking circle, doesn't it?"

"Better now than before," Mike said.

"True." If they'd come for me when I was younger, there

was no doubt I would be at the bottom of the ocean—or wishing I was while forced to work for them.

"What the hell is going on?" Keegan's clipped question caused me to turn to him. "There's something we don't know about you? Is that the bullshit you're telling us right now?"

I gave a partial nod. I'd fucked up in more than one way. My brothers would forgive me, but they would be mad as hell that I'd kept it to myself.

"Let's take a seat and let Hawk fill us in on Stan Jones," Jack ordered.

In my mind, Stan Jones would always be Porch Guy.

We moved back to the family room. Chris set the laptop on the coffee table. The screen showed the three guys' photos I'd blown up minutes before.

"Ready?" Jack asked.

No, but what choice do I have? A corner of his mouth lifted in silent support, and after a deep breath, I allowed the memories free rein.

"Most of you know a little about my mom and her husband, Lenny." Red didn't. She stayed quiet at my side, her hand on my thigh in an attempt to reassure me. But I knew her loyalty to family. I would have confirmation of how she felt when she pulled it away in disgust after I said my piece. She too would be repelled by the type of person I was.

"Anyway, Lenny gambled and lost more than he won at the track. As a kid, I'd hear bits and pieces of how much he owed, but nothing stood out to me. There were other things I was more focused on than the loan sharks he had to pay."

A few of the guys murmured their understanding. They'd grown up to be hypersensitive to sound. The subtle differences in body language could help us gauge if we were going to take a hit or could make it safely across a room.

"The night I left home, Lenny had a visit from two guys. They messed up both Lenny and my mom pretty bad. I was in my room, but they knew I was there."

"How did they know?" Stella asked.

"Lenny told them. He tried to swap me for his debt."

Stella sucked in her breath as Keegan lurched from his chair. Fury radiated from him. I locked onto his gaze and saw more than he probably wanted me to. *Fuck, he has secrets too.*

"I had to get out, and I did, just in time. They torched the place." *I'll never forget the sound when the flame caught.*

"They thought you died in the fire too?" Hayden asked.

I nodded because they must have. If they hadn't, they would have come after me. No one was supposed to get away when things went that far. We all knew that well. "When I was out and running away, I looked back and saw a man stationed at the front of our house. The other two had just closed the door behind them, shutting Lenny and my mom inside."

"That sucks, but I don't understand why you didn't tell us this before," Chris said.

"Because I *let* them die. I could have gone to the neighbors next door and called for help. They were still alive when I went out the window." *This is when she'll pull her hand away.* "I could hear their screams."

CHAPTER 18

HAWK

The memories were too close. I couldn't keep them at bay. Soon, I would be coming face-to-face with several of the goons from that last night with the people who'd raised me. My stomach churned. Flashes came in fast succession until I gave in and let them play out.

The crash had been explosive, dragging me from sleep. I had frantically sought where the sound had come from. The door to my room was closed, and I wondered if he was coming. With my gaze glued on the doorknob, I waited, praying it didn't turn. Heart pounding, I crouched and took stock of my surroundings. The only light in my small room was from under the door and the silvery glow the crescent moon cast through my window.

The door stayed shut, but I didn't relax my stance. I had to assess what was happening.

I counted how many pairs of feet scuffed against the floor. *Four people? Maybe five?* The slide of shoes closest to my door wasn't from Mom or her husband. I knew their tread well. Another step, and the squeak from the floorboard near the kitchen sounded more strained than if any of us had stepped on it.

The dull thud of a fist slamming into flesh echoed in time with the thump of my heart. High-pitched whimpers played under the violent melody of the beating. It continued until a heavy weight dropped to the floor.

"Time's up, Lenny," a smoke-ravaged voice threatened.

"I need more time," Mom's husband pleaded. His voice was thick with pain and desperation. "Give me a week."

"Already did that. You've got nothing for collateral."

"Take my wife or the kid. You know my word's good if you hold them 'til I deliver the payment."

My blood iced. The bastard was going to bargain with our lives. He was full of shit. He didn't care about us.

"No!" Mom begged. "Take the kid. He's a hard worker."

Fuck, her too? It crushed any hope that she cared. I was only thirteen, and they were going to use me to save themselves.

"Boss says this is it. Payment's due."

"I swear I'm good for it," Lenny pleaded.

I could hear the man walk around. I strained to hear if he was coming closer. His steps were tight. My guess was that he was moving in a circle, probably around Lenny. I visualized where they were. There was another by the kitchen counter, near Mom. I knew because that's where her muffled crying was coming from. I'd lost the third's movements while Lenny got pummeled.

"Please. I got a tip today for tomorrow's race. I'll have it then. I swear."

"Always something with you," the man said.

A dull thud sounded, and glass shattered. *Had the glass fallen from the counter? Was it thrown?* I couldn't be sure. I knew what the next sound was, another punch. *Lenny sold us out. Nothing good will come from tonight.*

I didn't need to hear more. It was time.

Something splashed against my door. The liquid dripped down and pooled underneath, seeping in. Footsteps crunched outside my window. With care, I slipped my pack over my shoulders as the acrid scent of gasoline burned my nose.

More splashing coated my window, some spilling in. A shadow moved past. I had to go. I waited a minute for whoever was out there to move to the back of the house.

As soon as it was safe, I inched my window up until it was open wide enough to crawl through. Perched on the small ledge, I swung one leg through at a time before lowering myself out. I pushed away and dropped with a small thud into the dirt under my window.

Weaving through the junk strewn about the miniscule side yard, I paused. Deadly awareness accentuated my already heightened senses, and I peered into the night. A large form leaned over the rickety railing of our sagging porch. With his arms crossed, the thug looked out into the night. A cigarette dangled from his hand, and smoke curled above him as two men exited the front door. He turned to look at them, and I got a good view of him.

He had squinty dark eyes in a cumbersome square face that reminded me of a boxer's. The image was seared into my mind's eye. I would never forget any of them. All three were large, their noses crooked as if broken one too many times. One had a slight hunch to his oversized body.

"They aren't going anywhere." The guy who spoke threw a plastic gas container inside and shut the door. With his elbow, he smashed a small window pane in the door. He took the cigarette from the guy stationed out front and flicked it through the hole.

"What about the kid?" the trio's lookout, or Porch Guy, murmured. "There can't be any loose ends."

"The house was thoroughly doused. You got the perimeter. He won't survive," the crooked-arm guy replied to the porch lookout.

Porch Guy grunted, and all three went down the stairs, heading to their car.

Like a sheet snapping in the wind, flames erupted. I turned and ran. *They're alive in there.* I doubted they could get out on their own, not after the beating and then the fire. Bile climbed my throat, and the agony of what I was doing nearly brought me to my knees. There had been no going back. My fate would have been the same if those men caught me.

I sucked in a ragged breath and blinked my way back from the past. There wasn't much that was good back then except my brothers, who were the only positives in a sea of hell. My stomach churned while waiting for the fallout, including Stella realizing I wasn't worth it.

I stood and went to one of the spare rooms. I needed space.

A hand gripped my shoulder, and I snapped my head up only to meet Jack's stare head-on. An unwavering mask of determination was stamped over his features. I knew that look well. "No one thinks any different of you, man. Stop beating yourself up." He squeezed my shoulder again before dropping his hand to his side.

"Maybe. It doesn't change the fact that I walked away. That says something right there."

"Mike and I know what your parents were like, and wasting an ounce of remorse or guilt to their memory makes no sense. Let it go. Walking away was the only thing you could have done after all those years of abuse."

Fuck. I got it. I did. But Stella… To her, family was everything. There was no way she would understand, yet a part of me had dared to entertain that something would come of us.

"The fact that you're in here and not up on the roof says something."

He was right. A small glimmer of hope remained, against my better judgment. The guys were used to me hanging out on the roof—they'd given me the nickname Hawk back in high school as a result. I'd always felt safer there, being able to see who was coming and going. And most people didn't look up. I scrubbed a hand over my face. "I'm not worried about the guys. I thought I was, but definitely not after seeing their reactions. None of us had it easy."

"No. We didn't, but we had each other then, and we always will."

"I should have told everyone a long time ago."

"Fear is a vicious bitch. Don't give it power. We know who you are, and no one's opinion of you has changed."

"Thanks, man."

Jack studied me for a moment longer. "We've got work to do. Shake off whatever this is."

I nodded, feeling like a jackass. He and Mike had known the details of my last night at home since it happened, and they'd still taken me in. I kept going back to Stella and that hand on my thigh. I'd stood and walked away before she could pull her hand off me. I shoved away from the wall I'd been leaning against then went into the kitchen to get some coffee. I had a feeling it was going to be a long night.

As I stepped into the kitchen, Stella collided with me. With a hand on her elbow, I steadied her then moved around her to the coffee machine. I avoided making eye contact. I couldn't deal with her judgment or rejection.

"Hawk."

I didn't want to have the conversation. I dropped a pod into the machine, put my mug in position, and waited for it to heat up. "We're talking strategy soon, Red. Do you want any coffee?"

Her small hand gripped my forearm, and she tugged on it insistently.

"No. I want to talk to you."

Crossing my arms, I leaned back against the counter and waited for her to tell me what was on her mind.

"I know there's more to your childhood than the fire. I've shared a lot about my life, and I'm trusting you with, well, everything. My brother, the letters my grandmother left me, the possibility of finding heirlooms. I'm hoping you'll do the same and let me in."

Anger burned through me. *No, it isn't the same. She had a loving family, even if her brother is fucked up.* We weren't the same, and I didn't understand how she could ever relate. I spoke through clenched teeth. "It's not that simple. There's nothing pretty about my past. You come from a very different world. My sharing anything about that time won't bridge the gap to common ground for us."

Her eyes shone with a fine mist of tears. "I refuse to accept that. The man I've gotten to know is strong both inside and out. You have integrity and a deep sense of loyalty to the ones you've let in. Your past doesn't matter to me, but your future does." She stepped closer, placing a hand on my chest. "Please let me in."

She had no idea what she was asking. Our being physical was one thing. But her heart was pure, and I didn't want to risk harming her. I came from a shit life and had been told on a daily basis I wouldn't amount to anything. She would come to see all my shortcomings, or I would screw up somehow, and she wouldn't want me anymore. But most of all, I didn't want to hurt her.

It had to end even as my hands ached to brush across her soft skin, to pull her close and feel her lean on me. It would have been selfish. So I did what I had to do and said what needed to be said as I moved aside, coffee in hand. "There is no us, Stella."

STELLA

DARKNESS BLANKETED MY ROOM. THE LATE HOUR TAUNTED ME, and sleep was elusive. The guys had stayed until close to midnight and had worked out a tentative plan. While I was terrified for Max and wanted to get him as soon as we could, I trusted the guys—well, I had faith in them to look out for me. They knew what they were doing. I wasn't entirely sure regarding Max.

Instead of obsessing over my brother's safety, I fixated on what had happened in that kitchen. Hawk saturated my mind. I couldn't stop thinking about what he'd said to me, and as the hours passed, I got angrier.

The guys had gone back to their cabin, whichever one they were in. I didn't care, not in that moment. I couldn't believe what he'd said. We hadn't said one word to each other after he declared that there was no us, and eventually, I went to bed mad.

The sheets were holding me hostage in a straitjacket of a mess. I squirmed and kicked free only to flop onto my stomach. With every second that ticked past, my temper notched higher.

Screw this. I flung the covers off and tiptoed to his room, wearing a tank top and small pajama shorts. After what he'd shared, I wouldn't let him shut me out. His touch said one thing and his words another. I wanted them to be in alignment.

Stepping quietly, I pushed open his door. It was pitch dark in there. Waking him could be tricky. He was trained to take down targets. The last thing I needed was a broken nose or a black eye.

I neared his bed and could hear his slow, even breaths. He was asleep. I wanted to rub my hands together. Maybe it would be the best way to slip past the walls he insisted on hiding behind. A half-asleep man would have his barriers down and might admit things, such as the fact that he wanted me.

My fingers curled around the sheets, and I pulled them back. Hawk lunged, a dark form towering over me. I blinked. My back hit the mattress. A large hand wrapped around my throat.

I squeaked. Adrenaline flooded my body in fear. My hands slammed flat on his chest. I pushed—he didn't budge. His fingers loosened. *Holy hell.* "It's me! I heard a noise." Maybe I should've let him know when I was by the door. It would have been a much safer distance.

My heart thudded against my ribs, feeling as though it could break a few of them. My anger fled. *Coward.*

"Goddamn, Red. I could have hurt you." His hands fell away only to return to rub the spot he'd grabbed. "Are you okay?"

I swallowed. "Yeah. I think you scared a few years off my life, though."

He leaned over. *Why? Is he turning on the lamp?* I gripped his incredibly sexy arm. *So much muscle.* I skimmed over the dips and ropes of his forearm to explore his bicep, which felt like skin stretched over steel. He froze. The light stayed off.

I bit back a moan. My heart let go of fear's percussion and took up the tempo of desire .

The bed dipped again, and he dropped onto the mattress next to me. I tucked myself closer. *I can pretend to be frightened.* It wouldn't have been a total lie—he scared the hell out of me with how fast he'd reacted. And seriously, he was so freaking hot.

"What noise did you hear?"

Huh? My body was betraying me, confusing me. "Oh." *Shoot.* "It was probably nothing. The pipes, I think. It startled me. I feel safer with you than in a room by myself." That was true.

He sighed then pulled me close. With my cheek resting on his bare chest, I molded against his side. *Yep, no shirt—score for me!*

I splayed my hand over his heart and grinned at the elevated beat. I affected him too. Good. "We need to talk about what you said to me."

Seconds ticked by. I waited. He cleared his throat. "What did I say to you?"

Oh, we're playing that game? Ignorance? Did the color of my hair not register to him? It was a clear reflection of my legendary temper and stubbornness. He must have needed a reminder. I wasn't going to play along with him. "You know what I'm talking about," I snapped. "Your comment about how 'there is no us.'"

More silence. I wanted to roll my eyes. *Fine.* I could talk. He would listen.

"We shared something pretty incredible in this bed not too long ago. Every time we touch, it's like a thousand sparks of energy. So what you said about there being no us is a load of crap. Stop shutting me out. You like me. I don't understand why you won't let me in."

"I don't deny we have a physical connection."

He better not go there.

"That's all there can be, Red," his deep voice rumbled.

Yep, he's going there. I pressed my lips together before I told him to go to hell.

"After what you heard I did to my mom and her husband, you should be running as far away from me as you can."

Oh. Some of my anger dissipated. "Why? Because you saved yourself and got out of a hellish situation when you were a kid? I said it before, and I'll repeat it as many times as you need me to—that was your past." I laid my hand on his chest. "You're a good person, Hawk. You rescued me and are trying to do the same for my brother too."

His body was like stone beneath my hand. My heart broke for him. I couldn't relate to what was going on in his head, but I could try to help him overcome his fears. *We* deserved a chance.

"I'm sorry I hurt you." He paused again. "But relationships aren't my thing. I don't want to do something that causes you pain."

"That's crazy. Look at what you have with the guys?"

"That's different."

"No, Hawk, it's not. It's a bond you have with them. They

accept and love you for who you are, flaws and all. And you do the same with them."

"I just… I've never been involved with a woman, aside from casually."

He had some extensive damage inside if he thought he couldn't have a relationship with a woman. I hated everyone who'd contributed to his shredded self-esteem. "What you did and endured in the past is not the man you are today. You rose above a horrible time in your life, and you've got a pretty incredible future. You did that."

"Stella," he grumbled.

"No, Hawk. I want to see where this thing between us goes."

He didn't answer me verbally, but I was more than all right with the toe-curling kiss and everything that came after. *Maybe we'll be okay.* I would find out in the morning if he still held me at arm's length.

CHAPTER 19

We'd been up most of the night, and a plan was in place. Red would stay at the cabin with Hayden and Keegan. Hayden would keep her distracted and entertained. He was like that—he made everyone around him happy. Keegan was a mean son of a bitch, which made me feel better about the possibility of someone finding out where she was and trying to come within visual distance of her. Keegan would gut them before they even knew he was there.

We were all trained to be ghosts, but Keegan had even been that way when we were kids. None of us knew what had happened to him—it had to be bad, even worse than my story. We were damn lucky he was with us. Whatever it was, he projected a predatory deadliness derived from his hellish past. Someone had taught him well. From his reaction to my story the night before, I knew his mentors had to have been even bigger monsters than the ones who'd molded me.

I waited as long as I could with Stella snuggled beside me, her head on my chest. She'd slipped into my bed last night, saying she felt safest by my side, and I wasn't going to complain. I'd tried to resist but couldn't after she reamed my ass for being self-centered. I was glad she did it and grateful for what happened after. Later, she'd curled against me again and fallen asleep. She was soft and smelled so good—vanilla and cinnamon warmed my nose. I held her while she slept through the night, and I dared to hope.

The night passed way too quickly. I untangled myself from her, got up, and tucked the covers around her. I grabbed a quick shower, got dressed, and went to the kitchen to make coffee and bacon and eggs. The front door opened, and Keegan came in and sat at the table.

"You eat?"

He glared, and I couldn't help but grin. *That would be a no.* I dumped the food on a plate for him. I mixed up more eggs, enough for Hayden and Red. When everything was ready, I dug in just as Hayden came in and fell into the chair next to me. I needed sleep.

Stella rounded the corner and smiled. "Good morning."

Hayden grinned while Keegan and I grunted our responses around mouthfuls of food.

"Well, it's nice to see at least one of you is a morning person." She winked at Hayden and took the plate he handed to her. "So, today is the day?"

"Sure is." Hayden passed Stella the bacon. "What do you want to do? We could play cards, video games, watch movies. Maybe boating?"

"No," Keegan and I both snapped. "Stay inside and out of sight," I added.

"Whatever, Dad." Hayden thought he was funny. Stella did too, if her laughter was any indication. "Eat up. The rest of the guys are ready to move out in five minutes."

I shoveled the remaining bites into my mouth, rinsed the dishes, and headed for the front door.

"Wait!" Stella rushed after me. She wrapped her arms around my waist and pressed against my back. "Please be careful," she said in a voice thick with emotion.

I squeezed her hands before disentangling myself, brushed

a kiss across her lips, then went out the door. *What am I doing?* Any thought about a future with Red was foolish. She was into me because I was helping her. After the stuff with her brother was settled… I was worried I would end up breaking her heart.

"Look who's finally awake." I slapped my palm against Mike's shoulder.

Mike shoved my hand away. "Screw you. I've been up for hours. We ready to do this?"

"Hell yeah," Chris, Jack, and I answered.

Mike got behind the wheel of our black Range Rover, and the rest of us settled in. Chris pulled out his laptop and got to work tracking several of the guys not too far beneath Stan Jones on the food chain, aka Porch Guy and the northern California regional lead, before settling on Billy Williams, one of Tridel's lackeys. Chris's hacking skills were terrifying, and each time I watched him, I was thankful he was on our side.

Several hours passed after he located one of the guys at a bar in the Tenderloin. We parked a few cars away from the entrance then sat in the Range Rover and staked out the place, waiting for him to leave. Chris's laptop was stowed away. With his head still resting against the back of the seat, he turned toward me. "You know we can't do this blind any longer. Rich needs to be brought in."

He had a point. Tridel was big, and there were probably feds who had a stake in their takedown. Our CIA contact, Rich Stevens, would want to know what we were doing.

"We could have Billy arrested afterward. I'm sure he's packing and possibly even has drugs on him." That was weak. I knew it, but I felt like I had to give Red and her brother as much of a chance as I could. While I didn't think it would be an issue to keep Max out of what we were about to do, there was a possibility he was in deeper with this group than any of us knew, and that could pose a problem. Red would be heartbroken if her brother landed in jail.

"Billy will be bailed out in a matter of hours and will spill to his boss, David Malone, the head of Tridel Corporation. You know we can't take that risk," Jack interjected.

"I do, but why wasn't this discussed last night when we strategized for this?" I hated doing that to Red.

"Because of Stella. We like her too, and causing her pain isn't the objective here," Mike said. "Jack called in a favor with Rich. After we're done questioning Billy, Rich will have the guy picked up and tied up in red tape for a few days. It should be enough to give us a small advantage."

"Thanks, man." That would work. After a while, we would have the situation under wraps. That was the goal, anyway, unless something new popped up and messed with everything. Unfortunately, it usually did.

"There he is." I squinted out my window, trying to catch sight of the guy.

Billy left the bar, laughing with two other guys. When he went his separate way, I slipped from the car. I'd offered to take point.

The day had passed in a blur, and dusk was settling. Street lamps flickered on, casting a soft glow over the pavement and parked cars. The Tenderloin was a run-down part of town, and there wasn't a lot of foot traffic. The people that were out would turn a blind eye—that was the type of area we were in.

Billy turned the corner, heading for his car. I fell in step with him, shoved my hands in my pockets, and kept my head low, making my posture as unthreatening as possible. He looked over his shoulder and dismissed me.

When he took his key fob from his pocket, I chopped my hand hard onto his wrist. His keys fell. He turned, his mouth open on a growl. My fist kissed his jawline. His eyes rolled back. He was out cold. As he crumpled, I moved forward and grabbed him.

Hefting him over my shoulder, I stepped into the street as Mike pulled up. Chris opened the door. Tossing the guy onto the floor of the SUV, I climbed in, and we sped off.

"Nice hit." Jack grinned back at me.

I matched his grin. "Not messin' around."

"Let's get this done." Mike drove several blocks until we arrived at a storage facility. We'd rented a back-corner unit that was large enough to park the vehicle in. The place had undergone a renovation, and there was even a drain in the larger section, which was useful for situations like this.

After the garage door was shut and locked, I dragged Billy from the car and tossed him into a chair, where Mike secured him with zip ties.

We had a single bulb we'd hung for necessary interrogations. Its pale light illuminated Billy and shrouded the rest of the area in darkness. I stepped closer so he would see enough of me to be intimidated.

"Wake him up," Jack commanded.

Mike, Jack, and Chris stood behind him, so the only one he would get a visual on was me. Several of these guys should've already seen me around Red. I saw no need to give them extra intel on my team.

I slapped the guy on the face a few times until he started to come to. After a few seconds, he jolted in his chair. His wide-eyed gaze locked on me then darkened with fury. I let him struggle for a few minutes so he would realize he was secure and not going anywhere, at least not until we got what we needed from him.

"What the fuck do you want?" he growled as if he had power.

I chuckled. He had none. "You have information I want."

"I got nothing for you."

From behind my back, I pulled a seven-chamber revolver from the waistband of my jeans. We didn't use these types of guns unless we wanted to play Russian roulette during an interrogation like the one we were undertaking.

With a click, the cylinder slid out, and I spun it for effect. There were no bullets in it. From my pocket, I retrieved two and put them in randomly before popping the chamber back in place. I spun it one more time so we didn't know what position they were in then pointed it at his leg. "We're going to play a little game."

"Fuck you! You have no idea who you're messing with. You're a dead man."

I laughed. "Who's the one holding the gun, and who's tied up? Think you've got that wrong, Billy. I know who you are. Do you know who I am?"

"You're the dude helping the girl. You're on our hit list too. Only a matter of time."

"Let's get started." I was tired of his game and ready for one of my own. "You know how this works, right? I ask you a question, and you answer it truthfully. If you don't, or you lie, I pull the trigger. You may or may not get lucky."

He glared at me, his body straining against his restraints.

"What's the plan with Max?" Ultimately, I knew they would kill him. I couldn't believe they had any use for him beyond getting to Red, but I needed to know all I could find out.

Silence met my inquiry. I raised the gun, aimed it at his right thigh, and pulled the trigger. The click echoed off the metal walls.

"Let's try that again. What do you want with Max?" We already knew he owed money. How much was the question, and why he wasn't in the hospital, missing digits, or dead was the other.

Sweat beaded on the guy's upper lip as a drop rolled down his temple. "We didn't do anything to him yet. Not really."

Except beat the shit out of him.

"He owes over a hundred k and is late on payments."

I lowered the gun. That helped. Max owed a lot, but there would be time for him to run into luck and make a significant payment—that's probably what they were holding out for. "And now? Plans must have changed. Why is that?"

"Go to hell."

Huh, he was getting brave again. I raised the gun and pointed it at his thigh once more, just right of the femoral artery. There was no sense in shooting him and having him bleed out. We needed answers.

In slow motion, I pulled the hammer back, giving him every millisecond to change his answer. The bang from the gun was louder. "Look at that." His mouth hung open as blood bloomed through his pants. "There was one bullet."

I slid the cylinder out, inserted another bullet, and gave it a spin before popping it back in place. "One more time. What are the new orders?"

Billy laughed, the sound maniacal. "You. You're the target. We're to take you out and secure the girl."

"No shit. Last chance to tell me something worth my while."

"Fuck you." He spat the words, spittle hanging from his lip. "I'm not telling you anything else."

I aimed at his right shoulder and pulled the trigger fast and hard. The click emitted a hollow sound. "Why the girl?"

He reared back and launched a wad of spit. I fired the gun again. Another empty chamber. *Fucking hell.* "We can do this all day. I've got more bullets in my pocket and easy access to a scalpel. What'll it be?" I raised my eyebrows, waiting.

"I'll see you in hell, motherfucker."

I squeezed the trigger, not caring that my temper was leading the interrogation. Worry for Red overrode my sense of what was right. The explosion from the barrel hurled a bullet and struck his shoulder with a pop.

Instead of firing off another question, I let him stew in pain for a few minutes. He would survive. I had been careful not to hit anything vital.

"Let me tell you what I know as fact. You're muscle, four men beneath Stan Jones, the top man for Tridel's northern territory." *Porch Guy to me.* "You think you have more brains than the men ahead of you but haven't had a chance to prove it and move up. You're stuck in the same position, being a lackey and answering every call that the guy above you doesn't want to do. It pisses you off, doesn't it?"

Fury burned in his red-rimmed eyes. I watched with fascination as a vein throbbed at the base of his neck. "You're ambitious, and being hired muscle isn't enough. What is it you want? What'll you do to surpass the others that are in your way to the top? Will you defy orders? Grab the girl and what?"

He laughed, and I waited. I knew I was on the right track because Chris had filled us in on everything he'd uncovered on this arm of Tridel, including personality profiles and anything out of the ordinary.

The guy had been doing more than collecting money owed. He'd somehow found out what the orders were ahead of time. Then he usurped the person above him, taking several of the jobs on and completing them before his superior could. It made the next guy in line look bad. Billy planned to move up. It made sense that Red was his ticket.

I needed to stir things up, get his emotions involved, and amplify his fear so he would slip up. With a pop and spin, I rotated the cylinder again then raised the gun, aimed at his abdomen, and pulled the trigger.

"What the fuck!" Billy sputtered. The hollow click saved him. A stomach wound just sucked. He would be lucky to survive it, and we both knew it. I'd seen where the bullet was before I'd locked the cylinder, but he hadn't.

"Tell me what you know." I aimed at his stomach again. "Next one is your throat. Ever seen that? The bullet will tear through that soft skin, shredding the tissue. You would probably bleed out before help arrives. What do you think breathing would be like? Drowning in your blood? Would your esophagus be gone?"

Sweat poured off his face, drenching the collar of his shirt. "The brother blabbed, and our objective changed."

Max had talked.

"Grab the girl and kill you." His lips pulled back in a mocking grin. "You're a loose end that was supposed to be snuffed out years ago. Stan was pissed when you turned up with the girl."

Porch Guy had recognized me. "Still not enough. I already know that." There was no way I would have clued him in to my surprise that they'd figured out who I was. "What else you got?"

I'd made him mad. He pressed his lips together, probably to stop from swearing at me. "The orders trickled down from Tony, and I only know what I told you."

Tony was one guy above him. He had another source. I raised the gun higher and pushed it against his neck. I was tired of playing around.

Panic flashed in Billy's eyes, along with an innate sense of self-preservation. "That's all I know, I swear. His directive to kill three birds with one stone was divided up on a need-to-know basis to get the job done."

CHAPTER 20

HAWK

Stale air greeted the seven of us as we crowded into the small, dark columbarium at the Bay Area cemetery where her parents and grandparents had been laid to rest. Somehow, Stella had talked us into taking a side trip rather than holing up at the lake and working on whatever the hell Billy had meant by "kill three birds with one stone."

Billy was in the capable hands of the men our CIA contact had sent. He'd received medical attention and was being detained by red tape, as we'd hoped.

Red tugged on my bicep to get my attention. Over the past few days, I'd been getting used to her constant touch, and I liked it. I was probably just as bad. We didn't have any alone time, and I wished we did. Being near her soothed a part of me I hadn't known existed. For the time being, I would go with it. In the back of my mind, I knew our relationship was temporary—she would realize I wasn't good enough for her down the line.

"Do you want to know how I figured out the clue?" Excitement radiated from her sparkling eyes and wide smile.

"Absolutely." Hayden had called us when we were halfway back with instructions to meet them at the cemetery. I could picture Keegan fuming at the change of plans in the background. But Stella was adamant, and I understood. It was about her grandma, a connection, and the chance to help her brother. We wouldn't let her part with any heirlooms found, and we also wouldn't stifle her hopes.

"Pay attention." She tugged on my arm again, and I focused on her. "That last note connecting to Oma's past and the one holding her heart referenced her brother or husband. I don't think it was about her parents. That doesn't feel right to me. She grieved all her life for Stefan, and my grandfather was the love of her life. She told us that all the time."

"And you eliminated the brother as a possibility because?"

She turned a little green. "His body wasn't, ah, laid to rest in the States."

Realization dawned, and I wrapped my arm around her. I'd forgotten that her uncle had died during the Holocaust. He was a part of a group of German teenagers who'd opposed the Nazis through music—at least, it had started that way.

"So it has to mean my Opa, my grandpa. Especially since Oma told me her mother had her carry their family heirlooms to misdirect suspicion when they immigrated."

I nodded. That made sense. Going through a child's possessions might not have been a high priority.

We walked farther in, our flashlights illuminating several niches that held urns. Stella directed us to where her family was. They had all been cremated, and she had the keys.

Silence fell as we stood before the openings. Each family member's name and dates were below their respective urn. Her parents and grandparents had been put to rest side by side in order of when they had been born: grandfather, grandmother, mother, father. There were two empty spots in the same row for Red and Max.

Stella raised a shaky hand and inserted a key into the door that housed her grandfather's ashes. With a turn and pull, the door swung open. I angled my flashlight for her to see what was inside. Carefully, Hayden lifted the urn out in case anything was behind it.

The cubby went deeper than expected.

She gasped and reached in to remove a dark, rectangular object. She set it on the ground then paused to give me a watery glance. Hayden put the urn back, and we all hovered around her, waiting.

After a deep breath, Stella opened the lid on the wooden box, which had a bouquet of flowers painted on the top. An antique mirror on the inside of the lid caught and reflected her face. Nestled in the velvet-lined interior, along with a ribbon-tied stack of letters, were several small bags.

One after another, she opened the pouches to reveal various antique rings and necklaces. Sapphires, emeralds, rubies, and pearls lay against the dark-red lining of the jewelry box. There was a handful of large gems, several karats in size —they were extravagant. "Those are pieces you would find in a museum."

"They must be my great-grandmother's." Tears rolled unchecked down her face. "I can sell one and save my brother, paying off his debt. I bet one of these emeralds alone would bring in enough money if there were few infractions."

I shot a sharp look at Jack and Mike. All of our expressions said *hell no*. We would end it another way. The jewels were Red's and her brother's. She would keep every single one of them.

Hayden locked the door that held her grandfather's urn and handed Stella the key. With great care, she replaced the jewelry into the velvet bags and closed the box's lid. As she raised her head and stared at the names of her family members, I decided to give her space. Stepping several paces back so she could have a few minutes to mourn her family, I turned to Jack, keeping Red in my sight.

"There is no way we're allowing her to sell any of those to

pay off a loan shark." Anger rolled in my gut. As I looked at each of the guys, I noted similar reactions in their expressions.

"Agreed," Jack stated, his voice hushed. "Hayden, you're going to take Stella's family heirlooms on the jet to Hannah and Liv. We'll tell her you're selling a single piece that she chooses, but in the meantime, Hannah and Liv will keep them safe."

"That will only work because she's aware of the danger here. I'm not positive we can get her to part with all of it. She may insist on selling one of the rings or necklaces herself," Mike added.

"Nah, she'll go along with the plan because she likes me best." Hayden winked at me, a silly grin on his face.

I snorted my response. *He would think that.* "It's because you're so pretty."

Hayden laughed. Not much fazed him. Call Keegan pretty, and he would answer with a fist to the face. It was strange how much they looked alike, though they weren't related.

"If she sells anything in haste, she runs the risk of under-valuing the piece," I said. "We'll make sure she knows the loan sharks have their hands in the pawnshops. What good would that do her family?" I would convince her that this was the best plan, even for her brother. We would have this wrapped up before anything else happened, I hoped.

Stella turned, and we fell into silence as she made her way over to us, the jewelry box cradled awkwardly in her arms. I took it from her, and she flashed me a grateful smile.

I explained everything that the team had discussed regarding her find. It took a bit of convincing, but she finally agreed to let Hayden take the box of jewelry to Maine. There, Liv and Hannah would catalog the jewelry. Then they would get back to her with prices—it helped that Liv came from money.

Liv had plenty of experience with heirlooms. She could help Stella determine which ones to sell, and they would handle it for her. Or we would let her think they would sell it. I knew it would break her heart to part with any of her grandma's history, so I wouldn't let that happen.

With the box secure in my arm, I placed my other hand on the small of her back to lead her out with the guys.

"Wait." We all paused for her. "I want to put this in there too." She reached around her neck and lifted the chain that held the ring her brother had given her, the one he'd said he had to take back for some reason. From under her shirt, the small silver ring with its delicate etchings flashed in the dim light.

Jack lurched forward, his expression stricken. "Where'd you get that?"

Eyes wide, Stella froze. "My brother gave it to me. He said it was to remind me that he loves me. Why? It's not worth much, or I would have sold it."

Pain lanced Jack's eyes, and Red gasped in reaction to the raw emotion. *Fuck.* I finally figured out where I'd seen that ring before—back in high school, on Jack's girlfriend's finger. *This isn't good.*

Jack took hold of the small silver ring with the infinity symbol and floral etchings and turned it until he found a small scratch. There was no longer any doubt in my mind, and Jack confirmed who it had belonged to, his voice clogged with emotion. "This was Jenni's ring."

CHAPTER 21

Back at the lake house, Jack paced from one end of the house to the next, a glass of whiskey in one hand and his Glock in the other. Our past was catching up with us, and not in a good way. When we were in high school, Jack had dated Jenni, Rex's younger sister. Rex had been the neighborhood drug dealer and had a gang of his own, and he hated Jack. Everything escalated and went to hell before we got out of there, thanks to a local detective who for some reason gave a shit about us.

Jack passed by again before pivoting to pace back to the other end of the house. He wasn't taking it well.

Everything was going to hell. We suddenly knew what Billy had meant when he said he was ordered to kill three birds with one stone. The objective wasn't Stella and Max, not really. They were bait, collateral damage. It went way back, and the presence of the ring could only mean one thing. Rex was out of prison.

Stella had tried to give it back to Jack, but he'd said no. It was better off with her.

I had no idea how Rex had gotten his hands on the ring.

One of his gang must have taken it off her finger after everything had gone to shit that night so long ago.

The rest of us shared uneasy glances while Chris typed furiously on his keyboard. "Got him." At Chris's words, every one of us stopped what we were doing and turned to him. "Rex is still in prison. Unless there is a new hearing I'm not seeing, he's not due to be released for another month." He leaned back and let hesitation cloud his features. "If that's the case, I'm not sure if the two are connected."

But we knew. Somehow, everything was connected. Besides, Rex had all that time in prison to hash out a plan to take us down. We'd fucked up, big time. After Detective Watters had struck a deal for us and we'd left our old neighborhood, we'd assumed Rex was out of commission.

That was the thing about assumptions, though. They inevitably came back to bite one in the ass.

STELLA

THE TENSION IN THE CABIN WAS THICK. WITHOUT understanding what was going on, I kept to myself in a corner of the soft leather couch, sifting through the stack of letters from my Oma. Every once in a while, I glanced at Hawk, but he was busy with Jack and the other guys. That freed up time for me to read.

I twisted my hair into a messy bun and secured it with an elastic band I'd tucked into the pocket of my jeans earlier. Shoving the sleeves of my favorite dark-gray T-shirt up, I made myself comfortable.

Most of the letters were to my Opa when he was away on business or sweet notes from when they were dating. There was even one from her brother. It was very old, so I took extra care in handling the worn paper and set it aside for later. For the time being, I would focus on the ones she addressed to me.

Her penmanship had turned shaky, as was common with the elderly. I wished she was there with me.

She'd written me three letters. I chose to open the one on the top first. After unfolding the letter, the uncomfortable atmosphere in the cabin faded away. I lost myself in what she'd penned, as if she were sitting next to me, telling the tale herself.

It started with why she left Germany, what had happened to her brother, and why that raised the stakes and sped up the timeline they'd set for her family's immigration to America. Part of her story I already knew, but not all of it.

My Dearest Stella,

I don't talk about my brother often. Last night, I was thinking of him more than usual, perhaps because of my advancing years and my pending reunion with him when I pass on to the next world.

As you know, my brother was a teenager when Hitler came to power. There were many ordinances that we were to obey as children during that time. I was much younger, but even I wasn't happy about it. The changes brought so much ugliness in their wake.

Teenagers never like to be told what to do, what to wear, or how to think. No one does, really. My brother had a particularly hard time with it, as did his friends. They'd heard of others their age who'd rebelled against the imposed conformity through music, which later turned into something else.

I've already told you what happened, about the beatings and public hanging. What I didn't tell you was that my parents went to be with Stefan in those last moments. They couldn't let him go without him seeing their faces as he left this world. He needed the support, loving faces to focus on during the atrocity that was being committed.

My parents would not let me accompany them, and I was made to stay with a family friend until they returned. Watching my brother's hanging broke my parents. I wasn't left unaffected, either, but I didn't witness what they had. We were never the same after that day.

Within the hour of being collected from our friend's home, my parents frantically packed small inconspicuous bags for us, and we fled the only home I'd ever known. They had received word that soldiers would be coming for us too.

My family was among the aristocracy. Our station protected us to an extent, but not from everything. Not from what mattered most.

Leaving everything and everyone behind was traumatic, but not nearly as horrifying as losing my brother. Hold on to those you love, my dear. Accept them for who they are. Always stand up for what you believe in, but be mindful—life is precious.

All my love,

Oma

Tears streaked down my cheeks unchecked. I knew the story—she'd told it to me before—but it broke my heart every time. The couch dipped, and Hawk sat beside me and pulled me to him. I buried my face in his chest, balled his shirt in my hands, and sobbed. I missed her so much.

He rubbed his hand up and down my back in a slow caress. Someone handed me a few Kleenexes, and I used them to wipe my face. My eyelids closed as his hand moved to the back of my head, holding me close. The comfort he offered reinforced how much I cared for him. Scars and all, he'd slipped into my heart, and I didn't want to let him go.

I knew he was hurting. The thing about internal scars was that the damage wasn't always easy to see. It was a minefield I would have to walk if I wanted to remain by his side. I did, and I would.

"Stella?" Hawk's deep voice rumbled through his chest and vibrated along my body. "Hayden is heading out. Did you want to put any of the letters in there, or are you keeping them with you?"

I sighed as I disentangled myself from him. "The one I read can go in there. I haven't had a chance to go through the rest yet." I handed it to Hayden, who tucked it into the jewelry box. He pulled me to my feet and hugged me before saying goodbye to everyone.

"This will be over soon, Red, and then we can binge watch the next season of *The Walking Dead* or *Game of Thrones*."

I grinned. Hayden was so much fun. I was looking forward to hanging out with him again. All of them, even Jack, although he was dealing with something I didn't understand, were there for the other guys—and for me. Jack, Chris, and Mike had dropped whatever they had been doing to be there for Hawk. Through Hawk, they were there for my brother and me. They were incredible men, though Keegan was a bit of a mystery.

"Come on." Hawk tugged me behind him. "Let's get something to drink. Do you want coffee or something stronger?"

"That whiskey Jack has been steadily making his way through looks good."

"Whiskey it is." Hawk snatched it out of Jack's hand when we found him in the kitchen. After he handed the bottle to me, Hawk gripped Jack's shoulder. A look passed between them that I couldn't decipher. "If you don't pull your shit together, Hannah threatened to come here and do it for you."

Well, hell. Jack laughed at that one, and some of the tension seemed to fall away. "Can you imagine?"

"No, I'm a little afraid to. That woman is frightening. Makes sense she's with you."

"I'll be sure to tell her that." Jack grinned, his tired eyes looking a little more alive than before.

I leaned against the counter with two fingers of whiskey in a glass and smiled at their interaction. They were all lucky to have each other. It made me long for my family even more. The ring of a cell phone pierced the semi-quiet, and Jack's grin grew as he glanced at the screen. "Speaking of Hannah…" He went into one of the bedrooms just as mine rang.

Hawk held my gaze, and I sucked in a breath.

"I'm sorry!" Shit. I was supposed to keep it in that signal-blocking bag. It wasn't a normal thing for me to do, and it didn't fit in the pocket of my jeans.

Hawk shook his head. "I should be a helluva lot madder than I am. But if they come to us now, we'll handle it."

I bit my lip and nodded. The only person other than the guys who had my new burner phone number was my brother.

"Go ahead and answer it," Hawk said with a sigh.

Fear licked my body as I pulled the cell from my pocket.

Max's name flashed across the screen, and I pressed the button to answer as I raised it to my ear.

"Stel?"

Shit. His voice is weak. "It's me. What's wrong?"

There was a small rustling, and Max swore under his breath. His breathing sounded labored. Then I heard the steady beep in the background, and my alarm tripled. "Where are you?"

"I'm at Mercy."

"The hospital? What happened? Are you okay?"

"Yeah, I'll be fine, but I can't talk long. Goddamn pain pills make it hard to think. Had to warn you. They know."

"What?" Adrenaline laced my blood, and my fingers went numb. Hawk grabbed the phone and hit the speaker button. "What are you talking about? They know what?"

"I fucked up, Stel. Told 'em about you." His speech slurred, and the beeping in the background sounded erratic.

My hands shook as I held the phone. "I already know, Max. Did something else happen?"

"Oma's legacy—" A horrible rattling cough stole his words. Several seconds passed before he delivered the next bomb. "They know you have it and are coming to take the treasure from you." Then the line went dead.

CHAPTER 22

Red was beside herself about her worthless brother. I kept her close, absently running my fingers along her arm, while the guys and I planned what to do next. Hayden was already in the air and on his way to Maine with her family heirlooms. That was one thing we didn't need to worry about any longer, but the brother remained a concern. Max needed protection.

The sky lightened as the miles melted beneath our SUVs. Mike and Keegan followed in the other Range Rover. We would be in San Francisco within the hour, just in time for breakfast.

"I called in a favor, and guards will be stationed at Max's hospital door," Mike told Stella on speakerphone. "No one will get to him while he's there."

"Thank you. I want to see him."

Bad idea. "You will, just not yet. He's probably resting, anyway, and having you there will increase the danger he's in."

"Because they're after me?"

"Yes." What I didn't tell her was that they were keeping her brother alive so she would stay close and lead them to her family's treasure. Once they had what they wanted, both Max and Stella would be loose ends that needed to be taken care of. I had a feeling she already knew that. She was smart and processed things quickly.

I tucked her closer to me, so damned impressed with how she was handling everything. After talking to her brother, she had been in a panic, but she quickly reined that in and wanted to work with us on a solution. There was strength in her response, which assured all of us that she wasn't going to fall apart. None of us wanted to deal with that. Tears from a woman sucked because we weren't the best at knowing what to do beyond attempting to fix whatever had hurt them.

The compulsive drive I had to keep her safe and happy punched me in the gut. *When the hell did I start to think of her as mine? And when did I start to think of her as part of my family? Shit, I don't have time to psychoanalyze myself right now.* I caught Chris's gaze. "We're sure Rex isn't in play?"

"Of course not, but we don't have a lead on any of the other guys from the gang yet. Mole got out a few years ago but isn't turning up around here."

"That doesn't mean he isn't in contact with Rex," Jack said.

"No, but it's something," Mike interjected before addressing Chris. "Were you able to get the visitor records for Rex?"

Chris nodded. "Mole's name isn't on there, but that doesn't mean much."

True. Getting an alias wasn't hard. And while Rex's right-hand man wasn't exactly smart, I would have thought he had enough sense to lay low or use his criminal connections to start over.

Red fidgeted next to me.

"When Hayden lands, I want him to go ahead with selling the ring. The faster we get the money, the safer my brother will be." She held up a hand to silence our protests. "I know that's not the end of it, but that will buy us some time to get out of the country. We could start over wherever their reach isn't strong. Maybe Canada?"

"It won't help. These people will take the money but then decide they want more, and neither of you will ever be free." I shifted. I was looking directly at her, so she could see the truth behind my words. "They won't stop. It's not their MO. They'll bleed you dry until there isn't any more. Then they'll put a bullet through your head—if you're lucky."

"Like how your parents weren't as fortunate?" Her hands gripped mine, and she gave me a gentle squeeze. "I hear you. I do. But maybe this situation is different."

"It is, and it isn't." I didn't know how I could tell her without sending Jack into another tailspin. I glanced in the rearview mirror and saw him watching me. He gave me a sharp nod, telling me to talk about it. She needed to know. At least some of what we had been worried about was coming full circle.

"I've told you a little about my past"—I caught Chris's attention too—"and our history. You already know that the same organization that's after you and your brother killed my mom and her husband. What else is in play is that I'm a loose end they've just been made aware of."

She nibbled on her bottom lip. "So you're involved on a whole other level. I'm so sorry for dragging you into this and turning their focus to you too, Hawk."

I gave her a crooked grin. "I'm not. I got to meet you, and that's worth dealing with them ten times over. Besides, it's long overdue."

When she smiled, she chased the shadows away, and I was grateful to her for that. "There is more going on here, and we're trying to figure out exactly how much, who, and what we're going to face next."

"Okay, but I don't quite see what that has to do with

clearing my brother's debt. Aside from the greedy, corrupt bastards part."

Jack barked out a laugh. "You've got that right."

She had no idea how right. I needed to give her a glimpse into our struggles when we'd banded together in the warehouse so many years ago. "When we were in high school, our neighborhood had an aggressive drug gang that harassed a lot of the kids."

"And several months after we'd graduated, too," Jack interjected.

That's right. Jack, Mike, and I had finished up our last year when things got bad. "Rex was the leader of the gang and had a major problem with Jack, as he was dating Rex's younger sister."

"That's putting it mildly," Chris cut in, and Stella's eyes rounded, the pieces probably falling into place around Jack's reaction to the ring.

"We took it on ourselves to police our neighborhood when it came to Rex and his followers. When Rex began talks with a larger drug lord or maybe a cartel—we're not sure about that —his personality took a turn for the worse."

"The guy had never been good, but the drugs he was sampling made him unpredictable," Jack said.

"Things went from bad to nightmarish before we all got out of that hellhole and into the military. We've never forgotten, and I'm sure he hasn't either, considering we're the reason he went to jail."

I paused as we entered a parking garage for the hotel we had decided to stay in. It was a strategic move, as we were sure it was being watched. After all, it was a casino owned by the Tridel Corp. We'd planned to take Malone, Tridel's owner, out from the inside if he showed up. Things were going to escalate, and soon. We would cut the head off the snake, so to speak. I needed to wrap this story up for her so we weren't talking about anything personal when we got out.

Stella's brows furrowed. "You think Rex is involved too?"

"We're not sure. There isn't proof that he is, but the ring posed the possibility. We're going to need to find out where your brother got that."

CHAPTER 23

STELLA

Hawk and I were in the room we were sharing in the casino's hotel… The same freaking casino owned by the people who were after my brother. I couldn't believe it. I got that they planned to take them down and thought this was the right place to capture the boss, but no. I was tired of worrying about those guys. My brother had been hurt. He was my priority.

And I finally had the means to get Max out of the hot mess he'd created.

Hawk leaned against the door, all broody and sexy like he always was. I couldn't let him distract me. He and his teammates had other priorities. *Yeah, to keep me safe. But what about Max?* It seemed as though he was last on their agenda, right behind taking down Tridel. Well, I'd made up my mind. If they weren't going to get my brother out of harm's way, then I was.

The guards in front of Max's hospital room helped to ease my mind. I pivoted and paced to the other end of the room. Hawk followed my movements.

My thoughts churned with how to handle what I had to do. I needed to test the waters.

Maybe appealing to Hawk would work.

I halted in my tracks and faced him. I pulled out the necklace I'd pocketed from Oma's heirlooms instead of sending it to Maine with Hayden. "I want to sell this and pay off those men."

A nerve jumped at the edge of Hawk's jawline. "No. It won't do any good. They know you have access to more, and they'll continue to use your brother as bait to get it."

"I have to do this. You're probably right, but what if you're not? There's a chance this could work. Shouldn't we try before going in with guns blazing?" I held out my hand, stopping his argument. "Max is my priority, even if he isn't yours." I had to take a deep breath and stop myself from saying something I couldn't take back.

Between us, the large emerald dangled on the end of a chain. "I'm selling this and taking the money to him now. I won't wait for those men to hurt him again." I choked on the last few words. Worry ate at me.

All the times I'd screwed up and taken my phone from the signal-blocking sleeve was because I loved my brother. I couldn't abandon him. It put us at risk, but I had to be there for him if he needed me. The guys he was mixed up with were serious. What if I'd missed his last call? I could never live with myself if that happened.

Hawk shook his head and took a step closer. I withdrew the necklace and put it back in my pocket.

"That won't help. No matter how much it seems like selling your family's jewelry is the answer, it's not."

"You don't know that!" I yelled. "We've been in situations like this before." I pressed my lips together and inhaled through my nose. I had to calm down. "Not exactly like this, but he's gotten into tight spots where Oma and I had to bail him out quick. After we paid, there was no fallout."

"No," Hawk snapped.

Shit. I could tell his worry was transforming to anger. I had to defuse him so I could do what was necessary.

"I'll be fine, and there is security at the hospital. I can pawn the stone then see Max. The guards will keep me safe while I'm there. Please, Hawk. I'll be back before you even know it, and all this will go away."

He crowded me, his pupils dilating in what looked like panic. "I'm telling you it won't help. Not anymore. They want their pound of flesh. They'll make you an example to your brother after they force you to give them the rest of the jewelry."

"Ahh!" I whirled around and shoved my hair back from my face. For a few seconds, I closed my eyes, trying to regain control of my temper. "That's never happened before, and this time will not be any different. Once they get the money, they'll leave us alone." I at least had to try. He didn't know everything, nor had he been in my shoes before.

I faced him again and placed my hand flat on his chest. Dammit, he affected me. I didn't want to do what I needed to. I softened my voice. "Don't worry. I won't tell Max anything about you or the rest of the team. I wouldn't put you in any additional danger or further on their radar."

Hawk growled and gripped my hips. "There is no way you're walking out that door and into their hands. The stakes are even higher since they know about me and my team, Stella."

"Nothing will happen. This is a separate issue." *Oh my God, this is killing me.* I didn't want to lie to him. I could do it. I knew I could sell the necklace in the pawnshop downstairs. I needed a hundred grand, and the piece I had was easily worth more than that. So long as I got enough money, my brother would be safe, and I would also be able to protect Hawk and the guys too. I would be back before Hawk knew I was missing. I had to try, even though the last thing I wanted to do was to hurt him or to shake the trust we had already established.

He didn't say anything, so I dropped my forehead to his chest partly because I wanted the connection and because I didn't want him to read anything on my face. "Okay. I understand."

He kissed the top of my head and wrapped his arms around me. Warmth spread through me at his touch. I wanted to stay like that, but I couldn't.

"I'm tired." I pressed a kiss to his chest, wishing his shirt wasn't in the way. I couldn't look at him yet. I had to get my emotions under control. "I think I'm going to take a shower."

"Take your time."

His hand traced up my spine and sank into my hair. He was killing me, but I had to do what I had to do. Max was all I had left of my family, and I had to put his well-being first, even over my own needs.

Hawk tipped my head back. I closed my eyes, and his mouth brushed across mine. I opened for him, needing him. We kissed, and it was sweet and raw, but I pulled back. He let me.

I slipped from his arms and went into the bathroom. Once the water was turned on, I waited. A few minutes went by before I cracked open the door. Our room was in front of the kitchenette. There was a very slight chance I could sneak out without being seen. Leaving the shower running, I inched out of our room and to the door.

The guys were crowded around a laptop, their backs to me. It wasn't exactly easy. I had to open the door of the suite and close it without any noise. It was my chance, and I had to take it.

I MADE IT OUT OF THE CASINO WITHOUT ANY OF THE GUYS spotting me—yet. My heart continued to protest with heightened speed. If I could get Max the money and return before they realized I was gone, I could prove to Hawk it was the right move.

The pawnshop ordeal hadn't been fun—it killed me to part with anything of Oma's history. But the money jammed into my jeans pocket could very well save Max's life.

I slipped through the doors of the hospital and kept my head down. The halls smelled of antiseptic and illness. Nothing was comforting about a hospital. There was always someone moving about. I'd stopped at the patient information desk and gotten the number for Max's room. He was on the third floor.

When the elevator doors pinged, I stepped out onto the ward, keeping my head down. A peek through my lashes showed which way his room was. I turned right and followed the arrows toward his room. The hallway forked, and I checked again, following the sign pointing to the left. *Has to be down this hall.*

I took a step and was jerked back. My mouth opened in a scream. A cloth slammed over my face. It was hard to breathe. I struggled, but an arm held me tightly against a body much larger than mine.

My head swam, and I took another breath through the cloth. The black dots floating in my vision multiplied.

Darkness greeted me when I awoke. My mouth felt cottony and foul, as though something had crawled in and died. It smelled of oil and gasoline. Curled in a fetal position, I was jostled around. The space felt tight and cramped. *Oh shit, I'm in a trunk!*

I tried to move, but my hands were bound behind me. So were my ankles. The motion of the car stopped, and I slid a little from the abrupt movement. Panic welled inside me. *Will they come for me now? Is it one person, or more?*

What had happened? I wracked my fuzzy brain, trying to remember. I was almost to Max's room. So close, but not close enough. I didn't see the guards, so his room must not have been around the corner as I'd thought.

Did they do something to my brother? Is he okay? The anxiety and anticipation of what would happen next spun out of control.

Sweat broke out along my hairline, but I couldn't wipe it away. My limbs trembled.

I heard a pop, then the trunk was opened. Light flooded the interior. I shifted my head. If they were going to kill me, I would look into their eyes. Because I would come back and haunt their asses. *This is so not okay.*

I went with anger. The flip side to my raging emotions was tears and terror, and I couldn't afford that.

A shadow fell over me, and I screamed. He slapped his hand over my mouth. I tried to bite him, but he cupped his palm. My eyes went wide. He was huge. And gross. *Ick.* He smelled as though he rarely showered. His hair was stringy and rather long. There was a big mole on his chin that his beard didn't quite cover. It was disgusting.

"Shut up. I won't hurt you if you keep your damn mouth closed."

I tried to nod with his hand clasped around my mouth. His arms slid under my legs and back. He lifted me as though I weighed nothing. In the low light, I looked around. The car was a brown sedan. We were in a run-down neighborhood.

Oomph. The world spun. He'd thrown me over his shoulder. My view was restricted to dirty jeans.

The trunk slammed shut, and his legs ate up the distance. One door opened, then another. We went down a flight of stairs. It was darker there and cold.

"You got her?"

The guy carrying me grunted.

"Throw her over there."

What? Throw? For a brief second, I was airborne. My hip and shoulder smacked into concrete. Dust billowed around me, and I inhaled it, which resulted in a coughing fit.

A foot dug into my hip then flipped me to my back. My tethered hands hurt. The plastic zip ties bit into my wrists. No… The guy who'd made me turn over was obviously strung out.

"Why am I here? Who are you?"

He snorted. "Gag her," drugged-out guy ordered my kidnapper.

"No!" I struggled, but kidnapper guy shoved a bandana in my mouth. Then he tied another one around my face to hold it in place. It was too tight. My eyes watered. I couldn't think about how dirty it probably was.

Once he'd finished, Drug Guy came back. There was a clang. Then I was dragged back. He grabbed under one arm and lifted me into a metal chair. It was awkward, and I started to fall. With a hard yank on my arm, he righted me. "I bet he wants you back."

Oh, shit. This guy is using me to get to Hawk.

"Smile pretty." He snickered and stepped back, holding up a phone.

Fuck you. I narrowed my eyes and dropped my head. I would not make it easy for him.

After only a second, pain exploded on my scalp. My head jerked back. Drug Guy's hand fisted the hair at the top of my head. My back arched, and I tried to get purchase with my bound feet to take the pressure off, but they kept slipping.

He slammed the barrel of a gun against my temple. I whimpered. I didn't want to die.

"Listen up, bitch. You'll sit and like it." His nostrils flared. "If you don't, I'll make sure your brother hears about it. Maybe I'll even bring him one of your fingers."

Where's Max? I wanted to scream at him and make him talk. I couldn't. The gag did its job. I thrashed again.

The cold from the metal chair seeped through my clothes. I sat there. I didn't want him to shoot me.

Mole Guy stood next to the other one. "I'll take the picture, Rex."

"No," Rex snapped.

Rex. I'd heard that name before. I would have to remember to tell Hawk if I made it out alive.

The light on his phone flashed. He'd taken my picture. I sagged a little when his gaze swung to Mole Guy. "Move her after this. They'll come here first."

My heart rate spiked as he stepped closer. He yanked my head back farther, and I glared into his dark, pupil-eclipsed eyes.

Spit sprayed my face as he yelled, "You heard right—I've got Max by the balls! He's nothing but a bargaining chip." His mouth moved into a sinister grin. "So are you."

I couldn't move. I whimpered. He took that as a yes and released me. Tears streamed down my face. Hawk was right. I should never have left.

CHAPTER 24

HAWK

I grabbed Jack by his black T-shirt. "Have you seen Stella?" He didn't flinch or pull back even though wild panic coursed through me and had to have been visible.

"Not since breakfast. I'll check in with the other guys. Maybe they have."

I let go of him and paced the length of the room we were all occupying. Keegan was staking out the roof of the hotel and surrounding area, mapping exit strategies. We didn't think they were aware of our presence because only one of us had checked in. The rest of us met in the back stairway to get to the room with our heads down and hats on. We stayed off the cameras as much as possible.

The argument Stella and I had in the room played back in my head in excruciating detail. I had denied her the right to sell the jewelry, which I should not have done, but my fear for her safety had been paramount in my mind, as I knew the nature of Tridel firsthand. True to the color of her hair and what I'd learned about her personality, her temper had erupted.

I'd dropped my guard when she'd rested her forehead against my chest. She'd outwardly agreed with me that we would wait, though I was skeptical even at the time. When I'd kissed her, all I could think of was how soft her lips were and how perfectly we fit together. When she'd pulled away, wanting to take a shower, I'd put our argument behind us as resolved. That was my first mistake.

When I'd heard the shower running, I went to talk to Chris to see if he'd spoken to Rich, our contact at the CIA. The favor we'd called in with him to hold off Porch Guy's underlings, including Billy Williams, came with strings attached. Rich had fired back a request of his own.

Actually, it was more of a demand. He wanted the head of the Tridel Corporation, David Malone. The whole situation had crossed from personal mission and into a job, one we needed to execute quickly.

She'd been in the bathroom too long. I went to check on her, and terror detonated in my gut when I found the shower empty. It had been a half an hour, so she had a major head start on us, assuming Keegan or Mike hadn't spotted her leaving the hotel. I ran my hands through my hair, desperate for news. Someone had to have seen her.

Something caught my eye. She'd left her cell, still in its sleeve, probably because we had been too close for her to grab it off the couch. We couldn't even track her that way. I held the burner phone up for the guys to see and noted the heightened worry reflected in their grim acknowledgment.

"We don't know where she is!" Jack shouted as he strapped his gun on and shoved a few clips into his pockets. "Chris is going through the security cameras in the hotel to see where she exited and the direction she went." His hand gripped my shoulder in a hard squeeze. "We'll find her."

Damn right, we will. I locked down my overactive imagination to focus on that thought alone. I wouldn't allow myself to go back to the night my parents were murdered, to the possibility of Stella being beaten, or to the image of flames devouring her soft skin, stealing her beauty, the light from her eyes, her soul. No fucking way.

I relaxed my fingers around the gun I hadn't even realized I'd pulled from its holster. After taking several deep breaths, I returned it. As Jack had done, I shoved many clips into my pockets, anticipating needing an endless supply of bullets.

Mike and Keegan burst into the room with matching expressions riddled with worry and determination. In a flurry of efficiency, we all geared up with Kevlar vests, guns, knives, extra ammo, and a grenade or two. *You never know when you might need to toss a grenade into a nest of enemies for maximum damage.*

"Got her," Chris reported, and we all crowded around the screen.

Stella had wrapped her head in a scarf that knotted on the lower left side by her neck. She wore oversized glasses and—*is that my shirt?*

"She went into the shop in the casino. Then I picked her up leaving through the service doors." She'd turned and headed in the direction of the hospital where her brother was.

"Call the guards. Keep her there," Jack ordered as Keegan pressed a number on his cell.

We filed out of the room before Keegan ended the call. "She never showed."

"Fucking hell." My heart slammed against my ribs. "They've got her."

We sprinted to the stairs and then to the garage. Once there, we piled into one of the Range Rovers. In the SUV, I felt a single vibration from her cell, which I'd slipped into my pocket. I pulled her phone out and almost threw up from what I saw.

Stella sat gagged and zip-tied to a chair.

"We've got a bigger problem." I showed the picture to the guys. That wasn't all. There was a text accompanying the image: *want the old crew.*

There was only one person who held a grudge big enough

to take Red to draw us out. *Mole*, Rex's right-hand man, whose real name was Blaze. We'd mocked him at every opportunity, even calling him Mole to his face.

I knew we weren't going to find her anywhere along the way to the hospital. As I met the gazes of my crew, I could tell we all knew where we'd have to go. Mike executed a sharp turn around the next corner, and we were on our way to where the showdown would inevitably happen: our old neighborhood.

Fury and fear warred in my body. They were using Stella as bait to act on their longtime grudge.

Jack had just gotten off the phone with Rich Stevens. We'd found a motel close to the school and our old warehouse to hole up in. True to his word, Detective Watters from our old neighborhood had cleaned the town up, at least regarding Rex's reign. The streets weren't desolate, and several new businesses had moved in where abandoned storefronts and factories had been. It still wasn't a great place by any stretch, but it was better than the ghetto it was before.

We couldn't go to the warehouse, as Jack and Mike had turned that into a teen shelter, the reason we were in San Francisco on business in the first place. We all were involved in the shelters.

God help that son of a bitch if he messes with the kids who stay there. Jack's first priority was to have Rich station security around the warehouse, and Mike had called the staff and put them on high alert. The kids would be told some of what was going on, just enough that they would stay out of the line of fire.

Chris connected the feed to his phone so that he could access the cameras or database search he'd continued to run for any hit on Rex, Mole, or Tridel Corp. We were ready, never having divested ourselves of the arsenal strapped to our bodies.

It was just past noon. We weren't waiting until dark, which

would have been a luxury we couldn't afford. Instead, we were going in hot. "Everyone knows what to do?"

We sounded off in the affirmative to Jack's question, which was standard after we'd settled on a plan of execution. We would surround Rex's old haunt then storm inside. The risk of casualties was there, but if we didn't do it that way, Stella would pay with her life. We had no idea what had become of Mole. He could have resumed whatever partnership Rex had initiated before we'd gone head-to-head on the street that night. I didn't even want to remember what had happened. I couldn't imagine the turmoil Jack was dealing with.

Mike parked several blocks away. We exited the vehicle then moved to the cover of the buildings nearby. On Jack's command, we split up. With earphones and mics in place, we could apprise one another as information came in.

I took point for a direct path while everyone else fanned out, approaching the old building from different angles. We'd recognized something in the picture Mole had sent of Red—a red knit cap, one we'd all remembered as Jenni's favorite hat, sat on a shelf in the corner. Stella was inside their old place.

The closer I got, the more focused I became. There was no way I would have been okay with covering from the rooftops. I had to be up close and personal. Keegan had offered to serve as sniper in my place, but Jack vetoed that idea. We all had to be on the ground.

Even though every one of my muscles tensed, I analyzed, processed, and reacted as I'd been trained to do. A paper coffee cup rolled across my path as I sprinted to my next point of cover on the side of a factory.

Since it was during work and school hours, there were minimal people out. The few who were got the hell out of our way.

My sights locked on the old, run-down house set between a factory and a junkyard. A lot had happened to the area, but it seemed that much remained the same. Poverty, despair, and danger clung to the time-ravaged house. Once a dump, always a dump.

We'd decided against tear gas. It wasn't a unanimous vote, but the satellite views hadn't shown men posted around the house. No activity in the past fifteen minutes could have indicated that there were several inside or only two, Mole and Stella. We didn't know. We were going in blind.

"In position" was repeated through our headsets until all of us had reported. I waited until Jack gave the command to go. When he did, we moved hard and fast. My foot connected with the front door with a loud crack. The wood splintered around the lock. As the door flew open, I jerked to the side in anticipation of a spray of bullets.

Silence. My heart stuttered. *That could only mean a few things.* With care, I checked around the corner. *No shots fired. No one in sight.* Gun first, I went into the room.

Empty.

Through a series of "clear" sounding through our earpieces, we came together in the main room. The chair was there, the ties cut and left behind, as was the red knit hat that Jack gripped tightly in his fist.

Mike and I spread out. I took the time to do a thorough search for cameras and bugs. We found a camera pointed directly at the chair and at us.

No one said a word as we left to regroup at the temporary motel. *We'll find her. There is no other option.* Rich was involved, as were his unlimited resources, which we would take full advantage of.

Mike got coffee started, and Keegan tossed each of us a protein bar. None of us felt like eating, but we needed to keep our energy up.

Chris dropped his phone on the table and turned to us, his face grim. Jack's cell rang as soon as Chris spoke. "Rex is out of jail."

Fucking hell.

Jack answered and uttered a few words into his phone before disconnecting. We didn't even have time to react before Jack swore a blue streak. "Rich has been monitoring the Tridel Corp's movements while we attempted to find and rescue Stella. The guards Keegan called in for Max's room are dead. Max has been taken, and no activity has been noted by the enemy yet. You all know what this means."

"They're working together." *At least in some capacity*. I threw my protein bar, and it hit the opposite wall with a less-than-satisfying thud.

It was clear as day. Rex and Mole had Stella and Max. Our old enemies and the Tridel Corp had to be interconnected. After what had happened to Jenni, my concern for Stella went through the fucking roof.

CHAPTER 25

It's too predictable.

The text from Rex—I assumed it was from him, although it came from a different number—taunted me as I wracked my brain to figure out where he could have Stella. We dispersed, checking weapons and gear as Chris scoured the locations for Tridel Corporation's four territory heads. I dropped down on the couch and pulled Stella's burner phone from my pocket, thumbing the picture back up. If there was anything there that could give us a clue to where she had been moved, I would find it.

Jack had placed a call to Rich, and we were waiting for him to pick up. I drifted closer when I heard Jack tell Rich he was going to be on speaker.

Rich stated the obvious. "It's clear that the target has help." By "target," he meant Rex and Mole. Without confirmation, he kept the finger-pointing to a minimum, but we wouldn't. We were positive they had her.

"We figured that, especially when his place was empty," Jack's dry tone voiced the thought we were all kicking ourselves over.

Rich cleared his throat. "You'll have several drones

dropped off within the hour, along with anything else you need."

I glanced at Chris and caught the grin that spread over his face. *Good, we'll have another way to track those guys.* Of course, we needed to figure out where they were first.

"What about Mole? How does he fit into everything?" Mike asked.

"Pretty sure I've found him," Chris said. "He's using an alias, as we'd suspected. He's operating under the name Vince Raymond." He chuckled. "He's got a full beard, which must cover that mole we used to give him shit over. From what I can tell, he mainly pays cash but popped up on the radar for unpaid parking tickets. At least we know where he's been, but that's not all. He's muscle for Tridel."

"Let's pick him up, then." I wanted it done. I would handle the interrogation, and if Mole survived what I had planned, he would be lucky.

"That'll happen, but I want you to focus on Tridel," Rich snapped authoritatively. "If you take them down, you'll strip Rex and Mole's access to power, their backing. Plus, you're on the clock for taking down Malone, Tridel's owner. You've got two days to cut the head off the snake."

"You're okay with putting Stella at risk by waiting two days to rescue her? Because I'm sure as hell not," I snapped. *I can't fucking believe this.*

"Not quite." Rich's voice was calm, while I wanted to rage. "Go after Stan Jones, Ben Anderson, Henry Garcia, and Landon Johnson, the men who run each territory, first. Interrogate them. One of them should know where Stella and Max are being held. If not, they should know where Rex or Mole is."

Mike leaned over to look at Chris's screen. "Just got your briefing document."

I couldn't think straight with the image of what they could be doing to her in my mind. *Hold on, Red. I'm coming for you.*

Keegan and I exchanged a look. Repressed fury burned in his eyes too, and it gave me a measure of calm. Even if the rest of our team was okay with following protocol on the mission, I knew he would have my back for the interrogations. Keegan was a mean son of a bitch. The smile that curved his mouth was one of dark intent. "Hawk and I will take point on the interrogations," he said.

A tic pulsed along Jack's jaw, but he nodded, his gaze straying again to the red knit hat that Jenni had worn. Mike snapped his fingers in front of Jack's face. "Hannah will be here in half an hour."

Jack's shoulders visibly relaxed. I got it. It wasn't that Hannah wasn't the one for him, but he was dealing with bad memories of those last few moments of hell. Rex, Mole, and Jenni's ring and hat had torn open old wounds that'd never fully healed. His fists clenched at his sides as he made eye contact with each one of us. "Rex is mine."

I had no problem with that and gave him a curt nod. All I wanted was Stella safe and in my arms, and I would mow down whoever I had to for that to happen. With respect for Jack, I would refrain from delivering a death blow to Rex. I didn't agree not to hurt him, though.

"They don't know Hannah." Mike calling her in was brilliant. "She can scope out the places Mole's been ticketed. Maybe she'll find where they're holding Stella before we do."

Jack grinned. "Chris, can you get a list and a map together for her?"

"Hawk and I'll use the storage unit for the interrogations." Keegan slapped my shoulder hard, and I welcomed the sting and especially his next words: "Let's get this show on the road."

"Don't kill the territory heads," Rich demanded. "We'll need them for information against their boss, the business, and for testifying."

I clenched my teeth. One side of me wanted to kill them all for being a part of my past, while the other snapped to attention at the order. Another glance at Keegan showed him bristling, as was I. We would have to walk a fine line.

"That'll work with Hawk and Keegan out of the action for today, but not tomorrow." Mike drew my focus. "Malone will be on alert if word gets out about his top guys missing. We could very well have an all-out war on our hands. We need you to take point as our sharpshooter."

I could easily slip into the skin of an assassin, and by the hard edge to Mike's voice, I knew he was thinking the same thing. We would have to wait for a go-ahead from Rich. The more we learned about Rex, Mole, and Tridel's owner, David Malone, the more it appeared as if several businesses were joining forces. Loan shark, money laundering, and drugs all under one management spelled a world of trouble.

"After you pull details from the four territory heads, we'll determine how to handle the ringleader."

"Everyone knows what to do?" Jack asked, and at our nods, he ended the call with Rich, promising to update him by midnight. Jack faced Keegan, and everything inside me settled at seeing our leader back under control. "You both have seen the headshot graph that Chris put together of all the members in the Tridel Corp. In the time we need to organize, I want you on the roof." Jack pointed at me. "If you see one, take the hit, but not a kill shot. We can begin interrogating with anyone who comes at us. Keegan, I want you down on the street. Keep to the shadows and do your thing."

Keegan's grin was dark, and if I didn't know him, I would be wary. He was the best of all of us when it came to blending in. No one heard him approach. I suspected it was something he'd learned before we all met. It was a skill I worked to master —it came in especially handy when assassinations were required. He and I had been a team on many of them. He took the up-close, hands-on targets. I took the ones from a distance, using my sniper rifle. It wasn't our typical mission anymore, since we were out of the military, but if need be, it was easy to slip into the skin we'd worn then.

Sometimes, I thought Keegan had never shed his.

The past was a vengeful bitch, and I hoped like hell it wouldn't repeat itself with Rex harming Stella.

CHAPTER 26

HAWK

Jack's cell phone was ringing, and he motioned us over. I crowded the motel's dinged-up table alongside Chris, Keegan, and Mike. We knew who it was and had been waiting for Rex to call. He and Mole were as resilient and persistent as cockroaches.

Jack set the phone on the table and put it on speaker.

"What?" Jack barked into the air above the phone.

The laugh that followed wasn't a sane one. It was dark and menacing with an underlying edge of mania. "Jack," Rex spat. "You should have stayed away. This is your fault, you know."

"How the fuck do you figure?"

"My sister's dead because of you."

Jack's head reared back as if he'd been punched. My jaw clenched at the low blow. That wasn't true, and each one of us knew that. Mike, sitting across from Jack, slowly shook his head to convey that we were behind him and that the fucker on the other end of the call was a goddamned liar.

"Bullshit." Fire danced in Jack's eyes, and I was glad to see its return. "You pulled the trigger. It's *your* fault. Those were *your* actions."

"If your guy on the roof hadn't fired the shot, I wouldn't have had to up the stakes. He raised the bar."

I couldn't keep quiet any longer. What he said didn't faze me one bit. "You're full of shit." We'd weaponed up because he'd forced our hand.

"Is that you? The one on the roof? Hawk, isn't it? Fucking fitting. Now, when we meet next, I'll know where you'll be."

"Shut the hell up. Everything that happened toward the end was on you." Jack shook his head at me. He had my back, as always.

I knew what we were dealing with. Rex wasn't all there.

"Keep telling yourself that, Jack. My sister wasn't supposed to be anywhere near you. She knew that. You knew that. But you couldn't help yourself. You kept taking her away. You increased the threat by invading her space and messing with her head. She was *my* sister. Not your anything. You fucked with that. You made her a liability."

"Jenni made her own choices. And you made yours, distracted and with a mind laced with drugs."

"Where's the ring?" Rex growled.

I guess we're done with that portion of the call. Stella had sent the ring with Hayden to Maine. There was no way we were getting it anytime soon, nor would we give it to Rex. That small part of Jenni was for Jack to hold onto, should he so choose.

Jack must have felt my urgency to find Red. I was done with the conversation. I wanted answers.

"Where's the woman?" Jack demanded.

"Why? You interested in this one too? What would Jenni have thought?"

Jack ignored the Jenni comment. "No. She's innocent in whatever you're trying to do."

"No, she isn't. If she's not yours, then she's one of your crew's. Which one?"

"Not playing this game, Rex."

"Oh, you'll play." The disturbing laughter pealed through the line again.

"Nothing's gonna happen until we know she's alive and unharmed."

Fucking finally. My gut tightened from the wait to find out if she was breathing.

Shuffling sounded before we caught a muffled cry. Rex growled, "speak, bitch," and then we heard her.

"Give him hell."

I grinned. *That's my girl.* Red was a fighter.

"You want the ring?" Jack brought the conversation back to a plan of action. "Fine. Bring her—that's the only way. Name the time and place, and you can *try* to take it from me."

"I want more than that."

"I don't have all day," Jack snapped.

"We'll meet up, your guys against mine. Just like back in the day. You know the place. Bring your crew, no one else."

This is a fucking nightmare. We knew what Rex planned, a replay of that last night back in the day. No way would that happen.

Jack met each one of our gazes. We were in. Once he had visual confirmation that we were all on the same page, he responded, "When?"

"Tomorrow night after sunset."

Jack ended the call, and we didn't waste time thinking about what the next day would bring. We had a job to do.

Now, we hunt.

CHAPTER 27

HAWK

Hannah arrived just as Keegan and I were leaving the room to take our posts. Having her there was a relief in many ways. She would help Jack hold his pain at bay until it was over, at which point I was sure they would deal with it together. The other reason I was glad she was working the mission with us was because she would attack Rex and Mole's location and activity head on. That way, we could focus on taking down Tridel, which would cut Rex off from the power he was undoubtedly siphoning from the company. No way would we let him tap into that and risk Stella disappearing forever.

What could they do to her? Death was one scenario. Bile climbed in my throat. I couldn't think about it. We needed to shut this shit down fast. *They'd better not hurt her.*

Under the cover of dusk, I peered through my scope, checking the terrain around our crappy motel for potential threats. So far, there hadn't been any, which was odd and could very well mean that Rex and Mole were acting independently of Tridel. It was also a possibility that we weren't an approved hit. That too gave me hope. It was small, but I would take what I could get.

I checked my watch again. It was time to go. After a final sweep to ensure nothing moved out there that wasn't supposed to, I abandoned position. Then I entered the stairwell that would take me down to our first-floor motel suite.

Keegan appeared as I was crossing the threshold to our rooms. Hannah, Jack, Mike, and Chris were at the table, surrounding two laptops. Jack looked up as Keegan and I approached. I left my rifle strapped to my shoulder, not quite ready to part with it.

"Nothing?" Jack's brows climbed high.

"No. All clear." Keegan answered, and I echoed his response.

"They may be working outside of Tridel, then," Hannah said, verbalizing my thoughts while on the roof. "That could buy us some time."

Time was what we needed. Chris hit a few keys on his laptop and pulled up a map. Hannah had one on the screen before her as well. We were keeping tabs on those guys with drones, satellite, cell phones, any electronic transactions, and facial recognition.

Chris pointed to two points some distance from one another. "We've located two of the territory heads, here and here." He tapped the screen. One point was east of where we were, and for the other, he scrolled to the next town and high-lighted a spot close to two intersecting streets.

There were two other blips on the map. Jack indicated that they were the remaining two guys we needed to pick up.

"We'll have to split up into two groups to hit these targets hard and fast." Jack indicated the two places on the map. "Hannah will scope the last couple of areas where Mole was ticketed with parking violations. The most frequent ones are where she'll start."

"What are the teams?" I wanted to go with Keegan so there wouldn't be any checks and balances to how hard we struck to obtain the target. Unfortunately, Jack saw through me.

"Hawk, you're with me. Chris, Keegan, and Mike will make up the other team."

"Any more contact from Rex?" Hannah turned to me, her light-blue eyes hard. There was a reason she was going in alone, besides being unknown to Rex and Mole. Trained as a spy since she had been a child in Russia, she could handle just about anything that came her way. She was one of us, a weapon all on her own.

Jack and I got into a nondescript vehicle that Rich had sent with the drones. Hannah got into a rental, and the rest of the team took the Range Rover.

The sun had set quickly, and the night was inky, with very few stars and a moon hidden by clouds. It worked to our advantage. Jack pulled away from the motel, and my gaze roamed in a restless sweep, looking for anything out of the ordinary.

"Chris give you a drone?" I didn't think we needed it, but they came in handy. There were often surprises on a raid like the one we were on. We had government backing and access to satellite photos and more intel than what we had when we began, but that didn't mean everything would go smoothly. We would have to adjust, as we always did.

Jack and I were going after South first. Our target was Landon Johnson—I liked to call him Lando.

"Yeah. We'll park a block away and come in from behind." Jack turned toward me for a second before focusing on the road. "You want to use the drone?"

"No. He's got a new wife. I'm sure he's distracted enough and making mistakes. If he's got guys watching his house, we'll find them and take 'em out." *Otherwise, it'll be one unsatisfying mission.*

The neighborhood changed from city to suburbia. *I wonder if Lando's neighbors know what's living next door to them.* The houses became larger and more spaced out the closer we came to the target. Five minutes later, Jack pulled over. We slipped from the vehicle, not bothering to lock it, then set off at a fast pace between two homes. Due to security and potential motion-sensor lights, we stayed far enough from the perimeter of each house that we wouldn't trip anything. A little over an acre, and we would be in position behind Lando's house.

Nothing moved. The night was silent. It was too easy. But a man recently married to a hot young wife would be distracted. Even so, it was surprising not to have any guards stationed nearby. From what we'd learned, Lando was intensely jealous —having anyone around his bride wasn't going to happen.

There was another vein of thought about his wife. Maybe she didn't know what her husband did. That was cause to keep up pretense, and guards would alert her to the fact that he was involved in questionable business dealings.

All of that worked to our advantage.

Using hand signals, Jack and I moved as a unit to the east side of the house, intent upon entering through a window of one of the guest bedrooms. Since we'd contracted through Rich, Chris had been able to give us a diagram of the house. Even though Chris could have hacked his way into anything he needed, it was easier to use our government intel, and saving even a small amount of time helped.

Focused like a laser on the task at hand, I kept a hard lock on worrying about Red. *These guys need to have answers.*

With our backs to the brick, we raced along the side until we reached the guest bedroom window. "In position." Chris had remained in the vehicle until he heard from us. Mike and Keegan would apprehend West while Chris shut off the alarms to Lando's house on our ready. Then he would help Mike and Keegan to secure West.

"Disarmed."

We didn't wait another second after Chris confirmed the alarm was off. Jack stuck the suction cup to the window and depressed the laser that circled it. With a soft pop, he pulled the circle of glass out, reached in, and flipped the lock. I pushed the frame to raise the window.

Going in and out through windows was something I'd done since I was young—it was a piece of cake to get in without any noise. We moved quickly through the empty bedroom to the hallway. The noise from the refrigerator door closing told us where to go. Hopefully, that was our target.

The house was dark, save for a lone light. On quiet feet, we clung to the shadows, moving quickly toward the illuminated room. The clink of silverware against glass was the only sound. We were banking on the wife being asleep, given how late it was.

Guns raised, we rounded the corner. *Too easy.* A large man was bent over the counter, eating, his back to us. Jack flicked his gaze toward me, and I clenched my teeth. We crept along the hall at a fast pace. The soles of our shoes didn't make a sound. We were the ghosts we were trained to be.

In place behind our target, Jack withdrew a syringe and popped the cap. I got into position behind South, aka Lando. I curved one arm around the big man and immobilized him, banding his arms to his sides so he couldn't use the knife and fork in his hands. My other hand covered his mouth and pulled tightly.

Lando jerked hard and tried to shake my hold. I tightened my grip as Jack jabbed the needle into the man's neck. His struggles slowed, and the fork slipped from his hand. Jack plucked the knife from his other. We slapped duct tape over his mouth and a hood over his head then made sure he was secure.

I hefted him over my shoulder in a fireman's carry. *Fuck.* He weighed a ton, a bit of a doughboy. He must have gotten lazy at the top with no need to exercise. His guys did all the dirty work for him.

We left through the back sliding door. I would have preferred going back through the window and tossing him to the ground first, but Jack had other plans. I looked forward to apprehending East, also known as Ben Anderson, anticipating action from him. From his dossier, the boss liked to get his hands dirty and throw his weight around. He wasn't out of shape or lazy by any means. He was a mean bastard, exactly the sort I wanted to take some aggression out on.

We hightailed it to the vehicle and dumped Lando in the back, where we secured his hands and feet with zip ties then tossed a dark blanket over him. The sedative had been a large enough dose to buy us at least two hours. Too much, and we would have had to give him a shot of adrenaline to wake his sorry ass up.

The ride took way longer than I wanted it to. It was already one in the morning, and the bars would close in an hour or so. We tried to get there before that happened to avoid patrons leaving together. The goal was to get each guy alone.

I shut my eyes as images of Red played through my mind. In the face of her abduction, I couldn't deny my feelings any longer. I admitted to myself that I cared for her, but it was so much more than that. I liked having her around, her soft body curled against mine when we fell asleep. I even appreciated her sass. She made things lighter and not so serious. She gave me hope that I could have what several of my brothers had found with their women. I'd never thought it would be an option for me, but without her by my side, I wanted that more than anything. I was prepared to fight for a life with her.

"This is it."

My focus snapped back to our current reality of seedy bars and stumbling drunks, which was more the scene I'd pictured when thinking of the territory heads.

The bar was a few buildings up the block, and Jack had parked in the alley behind it. Lando would be fine sleeping in the back. We would lock the car that time. It wouldn't stop anyone if they were dead set on breaking in, but it would deter the drunks.

For the time being, we waited near the back door of the bar, where East—or Anderson—was. We took position in the darkest part of the bar, out of view of the single light above the rear exit. From our intel, he often left that way.

Twenty minutes passed. That would have been nothing for me, but with the stakes as high as they were, I wanted to bust down the door and drag Anderson out. *To hell with stealth.*

I signaled at Jack: five more minutes. If Anderson didn't leave, we would go get him.

The rear door burst open, and men poured into the alley, looking as though they were coming to us. They were unaware of our presence, and we slipped behind them seamlessly.

Surrounded by five linebacker-sized men, one in front, one on each side of him, and two behind, Anderson walked toward a row of black cars. Smoke curled in the air from his lit cigarette. His guards were obviously packing. We needed to take out as many as we could before guns were drawn.

We would start with the guys in the rear. Then our surprise attack would end. The butt of my gun thwacked the back of one of the thugs at the same time that Jack struck another. The men fell, and we stepped around them to make ourselves parallel with the guys on either side of Anderson.

My guy raised his gun. I grabbed his wrist, crowding him. With a twist, my elbow smashed into his nose. He gripped his gun tightly and squeezed off a shot. I rammed my shoulder into him as the front guy came around. Another shot exploded. The front man missed. Side Guy covered me, and the bullet went wide.

Twisting Side Guy's arm away, I moved to kick Front Man in the gut. Jack fought both Anderson and the other side guy. He was holding his own. I focused on taking my two down.

I slammed an elbow into Side Guy's face. He recovered faster than I liked. Another shot rang out. Front Man was standing again, even after the hit to his gut from my foot. Side Guy was a pain in the ass.

With a punch to the gut, Side Guy doubled over. I twisted and wrapped my arm around his head. My hip jammed into him, and with a tug, he sailed over my shoulder. The two men crashed together.

I froze. The barrel of Anderson's gun was pointed at my head. He was too far for me to grab it—not Jack, though. Jack kicked his elbow, and the shot went wide.

Front Man recovered and stumbled to his feet.

Jack's guy was out cold. He took over Anderson again. My head snapped back, and I grinned. Front Man got in a good shot. Anderson was also a pain in the ass. He shouted orders the entire time. *Watch the gun.* Anderson waved it around.

I grabbed Front Man and flipped him around like a human shield just as Anderson took aim and fired. My shield jerked as the bullets struck his chest and gut.

Jack kicked out and connected again with Anderson's elbow. This time, a crack sounded. I flinched. *That has to hurt like hell. Probably broken.* The gun fell and clanged against the pavement. Without waiting a beat, Jack delivered a solid punch to Anderson's face and then his gut.

Anderson dropped to his knees, moaning. *Fucking baby.* We barely touched him, except for the elbow. *Wait until later.* Jack slapped duct tape over his mouth and a black hood on his head then finished securing him with zip ties.

Although it was satisfying fighting Anderson's bodyguards, I would have preferred to get to the storage unit so we could extract information. Irritation coursed through me at the delay in finding Red, and I lashed out at Jack. "This would have gone a lot faster if I'd taken point on the roof."

CHAPTER 28

HAWK

The door to the storage room slammed shut behind me. Jack was already through with South, aka Lando, a deadweight over his shoulder. My steps faltered when I saw the arranged room. Hannah must have stopped to set it up. She had even more experience than Keegan—we would probably never get her to tell us how much she knew about torture. After all, Hannah had lived through many sessions at the hands of her Russian trainers.

Four chairs faced the corners. None of the territory heads would be able to see each other, but they would be able to hear one another. Maybe it would speed things along.

Intense information extraction wasn't what we usually did, but Rich had a point. We would learn where Red, Rex, or Mole was. Not only that, but Rich wanted any news we got about Tridel so he could use it in his federal investigation.

East, aka Anderson, bucked against my hold. I tossed him onto the metal chair, and it tipped over. The thwack of his head against the cement was a sick sound, and he stilled for a few seconds. It had to have hurt like hell.

I righted the chair. Working fast, I sliced through the plastic that previously held his ankles and wrists together before pulling out new ties. Both front chair legs had a foot secured, and I yanked his arms back and re-tied them to the metal arms. I wrapped a nylon rope around his chest and waist to tether him further, since he was such a squirrely fucker.

Lando hadn't woken yet, and Jack got him secured before I finished with Anderson. I kept the hood over his head—there was no need for him to see either of us. The door crashed against the metal wall, and Keegan walked in with a sinister grin and eyes that sparkled with dark intent.

Each corner station had its own set of tools—mine had a tray with different knives. I looked over and saw that Keegan had a similar setup. He dumped North, or Stan Jones, aka Porch Guy, into the chair and delivered an immediate punch to his gut, stilling him long enough to get the zip ties in place.

Oh, hell. Keegan picked up a curved blade that looked like it could have been a Middle Eastern Shotel. "Why do you get that?" I had knife envy. Not for torture, but because it was cool.

"Because I know how to use it." His eyes narrowed to slits, and if I were Porch Guy, I would have thought my time was up right then and there. Keegan finished securing his guy, as did Mike.

Chris was the only one not manning an interrogation station. Mike grabbed his guy's face, tilting his chin way up. "You're in for a treat. We have someone else coming to take care of you."

Hannah would be taking over for Mike. That's why Mike's guy was stretched out on the floor, his hands and feet secured and tethered. There was a bucket of water with what looked like an extra-large plastic cup bobbing around the top. That would suck. We'd had to endure that during one of our SEALs training exercises.

"You were contacted?" I directed my vague question to Mike. If Hannah was coming, that meant she must have let him know. *Had she learned anything?*

"Yep. She'll be about ten minutes."

I turned to Jack. "We having a meeting, then?" I wanted to know if Hannah had found Rex, but most of all, I wanted to know about Red.

He nodded, his focus still on Lando. Impatience churned in my gut. I wanted to get started. A scream sliced through our triple-sized storage unit—it appeared that Keegan had the same thought. His prompts to gain intel weren't heard. There was only a low rumble of voice. Extracting information wasn't my thing. It was Keegan and Hannah's. But I had no problem getting my hands dirty today.

With deft fingers, I loosened the hood and tore the duct tape from Anderson's mouth. Bloodshot eyes glared at me. His chest heaved, but he didn't utter a sound from the discomfort of the adhesive tearing off a fine layer of skin.

I looked over the tray and chose a small three-inch blade. I stepped closer, leaning by Anderson's ear, close enough that only he heard me, but with enough distance that he couldn't attempt to shift and hit me. Not that the ropes had give, but his head wasn't secured.

"We're going to start with three questions. If you answer the first truthfully, your punishment will be lessened a great deal."

Tucking the blade against my palm, I grasped either side of his button-down sleeves and yanked until the fabric tore. They fell to bunch around his elbows. His arms weren't where I wanted to start, but misdirecting and confusing him would only heighten his fear.

"Where is Stella being held?" *Fucker had better tell me.*

Screams crested from Keegan's corner, and I forced myself not to look up. The guy had it coming. He took pleasure in people burning.

From the silence to my right, I figured Mike hadn't yet begun. Chris was in the other room—we'd opened two of the units to make a larger space. The third, we'd connected with a door through the wall to use as an office of sorts, should we need it.

That was where Chris had gone. He'd sent drones out and was scouring the city for any sign of Rex or Mole. It was dark, but the drones could pick up facial recognition, and Chris was on it. Hopefully, it wasn't too limited, and they'd pass through a streetlight or something. So long as Rex or Mole left whatever hole they were in, we would be good.

Silence met my first question, and I wasn't going to ask it again. The tip of my blade pierced Anderson's right thigh, and I shoved it in to the hilt.

Anderson panted, hissing through his teeth, but gave no other indication to the pain. *Guess I'll have to up things to get a better reaction.* With the knife still in his leg, I repeated my question. "Where is the woman being held?"

Anderson rumbled with a deep laugh. "Fuck you."

I grinned. *Let the games begin.* Before I asked again, I glanced to my left to see what Jack was up to.

Jack had removed Lando's shoes and socks. Gun in hand, he tied Lando's hands. Before he woke him with the smelling salts on his tray, he dropped a flat, narrow board on the floor that had nails hammered all the way through. One-inch sharp metal tips pointed to the ceiling.

Jack reached under the hood and held the salts to the man slumped in the chair. Seconds passed before Lando regained any semblance of consciousness. The guy was probably still groggy. *I bet Jack's getting impatient.* I grinned when I saw what was in his hand. Jack jabbed the needle into Lando's chest and administered adrenaline. Lando jerked, suddenly fully awake.

Then Jack jammed the barrel of his 9mm into the center of Lando's forehead. Even through the black hood, the immediate threat would register. Jack issued orders. It began for Lando.

"Stand."

Lando stood, his hands clenched into fists and his right arm thrust wide, missing Jack completely.

Jack pulled the gun back, and with a quick strike, he slammed the butt of it into Lando's temple. He didn't hit him that hard, as Lando remained on his feet. With the barrel back against Lando's forehead, Jack snapped, "Inch your left foot forward. Squat down." It took another disciplinary action for Lando to follow. It was interesting. I administered another stab to Anderson for not responding as I'd warned then checked to see what Jack was planning.

Blood dripped through the hood from the twist Jack applied to his nose. Once Lando was in position, Jack had him lift his right heel off the floor. Jack traded his gun for a wooden cane.

"Hold position." Jack slid the exposed nails beneath Lando's heels. "If you drop your heel, you'll impale it on a bed of nails. If your hands touch the floor, they'll be caned." He wacked the side of the wooden cane against the concrete for effect. "If you drop the squat, you'll be shot in the leg and forced to hold an equally painful position."

Damn, military squats were hell, and pain had to be spreading through Lando at that very moment. It never took long for the effects of the squat to hit. Once more, Jack stood, and the questions began. "Where is Stella? Where is your boss? Where are Rex and Vince?"

We weren't sure if they knew Mole's real name, Blaze, so we used his alias, Vince. The head boss may have been privy to it, but these guys were on a need-to-know basis.

Keegan was across from me, and I couldn't see what he was doing—I could only hear. It was enough to send chills through all of us. I trusted him with my life, but the guys we had were as good as dead. Keegan had never told us how he'd learned his methods. By unspoken understanding, I hadn't pushed. I had my secrets and my own shame, but it was all out in the open in that storage unit.

While Jack maintained vigilance with Lando, Mike stretched his guy, West, or Henry. Mike roped his arms and legs and secured them to a bolt in the wall. Henry's hands were extended overhead with the end loop beneath the metal chair Mike sat on, waiting for Hannah's arrival, which was about a minute later.

Hannah swept inside, her silvery-blond hair coiled in a tight bun as she unbuttoned her light coat. A small grin curved her lips as her gaze met Jack's. The cry to her right drew her attention, and she paused to see what Keegan was up to.

"You have North?" she asked Keegan.

I was thankful because North was the man who had been there the night the people who raised me were killed, and even though I hated to see people get hurt, he deserved it.

A crooked grin transformed Keegan's intense rage to a milder but more malicious one. "Yes. You can still tell?"

I repressed a shudder. The man was most likely difficult to recognize at that point. There was a puddle of blood around him, splatters across the floor, and more dripping at a steady pace to pool on the cement.

Hannah pursed her lips. "Make sure to find out what he knows about the girl." She tossed him a roll of gauze from his tray of instruments. "Good work, but we can't have him bleed out now, can we?"

Keegan's dark laughter trailed behind her as she motioned for Jack and me to follow her into the makeshift office. Mike would keep an eye on our prisoners. Once inside the sectioned-off storage unit, Jack shut the door.

"Did you find Stella?" *Please tell me you did.*

Jack leaned against the desk Chris occupied. All attention was on Hannah, the air thick with expectancy.

"I think so. At least Mole if not Stella," she replied. "There's a run-down apartment complex a few steps from where most of Mole's parking tickets came from. She could be in there. I went through the building but didn't run into them. I can go back and break into each unit, but it will take some time. I wanted to see what we could pull from our prisoners before I did that."

"Anyone learn anything yet?" Chris asked.

"Lando had a meeting with Malone two days ago. He doesn't seem to know anything about Stella or Rex," Jack supplied. "If I had to guess, I'd say he wasn't the most trusted."

It was my turn. "Anderson handles heavier drugs and gambling. A rougher crowd. He knows something about Rex. Maybe not where Stella is or even anything about her, but he might have some information we can use."

"I'm wrapping Lando. He'll be ready for transport. Just waiting on the others." Jack put an end to South's continued torture.

Chris shot Jack a wry look. "Wrap Keegan's up too, before he's dead."

Keegan walked through, smirking, his eyes devoid of emotion. On closer inspection, a torturous sea churned beneath the flat facade.

"Most of the cuts are surface. He'll be fine." Keegan directed what he said next to Hannah. "How did you find out he might know where Stella was?"

"I grabbed a few of the henchmen you boys left behind the bar and found out which territory had the most recent dealings with Rex and Vince. Not surprisingly, it was the northern one."

Jack's grin grew. Hannah was a badass, and I was glad she was on our team.

Hannah hadn't looked concerned when she'd relayed the info about the guys we'd left behind, and I couldn't have cared less. They were men from the night when my parents died. I recognized Keegan's guy from my nightmares. His associates were still out there, but Keegan took care of things in a way I didn't think I could have. My rage would have taken over, and I would have sliced his throat. Interrogation wasn't my forte.

"What are we waiting for?" I asked. Each moment that

ticked by was another reminder of what Stella may be facing. I didn't particularly care for her brother, as he was the one who'd brought this shit to her doorstep. She was innocent, and I wanted her returned unharmed.

"Hawk, wrap up our guys," Jack commanded. "Hannah, do what you need to do and find out where Rex could've stashed Stella."

Hannah stripped off her coat and rolled up her sleeves before she went into the large area that held the four men. I was close on her heels, and the sound of imaginary seconds and minutes ticked loudly in my ears. I helped Jack with Lando first.

Then, in one smooth motion, I hauled Lando to his feet, and he buckled under the pain radiating through his body. With the toe of my shoe, I stepped on the wood that held the group of exposed nails. He screamed as they withdrew from his heel.

Blood dripped from his foot. I shoved him into the metal chair, where he sagged, his entire body trembling from fatigue and pain. I grabbed the gauze then wrapped his foot and secured the end with tape. I didn't give a shit about his shoes and socks. With practiced ease, I re-secured his legs and hands with plastic ties. He would remain there until transportation came to take them away.

Jack wouldn't let anyone into our world. We would usher the four out, and Rich's men would take it from there.

Gurgling filled the eerie silence as Hannah gripped Henry's jaw and poured a steady stream of water into his mouth. Mike held the rope attached to the guy's hands taut. His legs stretched from the secured hook on the wall.

She leaned back on her heels while Henry sputtered and coughed up water. Nothing changed in her expression or the tone of her voice. Over and over she repeated the same questions and process. When he failed to give her the answers, he received another round of water torture.

Five minutes passed, then ten, before he begged for her to wait, saying that he knew of a few places Vince frequented. She didn't give him a chance to respond. Water filled West's mouth until it went down his throat and spilled over his face. Small geysers of water pumped from his mouth as he fought.

When she stopped, Henry threw up force-fed water. "Think isn't good enough. I'm aware you know what I'm asking," she said. "Next time, you may not pull air into your lungs. Where is the girl?"

Henry's speech was rushed, garbled, and filled with panic. I couldn't hear everything he said except for the words "north side." Hannah raised the water, and his hoarse voice rose.

"I know nothing about a girl! My sources told me Rex was planning to take power. They had a bargaining chip, but it wasn't a girl."

He was talking about Max. *Fucking hell.*

Hang in there, Red.

CHAPTER 29

I blinked in the harsh light of our storage-unit-turned-interrogation-and-office space. My eyelids were strips of sandpaper, rubbing my eyes raw. In the early morning hours, I slumped against the doorframe and readied myself for what would come next. We were all crowded in a circle, waiting to see what information had been extracted from our four captives after the first meeting.

Please, let us have found out where Red is.

Chris stood and stretched, abandoning his position by the computer. He'd been instrumental during the mission with his hacking skills, but from the restlessness in how he moved, we could tell he wanted in on the action.

"You all know Landon Johnson was worthless. There wasn't any information gained from him," Jack reported.

I cleared my throat. "Anderson, or East, had only heard of another expansion to Tridel, which included some heavy hitters in drug trafficking. Nothing new there."

Hannah was the spokesperson for her and Mike's tag team for West, aka Henry Garcia. "West was also aware of the change in business, with narcotics added. He didn't know the names of the people orchestrating the merger, only that Stan's area would integrate the head of the new arm." *Porch Guy.* "The two men would be demoted to muscle once the union was complete. My guess is that Rex and Mole didn't know that little tidbit."

Keegan snorted. "Not really, but they'd taken precautions. Porch Guy had a lot to say." He finished wiping his hands. Keegan was in on my nickname for Stan.

"I bet he did, from the looks of him." Keegan had worked him over within an inch of his life. We would have to wait and see if he survived.

"It was mostly superficial, shithead." Keegan tossed a pen at me.

I ducked, just missing the pen striking my forehead. "Don't keep us in suspense here."

"I'm almost done. I'll tell you what I've learned, then I'm back at it to make sure he talks." Keegan notched his chin in my direction. "He had a few things to say about you once they realized who was helping Stella. They knew you had survived the night they torched your place. That's when their plans turned urgent to take you out ASAP. News of that little slipup wasn't to reach Malone."

"It was his guys shooting at me, then, trying to sweep me under the rug."

"Yep," Keegan confirmed. "North was working directly with Rex and Mole, even behind Malone's back. His directives were that Rex and Mole's connections were to be obtained and incorporated, then the two would be demoted to muscle under North, as Hannah said earlier."

"So we haven't learned anything new?" Mike asked.

Keegan grinned. "Oh, we've learned a lot. North was a little too ambitious for his own good. He didn't like Rex much and was playing him. When they found out from Max about the treasure, unfortunately, Mole was present and told Rex later that he'd formed a new plan. They would work together to get whatever Stella had and keep it for themselves. Max would be delivered to Malone as promised after the issue with Stella was completed." He glanced at me. "You're not going to like this part, man, but hold out until you hear everything."

My jaw ached from how hard I clenched my teeth. "Just spit it out already."

"After they recovered the loot, Stella was supposed to go to Porch Guy. And before you ask, no, I didn't push to find out exactly why. That wasn't the objective."

"Does he have her stashed somewhere? Is she hurt?" I was going goddamn crazy waiting for him to finish.

"He doesn't have her, but I'm sure he knows where she is."

I exploded off the doorframe, every muscle strung tightly. "Where the fuck is she?"

Keegan shook his head, his mouth set in a grim line. "Give me a minute—I'll finish up. He's had enough time to think. I'll extract the information from him."

Dammit! I paced while the other guys tried to calm me down. It was pointless. They would have been in the same state if it had been Hannah or Mari in danger. The minutes ticked by. It didn't take long until Keegan slammed back into the smaller room.

"You're not going to believe this. You know that little place we used to play pool and eat?"

"Joe's Eatery?" Chris asked.

"Yeah, that's the one," Keegan confirmed. "Stella is being held in the basement."

Jack came into the room and gave us the hand signal to wrap up the cargo. Four men were tied with bags still over their heads to obscure their view and shuffled to the door. Someone called Rich, and their transport was waiting outside.

We'd delivered the men Rich had hired us to detain. In doing so, he had also agreed to help us in any way we needed when it came to the final showdown with Rex. Rich would coordinate apprehending Malone, Tridel's boss, with our pending meeting with Rex, stripping him and Mole of additional power. Maybe we would even find Max.

Someone pounded on the door to the storage unit. It was time—we were finished with the men. Through an exit to the side of one of the garage doors, we passed the four territory heads into secure hands.

We had to get back to work. We needed to rescue Stella.

We used the drones to get a wide-eyed view of the buildings and surrounding area, checking to see who was guarding Joe's Eatery. Rex planned the spot well, and I was shocked. He'd stashed her beneath our noses. I bet he pictured us eating there and never knowing she was below.

It had been one of our old haunts when we had extra cash, which wasn't often back in the day, but we managed a time or two. Watters had cleaned up the area in terms of drug gangs, but it still wasn't a great place to live—it was run-down and depressing.

Rex and Mole hadn't stationed anyone on watch, probably to deter any unnecessary suspicion or alert us that the restaurant could have been a possibility. We wouldn't have checked there otherwise.

Time passed faster than I would have liked. We had to get her back alive.

The morning was overcast, which helped us blend in. Jack spoke in my earpiece to move in on our target. I pushed off the brick building across the street from Joe's Eatery I was leaning against. There was no movement. The restaurant was closed for two more hours. We didn't think many people were inside getting ready for the eleven o'clock lunch. If there were, it would only be a few people—the place was small. On the side of the building was a single half window. That was our point of entrance.

With no scouts posted to watch for us, I had a good feeling.

We would be able to get in and out with zero to little chance of ambush. Even so, I pulled the device Chris had handed me to sweep around the window for any electronic devices. If there were wires attached, potentially to a bomb, the handheld would detect them.

No beeps or lights went off, and I turned the knob to shut down Chris's equipment before shoving it back in my pocket. With the glass cutter, I scored a circle and popped the suctioned piece out, slipped my hand in, and flipped the lock. It would be a tight fit to get in. I took the entire frame off to widen the space. My training was the only thing helping me to stay sane. I focused on my breathing and staying aware of our surroundings. *We have to find Red in there.*

Hannah covered me from the rooftop. Keegan was close by, as were the rest of the guys. Mike had stationed himself by the rear entrance. We were ready. In and out. That was the plan.

With a penlight, I searched the basement area directly in front of me. Boxes, broken chairs and tables, and several bags of flour crowded the floor. I whipped the light back to the bags. *Are those toes peeking past the sack?*

Fuck. They are. Not only that, but I recognized the copper toenail polish. Red. She was there.

Please be alive.

I kicked the frame away. I shoved my fingers into the crevices between the brick over the window and hung on while I dropped myself down through the opening. I landed on my feet with a soft thud. Even though I wanted to rush right to where she lay, I swept the area for any guards or trip wires.

What the hell? There were none. It was too easy. My gut tightened painfully. Either Rex and Mole didn't have the men to spare, or she was dead.

* * *

STELLA

No! SOMETHING CRASHED ON THE OTHER SIDE OF THE ROOM. They were coming back for me. I knew it. My heart beat faster and faster. My stomach churned and cramped as my ears strained to hear where he was. It had to be the guy who'd scared the hell out of me. His pupils had been dilated, and I couldn't predict what he would do. He said he would be back for me. The thud caused my body to shake uncontrollably.

What is going to happen to me this time? The guy who'd grabbed me before I entered my brother's hospital room was called Vince. I think? Or was it Blaze? My mind spun at a dizzying speed. He'd hurt me, but he didn't petrify me, as the other man had.

I sucked air through my nose way too quickly, but I couldn't stop the panic. Dark spots swam in front of my vision. A shadow fell over me, and my body started to convulse. I hadn't even heard him approach. He loomed over me. It took a second for what I saw to register. *Oh God.* Tears pooled then rolled over my lower lashes. *Hawk.* I'd never been so happy to see someone in my life.

"Red." Emotion infused his voice.

The rush of relief caused my body to go limp, as much as it was able. My hands and feet were bound, with the disgusting bandana stuffed into my mouth and another tied around to hold it in place. He would fix everything. With him there, I could relax.

"I'll get you free in a sec." Hawk pulled a knife and cut my feet and hands loose from the plastic zip ties. He helped me stand, but I fell back against the concrete. My extremities didn't have a lot of feeling, and I couldn't break my fall.

I just wanted him to hold me. His arm slipped around me and gave me the support I needed.

"I'm so sorry, Red." He cut the bandana away and helped remove the other one out of my mouth. "Are you hurt?"

I shook my head. I couldn't speak past the lump in my throat. I wasn't even sure I had a voice. They hadn't fed me. There was no water. I didn't think I'd been there too long, but I was weak and so incredibly thirsty. My body convulsed again, and I sobbed as his arms went around me. He cradled me against his chest. I let it all go and gave into the avalanche of emotions I'd barely kept in check.

He brushed his lips over my forehead and murmured over and over again that everything would be okay. I was safe, and he would never let anyone hurt me again. I believed him.

Those men who'd abducted me would pay. Fire kindled in my gut at the thought of what Hawk would do to them. I wanted to help. I wanted them to suffer slowly for the fear they'd caused me. And if they were the ones who'd also hurt my brother, I would make them scream.

I gasped, gaining control as Hawk lifted me high and passed me through the window to Keegan. I wasn't even scared, even though Keegan was the only one I was wary around. He handled me like I would break, and as soon as Hawk was out and standing next to us, he handed me back.

Keegan leaned down. We were eye level. "Don't you worry for a second, Stella. We'll take care of them so they never come near you again."

I gave him a closed-lipped smile. It was all I was capable of. But I was grateful, and I felt protected. I tried to convey that through my eyes. I think he understood because he winked before moving out of the way. We were leaving. Hawk sprinted with me in his arms, and I closed my eyes, hoping we would get to wherever we were going soon.

Hawk climbed into the back of the Range Rover without letting go of me. The rest of the guys piled in after him. It was a tight fit, but I wouldn't have had it any other way. Being surrounded by those guys guaranteed I would be safe.

"I'm sorry." I croaked. My throat was parched, and the dull throb in my head told me I was dehydrated. I tried to hold it in but couldn't, and sobs wracked my body. "I should have listened. I just thought—"

"Shh, it's okay. You're safe," Hawk comforted me, his hand running up and down my back.

"I was so close to Max." I hiccupped, working to regain control. "I wanted to end this."

"I know, Red. It'll all be over soon." His forehead touched mine before he brushed a soft kiss over my lips. "I don't think I've ever been so scared. I can't lose you. I need you. I'm so sorry I've been pushing you away."

I clung to him. I wanted that too, but fear clogged my throat. I wanted to leave that place. Hawk made me feel safe, but that place—*what if they came back?* "Please—I'm sorry." I was a broken record. My brain didn't want to work.

Someone handed me a water bottle. The painful tingles in my hands made it nearly impossible to hold. Hawk caught it in one hand and twisted the cap off with his teeth. His other arm held me tightly against him as he helped me take a few sips, cautioning me to take it slow.

"I don't want to hear any apologies, Red." His voice was low and intimate. He shifted me in his arms, and I rested my head against his chest. He wasn't mad at me. Another worry slipped away. Soon, I would have to tell them about the men who'd taken me and find out if Max was still alive.

CHAPTER 30

HAWK

*H*arsh fluorescent light shone down on Red, who reclined on the cot we'd set up in the storage unit's office section. She had barely let go of me since I'd first picked her up off that cold, dirty basement floor. I needed the connection too. It cooled the white-hot rage that threatened to consume me.

Her wrists and ankles were raw from the plastic zip ties. She'd struggled to get free—they'd cut into her skin. There was a bruise in a fat circle the size of a fucking gun on her temple. Small cuts ran across the corners of her lips, and bruises marred her hip and shoulder.

Fury popped and sizzled beneath the surface. My skin itched with anticipation to do damage to every person who'd hurt or scared her.

Until Mike had gotten what was needed to fix Red up, I'd curled around her body, both of us on the small cot, and held her tightly. After what had happened to her, I wasn't going to take any chances. We were off the grid there, and I planned to keep her that way. Because it wouldn't be long before Rex and Mole realized she was missing.

I tucked closer into her and whispered in her ear. There

were a few things I had to confess. "Red." I swallowed my previous terror back down. "When you were gone, when I knew they had you, everything became clear."

She turned her head so we were staring into each other's eyes. "What do you mean?"

"I want this."

Her gaze flared.

"No. That's not what I mean. Not this fucked-up situation." I ran a hand over my face. I was messing it up. "You missing was horrifying. It brought what we have together into focus. I want you. Us. A relationship."

Her hand fluttered to my face, cupping my cheek. "I do too."

I brushed a kiss over her mouth then pulled back. I had to tell her all of it. She deserved to hear it. "I won't hold back any longer and won't keep you at a distance. If you give me a chance, I'll put everything I've got into making our relationship work."

She smiled widely, and tears spilled down her face, but they were the good kind. "Yes."

The tightness in my chest loosened. Hannah motioned for me to get up. I pressed a kiss to her forehead. Red needed to rest.

We'd learned a lot in our extensive trauma training as SEALs. Mike hooked up a makeshift IV, and I reluctantly climbed off the cot. I moved by her side to clean her arm in preparation. Chris handed me the tape once I'd fed the needle into her vein. The IV was attached, and its steady drip gave me a measure of relief. I knew she would get the electrolytes and hydration she needed.

Hannah had gotten clothes from Red's bags, and I helped her change into clean ones that we'd brought from the casino's hotel. All of our stuff was with us. The only thing we were missing was a shower. Near the storage unit's main office, there were restrooms that we used if needed, and they would be good enough for the time being. Red wouldn't be going there alone. Hannah's presence was a balm to our worries surrounding her.

After the showdown with Rex, we wouldn't be there long.

I'd checked Stella over. She wasn't in bad shape, aside from the bruising on her arms and right hip and the rawness around her ankles and wrists that we'd put salve on and bandaged. The dehydration was a problem, but the steady drip of the IV eased the worry that was gnawing at my insides. She was safe. She would be okay.

Hannah reached around me and handed Red some lip balm and a small tube of lotion. Her hand dropped to my shoulder, and she squeezed it until I gave her my attention.

"Ask for what you need then back off and let her rest."

I nodded my understanding. Red's well-being had to come first. I would ask the tough questions later. "Do you need more pain meds?" I turned to survey the room to see if Keegan was back. He'd gone out to get her some soup.

"No. I'm okay." Her voice sounded better, less scratchy. "The ibuprofen is working."

Her eyelids were drooping. Hannah was right. We needed to hurry up and get answers—we could fill Keegan in with whatever he'd missed later.

"Did you find Max?" Her eyelids fluttered again, concern for her brother sharp in her voice.

Dammit. "No. Not yet, but we will. I need to ask you a few things, and then you can rest. Try not to worry about your brother. Right now, he's the only bargaining chip Rex and Mole have with Malone." Tridel Corp's leader wouldn't give Rex and Mole the position they wanted without a show of good faith.

What Malone didn't know was that Rex had already struck a deal with Porch Guy, aka Stan, the head of Tridel's northern branch. He wanted treasure and power too. "With you out of the picture, they can't kill him for that fact alone." Because

Malone wanted money, they would need to bring Max to him. Rex would want to be the one to do that, to prove his worth to Tridel.

Alarm flashed across her features, and I took her hand in mine "What do you need to know?" she asked softly.

"We're pretty sure we know who took you, but we need to know if there was anyone else there too." Specifically, we needed to ascertain whether any of Porch Guy's men or Malone himself had been there. "Where did they find you?"

She took a deep breath before she began. "I was so close to Max's room at the hospital. I had the money from the necklace in my pocket." A few tears rolled down her cheeks.

Keegan was taking care of retrieving the pawned necklace as we spoke. I'd given him my black Amex card to do so. It was important to her, and I wasn't okay with her leaving behind any part of her history. He would bring back something for her to eat too.

"I'm assuming you don't have the money anymore?"

"No. I think the one who grabbed me was Blaze. That's Mole, right?"

"Yes." I kept my emotions in check. We needed to hear everything. The guys were quiet behind me, and Hannah stood close to Red's shoulder.

"I fought." Fire flashed in her blue eyes. "I didn't make it easy for them."

I nodded. I couldn't help but be proud of her for that. I was sure that was how she had gotten some of the bruising. It was my turn, and they would pay for what they did. "Describe who was there, who took you, and if anyone else came by the basement where you were held. Even if you only heard a voice, that could help."

A cell phone rang. A glance told me it was Jack who'd picked up. I squeezed Red's hand, which was cold in spite of the blankets Hannah had laid over her, and waited for her to tell me everything.

"So that Blaze guy grabbed me from the hospital before I saw Max. He blindfolded me and threw me in a trunk of a car. When we stopped, I heard another man's voice."

A shiver coursed through her, and my anger notched up another degree.

"I saw him in the basement when they took the blindfold off. I tried to fight and get free again, but the other man hit me in the face, and I was disoriented. They tied me up and gagged me. The other guy, Rex"—she squeezed my hand tightly, panic flashing in her expressive eyes—"was on something. Drugs. He seemed crazy. When I got a good look at him, I didn't resist."

"You're safe now." I brushed a tear that'd fallen down her cheek with the pad of my thumb. My palm cupped the side of her face.

"I know. It's just that I thought he was going to kill me. He was so close to attacking me, but the Blaze guy distracted him. Rex was big with greasy brown hair and eyes. Mean."

Rex will die. I didn't think I could keep my promise to Jack—that he could take him out—and I caught his gaze over my shoulder. His mouth was set in a grim line, and he nodded. Rex would go down by whomever one of us got the chance. Jack understood.

"No one else came by?" We needed to know if Malone, the head of Tridel Corp, was there, or Stan, aka Porch Guy.

Red yawned, her eyelids growing heavier with each passing second. "No. No one else."

I kissed her on the forehead and tucked her hand under the blankets. "You did good. Try to get some sleep."

Her eyes widened as I stepped back. "You're not leaving, are you?"

"Not yet. I'll be here for another hour or two. You won't be left alone."

She nodded, her lips pressing together until she lost the fight to stay conscious. With a heavy heart, I moved away from Stella to find out who'd called Jack.

A headache was forming behind my eyes. *This goddamned light in here.* Why we hadn't changed the fluorescents out when we altered the lighting in the other section was seriously pissing me off. Everything was making me mad. We needed to move, not sit around. I wanted to end Rex and do serious damage to Mole.

"That was Rich," Jack answered before I had to ask. "He wanted me to convey his gratitude, Chris."

Chris smirked. "You can tell him I'll keep the drones in exchange for his thanks."

"Already did." Jack grinned.

We all knew what that was about without needing to ask. Chris had found and filled in the government's holes about Tridel Corp, including pictures. With that blueprint and any dirt he had been able to dig up, the CIA had a map to go after the corporation head on.

"We're off the hook with Rich now, right?" Not that it mattered, but I wanted to make sure we could focus on taking down Rex and Mole, not having to go after Tridel until Malone was apprehended.

"We are," Jack confirmed. "Rich is working with the FBI and local police to take them down as we speak. Malone should be picked up within the hour, along with Stan Jones's men."

Good. I wanted Porch Guy to pay for his part, even though I was better off without the people who'd raised me.

"Rich will need to focus on Stan's branch and take out as many as he can," Jack clarified.

If Rex continued to siphon manpower from Porch Guy, we would be severely outnumbered in our street fight. It was no secret that a slaughter was what Rex and Mole had in mind for our battle. "We're already down Trev and Hayden. That'll piss him off too, and it won't help us in numbers."

Mike dropped into a chair and checked his watch. "Rex did demand the original crew, but I doubt he has all the same guys so he'll have to get over it. We need to be in position in an hour. Let's head out and set up. Chris already has three drones in the air."

"I can control them with this device." Chris held up a small handheld electronic panel. "They're in place and will send an alert if anyone crosses the perimeters I've set. That way, we'll be warned if another group is sneaking up on us. It's an extra precaution."

"We'll take whatever we can get." It was an important addition to our defense, as we all had our sights set on taking down Rex and Mole.

"Hannah"—Jack motioned for her to come closer—"we need you to guard Stella so that Hawk's head is in the game."

"Already planned on it." She squeezed his hand then leveled her cool gaze at the rest of us. "Get this cleaned up so we can get out of here."

"On it." Jack circled his hand, and we grabbed the additional ammo on the table and stuffed it into our pockets before we headed out.

With Red safe and off the grid, I let everything fall away from my mind to focus on the objective of the street fight we were facing. Rex was going down.

CHAPTER 31

STELLA

I woke with a start. Dull pain throbbed through my body, though the medicine seemed to take the edge off. The discomfort didn't matter. I wanted revenge against the men who had Max and who hurt me. With a sweep around the room, my gaze landed on Hannah. "Where's Hawk? Where are the guys?"

Her lips twitched. "Good to see you're feeling better. They left to take care of the men who abducted you."

I shoved the blankets off and stood, only to stop when I realized I was still connected to the IV. "Can you get this out?"

Hannah was already up and moving toward me. She made quick work of the IV and covered the small puncture from the needle with a Band-Aid. Next, she gave me shoes and a hat, which I guessed was to cover my attention-grabbing hair. I would've put on a ski mask had she'd given it to me.

"Do you know how to shoot?" Hannah asked as she handed me a gun. A black stocking cap effectively hid her blond hair.

"Yes. My Opa taught me when I was younger. We used to go to the shooting ranges together."

Hannah flashed a small grin and handed me a weapon.

"Good. This is a Glock. It'll be easy to aim and fire, especially since you already know how to handle a gun."

I held it in my hand, getting comfortable with its weight. She moved behind me and repositioned my stance. Then she lined up my arm and showed me how to look through the sight. I was a little shaky, but I had just woken up.

"We're supposed to stay here, but I'm worried about Jack. I'd feel better if I could cover him and the rest of the guys. If you remain in the car and I shoot near it, I'm still guarding you. Are you okay with us going to where they'll be?"

"Yes." I wanted to make them tell me where Max was. Not only that, but I was concerned about Hawk. And if they learned where Max was, I wanted to go with them to be there for him when he was found.

"You'll be safe."

Maybe, but maybe not. I had an agenda. My heart thudded with the weight of the weapon in my hand. I would make it work to my advantage. I figured if I could get close enough, I could jam the end into Rex's body, force him to tell me where Max was, and then shoot. I wanted him gone. That was one nightmare I didn't want to relive.

"Let's go. I promised to guard you, but I gave no guarantees where that would be." Hannah winked then led the way out, and we got in one of the vehicles. As she pulled away, she picked up her cell phone and spoke into it. "We're coming in from the south. Don't shoot us."

"Who was that?" The guys trusted her, so I would as well—she was one of them, after all. Even so, I wanted to know who she'd called. My heart pumped, but I could have sworn it was pushing ice through my veins. I liked it, though. I didn't want to feel.

"Jack." She shot me a quick look. "If I had called Hawk, he would've been adamant that we go back. Not that we would."

"No way. Besides, we need to even the odds for them."

We drove in silence for a while until Hannah turned to me again. "For as long as we can, you'll stay in the car, and I'll shoot from the roof. If the situation changes and we need to jump into battle, you do what you need to do. I'll cover you and shadow you every step of the way. You don't need to worry about watching your back or anyone getting the drop on you."

With what I had planned, all hell would break loose. I only hoped Hawk would be okay.

***

HAWK

WE WERE IN POSITION, AND AS USUAL, I WAS ON THE ROOFTOP. Jack, Keegan, Chris, and Mike were on the pavement below. Even though Mole and Rex had demanded a rematch on our street, we'd moved it a few blocks over. Our old warehouse housed teens in the shelter whom Jack had spearheaded, and there was no way we would put them at risk any more than what they'd already faced in their young lives.

It was quiet except for the wind that howled and moaned as it raced down the roads and through alleyways. Heavy clouds rolled overhead with the threat of rain, but that didn't bother any of us in the least. *Bring it on.* The impending storm matched the ones that raged in our hearts. It was time to close that chapter from our past so it never came back to haunt us in the future.

"I've got fifteen heading our way. Two snipers broke off and are moving into position," I spoke into my mic, warning my team below. They stood, fanned out, and readied for the first wave.

"Old school, my ass," Keegan said, snorting.

"What'd you expect? A verbal fight first then a few punches thrown?" Chris's sarcasm was a deadly spark to Keegan's short fuse. "Of course they're playing dirty."

I waited for it then heard a smack to the back of Chris's head, or maybe a shoulder bump. When no retaliation came, a vicious grin curved my lips. I knew what Chris was doing—he was poking the bear. Keegan was always a live wire, but his barely checked fury and deadly fighting instinct only benefited our team.

"Got 'em in sight." The slightest movement caught my attention. On a roof less than a mile away, a shadow slipped from the doorway. He molded against the wall by the door. Then he inched forward with his body hunched. He was getting into position near the edge. Easy pickings. I aligned my sight, making allowances to the target within the small lines in the scope to account for the slight breeze. My finger squeezed the trigger, and I took the shot.

Across the street from sniper one, I caught movement. Sniper two had moved faster, already in position, rifle at the ready.

I shifted my sight, and in between heartbeats, I shot him through his scope. "Clear," I announced to the guys. In quick succession, I broke down my sniper rifle, packed it up, and headed to the stairwell. I identified no other snipers. Rex had demanded that the fight take place on the street. We wanted that too.

I flew down the stairs, and in record time, I exited the building to the sidewalk. I dropped my rifle by the door, intending to come back for it later. The fight required a 9mm instead. I'd filled every available pocket with clips.

We will finish this today.

Mike had confirmed that we would have a ten-minute delay from the time the confrontation was scheduled to when the police could respond to the reports of gunfire, and Rich had made sure to coordinate the bust on Malone's organization with our street fight.

The police had been apprised of the situation. We wouldn't have to explain or be detained.

"You brought fucking guns!" Rex yelled from a distance away. Thirteen men, including Mole, postured around and behind him.

"Nothing's pointed at you. What are you complaining about?" Jack shouted back.

I couldn't help it—I jumped in too. "You had snipers on the roof to pick us off."

"That's something you'd be familiar with, wouldn't you, Hawk?" Rex screamed, his temper notched up several degrees. "They were there in case."

"Bullshit," Chris sneered.

I echoed his sentiments. Rex and Mole didn't play by any rules, and trying to have a fight like we'd had from the old days was another clear sign that anything would go. We were ready. Our guns were accessible but not drawn. Nothing would stop us.

"We've got you outnumbered. You're missing guys, Jack," Rex taunted.

Rex and his group edged closer with confidence in their strides, given the difference in numbers. We were five against thirteen. Still, I wasn't worried, especially since they hadn't automatically pulled out their weapons and started shooting us. Rex wanted a show. He craved power. It was an illusion.

"You seem to be missing someone. Weren't you supposed to bring Stella? Wasn't that the reason for this meeting?" Jack casually threw out the fact that Rex had lost Red. She was safe in our storage unit with Hannah, and I could breathe easier because of it.

Rex's temper ratcheted up another degree as he picked up his pace, a maniacal sneer painting his face.

"Be ready," Jack said.

"All day, every day." I flexed my right hand. Rex would go for Jack first, and I would take Mole. Keegan would rain hell down on anyone in his path. Chris and Mike were more methodical, reading their opponents and striking where they thought it would bring them down the fastest. Watching them was like witnessing a choreographed fight.

Within arm's distance, the first punch was thrown with a satisfying thwack. I buried my fist in Mole's gut, followed by an uppercut. His eyes were dilated, and he didn't react to the pain.

The fighting around me faded. If an opponent came at me, I reacted. Otherwise, my focus was on Mole.

He pulled a blade. I did too. He swung his knife in a wide arc, and I jumped back. I threw mine, and the tip pierced then lodged in his shoulder. It caused the distraction I wanted. He glanced down at the protruding handle.

My fingers curled around his knife-wielding hand and shoved it. Once his arm was high, I struck his elbow, breaking or dislocating it. His knife clattered to the street.

Mole went to pull the handle of my blade out. I punched him in the nose. His head jerked back, and his arm hung limply at his side.

A body slammed into my side. With a grunt, I absorbed the hit. I lost track of Mole while the new guy and I exchanged punches. Then I heard a gunshot.

Yanking my gun free, I swung the butt of my weapon against the new guy's temple. He dropped, and I reassessed. *Where did that shot come from? Who was hit?*

Mole rushed me. Caught off guard as another guy slammed into my side, my gun fell from my hand. *Shit.* I froze. Mole's gun was pointed at my head. Noise ceased. His mouth opened. I heard nothing. The barrel held my attention. In slow motion, his finger squeezed. I dropped to the street. The bullet shot past my neck, barely missing me, but I could feel the burn from the heat of it.

Lurching forward, I lunged and tackled him. We rolled together, my hand on the one he held the gun with. All of my weight kept him on his back as I slammed his wrist into the street over and over until the gun fell from his grasp.

He cried out, his wrist likely broken. I lurched up to my

knees and straddled him. I put all my power behind my fist. I punched him in the sweet spot along his jaw. He jerked, lifting slightly off the ground then falling back, limp and unconscious.

I grabbed Mole's gun. Mine was missing. With a shove, I pushed off of Mole and jumped back into the fray.

Where is Rex? I wanted a piece of him. Keegan was decimating his way through four guys. Chris and Mike were fighting back to back. *There.* Jack's fists struck Rex in a fast combination.

The flash of steel in my peripheral vision had me reaching for my gun. *Shit.* The gun-wielding guy jerked back, and blood bloomed on one sleeve of his arm then the other. His gun fell to the ground.

I looked around, and panic spiraled through me. *Son of a bitch!* From the roof of one of the Range Rovers, Hannah was picking off the guys who'd pulled weapons. Her black stocking cap hid her platinum hair, and I knew Red was inside the vehicle.

Keegan's four thugs were handled and on the ground. Hannah took out five, who were alive but unable to use their arms. Mike and Chris were stepping away from the two they'd taken on. Mole was still unconscious. That left Jack and Rex. I badly wanted a piece of Rex. But they were engaged.

Another gun went off, and time stood still. Jack and Rex were locked arm-in-arm. The sound had come from them. *Fuck, no!*

Rex shoved, and Jack staggered back. There was blood on both of them. *Who'd been shot?*

Another of Rex's guys punched Jack, deflecting his attention from Rex. I took a step forward, seeing an opening to engage.

A car door opened. It registered in the back of my mind. I couldn't take my eyes off Rex. I shot a look at Jack, worried he'd been hit.

Sirens screamed in the distance. They were getting closer.

Jack twisted as he punched the other guy. The blood didn't seem to spread. Relief struck me hard. The shot hadn't hit Jack. The blood was Rex's. It wasn't a mortal wound.

The guy Jack fought went down. He took a step closer. Rex raised his gun at Jack. Time stood still. Then Rex's body jerked back. *What the hell?* Jack hadn't touched him. Blood bloomed at the top of Rex's shoulder, and his eyes narrowed.

I glanced over my shoulder. *Who had fired a shot? Hannah.* She stood over a man on the sidewalk. *Why is she here?*

My heart stopped. Red stood five feet away, her gun raised. My head whipped back to Rex while I pulled the gun from my waistband. It happened in slow motion.

I heard Red shriek, "No!" It barely registered. *Who'd given her a gun?*

Rex raised his gun and pointed it at Red. I lunged across the bullet's path. My body jerked. I fired. Then I crashed to the ground. My gaze stayed on Rex. His head jolted back, his body rippling from the bullet I put in his forehead. The gun in his hand fell, and his body followed.

A scream pierced the air. Then hands were on me. Turned from my side to my back, I blinked at a hysterical Red. That's when my heart started beating again. I scanned her body. *No blood. She's safe.* My God, I couldn't lose her. I knew without a doubt she was it for me. I would make it work—I would do everything in my power to be the man she needed.

Red's arms settled around me carefully. I pulled her close. Her hand pressed on my side. That's when I felt the burn. I'd been hit. When I looked at her hand, blood oozed between her fingers.

"I'm sorry." She hiccupped. "I saw Rex raise his gun. I thought he was going to shoot you."

"I'm okay. I think it's a scratch."

"I couldn't stay in the car. Hannah was fighting another man. She didn't see you and Jack. Well, she did. She shot him in the shoulder, but I wasn't sure she had. I'm so sorry. It's my fault you were shot."

"Shh. I'm fine. Promise." I needed her out of there. If any one of those guys had hurt her, I would lose my mind. I wasn't mad. I got it. Hannah would've wanted to be there for Jack. It was a clusterfuck of a situation.

All around us, men groaned on the ground. I scanned the scene and kept vigilant. If one of them had been able, they would have drawn a weapon on us.

I caught sight of Hannah. Her hands roamed over Jack. I waited but could tell from his face that he wasn't injured. We all wore bruises. We had all taken some hits.

Hannah helped to disentangle Red, and I stood with help from Chris. Keegan had a knife wound. The wound on my side hurt like hell, a burning path arcing up to my chest, but it didn't appear to be anything fatal—more of a graze.

We would be fine. Something inside me relaxed slightly at the knowledge that none of us had been mortally injured.

"Everyone good?" Jack asked.

Each of us responded that we were.

"No," Red replied. Her hand clasped mine. She stared at Rex's prone body.

"What's wrong?" I held her away, my gaze tracking every inch of her body. There were no signs of a new injury. No bullet holes.

She pointed at Rex. "That's the guy who took my brother. How are we going to find Max?"

Her brother. I cradled her face in my hands and held her gaze with mine. "Mole is alive. We'll get information about Max from him."

We were going to have to talk about her brother.

CHAPTER 32

I paced back and forth on the street where the battle had taken place. Blue and red lights flashed, painting the buildings around us as the crime scene it was. The officers left me alone after they asked me one or two questions. I wasn't hurt, only shaken. The blood on my hands and shirt was Hawk's. My stomach churned as the image of him being shot replayed in my mind.

For the hundredth time, my gaze sought his. He winked when he caught me looking at him, reassuring me once again.

"Hey." Hannah put her hand on my shoulder and a finger under my chin. She forced me to look at her. "Hawk is fine. Mole is being arrested. It's going to be okay. You didn't do anything wrong."

I swallowed the guilt as best as I could. It didn't work, and I spilled my concern to her. "But I was here when he wanted me to stay away. I caused Hawk to be shot."

Hannah snorted. "No. Rex would have shot either Jack or Hawk at that moment even if you weren't there. If I hadn't been fighting with another one of their guys, I would have laid Rex out sooner."

My gut eased a little. I wanted Hawk's arms around me. I

wanted him to be safe. Hannah squeezed me again before she stepped aside. I peered over my shoulder. In long strides, Hawk crossed the distance between us.

He pulled me against him, his arms wrapping around me. I was careful to stay to his right side so I didn't brush against where he was shot. One of his hands pressed against my back and held me tightly, while the other threaded through my hair. When I felt weight on top of my head, I knew he was resting his chin on me, smelling my hair. He'd told me once that touching me and inhaling my scent grounded him.

"Nice loophole, Hannah." He chuckled.

"Like that?" She snickered. "I'm off to pull Jack away. You two, behave."

Hawk shifted. When his arms loosened, I leaned back and looked up at him. "Are you in a lot of pain?"

A sexy grin curved his lips, relaxing his features. "I'm fine, Red. Stop worrying." He glanced back at the police officers. "They're clearing out, and Jack got a call from Rich. We need to head out. They found your brother."

"What?" Panic fought with relief and sent a volley of tremors through my body. "Is he… alive?"

"Shit. Yeah, I'm sorry, I should have started with that." His thumb caressed the side of my face. "Let's head out so you can see for yourself."

The drive to the run-down apartment building didn't take long. The men remaining from the fight were arrested and taken away by the police. An ambulance took the rest. The guys didn't seem worried about anything, so I let go of my anxiety over the confrontation. Hawk was incredibly skilled. I had nothing to worry about.

I shifted from foot to foot in front of the door to the apartment where Max had been found. His back was to me as the paramedics finished checking him over. Hawk's hand rested on my hip, and I was grateful. I needed his support.

The paramedic stepped back, and Max turned toward me.

Relief made my knees buckle. Hawk held me up. The same emotions were reflected in my brother's eyes. I bit my bottom lip. He looked like hell. He was too skinny. Bruises marred his face and arms. There was a nasty cut along his hairline and another on his dry and cracked lips. Deep purple half moons hung beneath his eyes.

Dammit. He did this. After the first wave of relief passed, my temper sparked. I broke away from Hawk's side and stomped over to my brother. I gave him a careful hug, holding in the words that threatened to fly out of my mouth. A few seconds was all I could hope for before I let him have it. "You're okay?"

"Sore and likely dehydrated, but yeah. I am." Max's lips curved into a small smile.

He's smiling? After all the shit he put us through? I trembled, and the words I tried to hold back exploded. "Do you have a single ounce of remorse?"

Max held up his hands, his eyes taking on that wary look he wore whenever I lost my mind on him. "Stel, things got out of control, but everything worked out."

"You think? It wasn't because of you." I flung my hand into Hawk's direction—he'd moved to talk to a few men I hadn't noticed before. I adjusted my arm to point at him. "It was because of him and his friends. They were the ones to handle your colossal mess. Do you have any idea what a nightmare you caused?"

"I do, Stel. I get it. Gambling's a problem for me." He hung his head. "I tried to get my problems under control. They spiraled."

"You should have gone to the police or checked into rehab. Instead, you did what?" I tapped my foot. *What is wrong with him?*

"I know. There were so many temptations. Then… I got involved with this new guy who was being brought on to work with my bookie. They offered me a few lines before I left. Things got even worse after that. That's when I saw the ring."

I shot a glance to Hawk. "Oh shit. That's where he got Jenni's ring. He went to Rex or Mole." Hawk's lips were pressed into a tight line. He'd heard. Good, he needed to know. It was something all the guys had wondered about. I focused back on my brother. "Between drugs and gambling, you have a major problem."

A muffled sob escaped his hands, which covered his face. "Stel—"

"No," I snapped at him. I knew he was going to fall back on old habits and excuses, but that wouldn't work anymore. "You risked your life. You sold me out. Not only that, you'd be dead if it wasn't for Hawk and his team."

"Shit. I know. I know." His shoulders shook with each sob he held back. "This time was different."

"Why? I don't understand what changed or why you gave me up to those men. Do I mean so little to you?"

Max banded his arms around me and squeezed. "No, Stel."

"I don't get it. You have to explain." My voice was muffled against his dirty shirt.

"There were drugs, and they—it was different. I don't ever want to fall into that hole again." His arms loosened, and he fell back against the couch. "I don't deserve it, but please forgive me. I fucked up, and I swear I'll never do that again. It left a lasting impression. I swear."

It wasn't enough. "You need to get help. We can't keep doing this. This time has to be the one that sticks. You have to uphold your promise to me."

With awkward movements, Max got to his feet. The weight of his hands fell onto my shoulders, which felt fitting, as it was how I'd felt since Oma passed away. It had been a huge freaking weight I had to carry around.

"I know." In slow increments, Max pulled me closer. "I'll do it this time. I'll go to rehab."

Tears ran down my face, washing away the last of my

anger. So many times, growing up, he'd comforted me. He'd stood up for me when we were young. He'd taken the fall when I'd screwed up a few times. It had been nothing big, but still…

"You're the only family I have left. I can't lose you."

HAWK

RED AND HER BROTHER WERE DEEP IN CONVERSATION WHILE Jack and I talked with Rich. We needed to wrap up the details. I overheard Max tell Red where he'd gotten Jenni's ring. Jack must have too, because he flinched. It was one thing that I hoped would be off his mind and put to rest. It was over. Rex was dead, and Mole was in jail.

"Is Tridel going to be a problem?" I needed to know. If Red continued to live in the area, I might have to move back to make sure she stayed safe.

"No," Rich answered. "Tridel is in the process of being dismantled with all their properties seized."

I snorted. *That would be interesting.* "Guess the casinos are up for new owners." I couldn't see the government running them.

Rich grinned. "Seems that way."

We must've had the same thought. "You guys did great work. We apprehended Malone and most of the men under him. Several have already talked. With their testimonies and the in-depth data Chris collected, he's going away for a long time. In addition to all that, we have Tridel's books."

"Were you able to find out if Malone had any knowledge of Stella?" I had to ask. If he had been involved, things could get stickier.

"From what we've learned, he did not. Stella was an exclusive target to the northern territory head, Stan Jones, and Rex."

"And Mole." Rex and Mole had always worked together.

Rex being dead didn't mean that Mole would be out of commission. He would want revenge. It wasn't something we could dismiss, not after everything that had happened and the past coming back with a vengeance. I had to find out what would happen to Mole.

Rich pulled something from his pocket. "He'll be going away for a long time." He gave Jack a quick look then focused on me. "Jack told me about Stella trying to pay Max's debt. We took this off of Rex. I thought you would want to give it back to her."

I nodded, feeling grateful. The necklace had already been secured. They hadn't known the full value at the pawnshop. We'd gotten lucky. I had a better plan for the money I would return to her. "Thanks, Rich."

Jack drew Rich's attention. "Sounds like our job's finished."

I hoped so. I needed a few days of relaxation with Red.

Rich clapped Jack and me on the shoulders. "Job well done. We don't need anything more from your team in this case."

We said our goodbyes, and Jack left to find Hannah and the rest of the guys. I would too, after I figured out what was going on with Red and Max.

Her brother was a big problem. While I was glad he was safe and that Red was happy, his addiction wasn't going to disappear because he'd been rescued.

When I reached Red's side, I wrapped my arm around her. My hand curled around her hip, anchoring her to me. Max noticed, which was what I wanted.

Max extended his hand, and I shook it. He at least had the decency to look ashamed, as he damn well should have been.

"Stel was telling me about what you did for her. For us. I wanted to thank you and the rest of your team."

I nodded, accepting his apology.

He took a deep breath. "I won't put my sister in harm's way again. I promised her I'd get help. This time, I'm going to do it." Determination shone in his eyes, even as he swayed back and forth.

The paramedic noticed and approached Max. He needed to go back to the hospital.

"I'm glad to hear it." I had to get the last part in before Max left in the ambulance. "I'll help her find a good place for you to get treatment. You put her in danger. That can't happen again."

Max hung his head, and Red squeezed his arm. The paramedics interjected before anything more could be said. They got Max settled on a stretcher and headed out. There was nothing more for us to do except spend the wad of cash burning a hole in my pocket.

We moved away from the medics and the few policemen that remained. "I meant what I said to Max. I'll help you find the right place for him to get help." Her eyes misted, and before she could hug me, I pulled out the cash and put it into her hand. "Rich was able to recover the money from Rex."

"Oh my gosh! I can't believe it." She clutched the money tightly in her hand. "I could buy back the necklace. Will you go with me?"

"It's not there anymore." I couldn't tell her I had it, not yet. There was another reason I wanted her to accept the money.

She flinched, and I could only imagine she felt as if she'd lost that piece of her history all over again.

I took her free hand and threaded my fingers through hers. "You should use the money to give your design career a shot, full time." I wanted that for her, but that wasn't my only motivation.

Her mouth formed a small o. "I hadn't thought about that, but…" She paused, thinking. "That would be a good idea. I'd love to get going on designing a new line. With Max starting over, I could too."

"Good, it's settled, then." I didn't want to give her too much time to think about it. "Since you won't be waitressing, we could take a vacation." We both needed the break, some downtime. "Bring your supplies because you can work on your jewelry designs anywhere."

The sweet sound of her laugh enveloped me. We could spend some time together alone, without any threat to her safety foremost in our thoughts.

"What did you have in mind?"

So very much. I grinned. I'd already promised her some time back at the cabins. Once she quit her job, I would surprise her with the necklace.

CHAPTER 33

STELLA

ONE MONTH LATER

The sun beat down on my skin. We had been spending some time at the cabin in Kirkwood. Hawk had said he would take me back when we'd first stayed there, and as soon as everything was squared away with my brother and my job, he'd delivered on his promise. I wanted some time off and was taking it. I'd turned in my notice.

I held the last letter from Oma in my hands. Hawk had given me some time alone to read her note, claiming he was hot and needed to get in the water for a few minutes to cool off. That man could read me better than anyone.

My Darling Stella,

The love your grandfather and I had was enough for this lifetime and every one after. The first time I saw him, there was a spark of recognition, and I knew at that moment that he was the one for me. When we'd talked about how we'd first laid eyes on one another, he'd discovered we both felt the same way.

After going through what we had before and during our defection from Germany, I hadn't dared to hope I would experience a love like my parents or what my brother had for that brief period before his fiancée was sent to the gas chamber for being Jewish. And then my brother was gone shortly after, and it tainted my expectations for my life.

Coming to the States, we were given another chance for happiness. I'm sharing this with you so you won't take anything for granted. The day you meet the man you're destined to spend a lifetime with, grab hold and live. Appreciate the little things. Weather the storms together and bolster one another when needed. Do not try to change each other, but cherish one another for the individualities that are uniquely your own. Life is messy. Find the good and be happy.

All my love,

Oma

"I found him, Oma," I whispered, and I knew she heard me. I felt her with me as I read her words.

I wiped at a few tears then tucked the last letter back into the envelope. There was no doubt she watched over me from wherever she was. There were so many times I could sense her comforting presence. The sensation faded, and I slipped the paper into my bag so nothing would happen to it.

I plopped sunglasses on my face and flipped over on the lounge chair. With one hand, I reached behind me and leaned forward to readjust the chair's angle. It was a much better way to enjoy the view.

Hawk rose out of the water, and I sucked in my breath. I would never tire of looking at him. Sun-kissed brown skin rippled with muscle as he moved. I was glad no one else was there to share my view. My former-hot-neighbor-turned-hot-boyfriend would have drawn way too much female attention. Drops of water rolled down his chest, sparkling in the sunlight. *Huh. I think I'm jealous of those beads of water.*

My gut tightened at the sight of the bandage at his waist that covered the bullet wound. He'd jumped in front of me, saving me again from Rex. The transparent adhesive over the dressing was waterproof. He was healing well. Still, guilt hit me every time I looked at it.

After Max had been recovered from the apartment complex Mole had stayed in—yep, really original hiding place —we'd tied up loose ends. We got my brother settled into rehab for his gambling addiction then hightailed it back to the cabin. Hawk needed to decompress from the in-your-face encounters from his past. I didn't blame him. I wanted a little time away, myself.

My phone chimed, and I ignored it. The view before me demanded all my attention. A knowing grin spread across Hawk's face, and his smoky-blue eyes sparkled. Yeah, I was staring, but there was no secret there.

I was pretty sure the ringing that I'd heard was from a Skype call. I'd been talking to Liv, Mari, and Hannah more and more. I liked them a lot, and Liv was a sculptor. She was interested in the jewelry I made, saying it reminded her of David Yurman's style but with my unique touches. Another line hinted toward Steven Lagos in the whimsical way the pieces flowed. It had meant the world to me, and she'd convinced me to start working on designing my line again. What I wanted to do was a vintage design, reflective of my family heirlooms.

I worried my lower lip with my teeth. The time alone worked wonders. Hawk was relaxed and happy, and the darkness that shadowed his eyes eased the more we talked and the more he put those memories to bed.

Hawk needed all the love his entire family showered on him, given everything he'd endured as a child. Someday, I hoped things would be easier. For Keegan too. He was another puzzle that Liv, Mari, and I discussed.

They'd told me that Trev—he was one of the guys I hadn't met—was heading to Maine soon. Mari had rolled her eyes when she told me that there'd been some drama about what the guys had referred to as a "babysitting mission" Trev had been on. Apparently, it had turned into something they'd never seen coming.

Hawk had dropped hints about my going to Maine to vacation. I hoped that would happen. I was curious about meeting the rest of his group. But most of all, I wanted to be with him.

The chime sounded again.

"Aren't you going to answer that?"

"Huh?" Seriously, my brain was scrambled.

Hawk dropped onto the lounger beside me and handed me the phone. I answered it immediately, recognizing who was calling.

Liv and Hannah's faces filled the screen when I hit Accept.

"It's about time," Hannah said.

"We found something. That's why Hannah is impatient," Liv explained.

Hawk moved behind me to see the screen. Not even a second later, he straddled the lounge chair I was sitting on and tugged me back. I rested against his chest then readjusted my hold on the phone so we were both in the frame.

"Hi, Hawk." Liv smiled. "I'm glad you're both here. As Hannah said, Stella, we found an inconsistency with the jewelry box you recovered from behind your grandfather's ashes."

My Opa and Oma had larger niches than my parents in the columbarium, including the members of their family they'd lost to the war in Germany. Even though their relatives' ashes weren't there, their names were. It tethered them all together.

"The mirror wasn't an antique, which wasn't consistent with the rest of the box." Liv held up the box so we could see. "If you are okay with it, we'd like to remove the unoriginal glass and see if there is anything behind it."

"Of course!" The line in one of Oma's letters popped into my mind: *Not everything is visible from the surface.*

"Just let me," Hannah mumbled as she repositioned the laptop screen to capture what they were doing with my Oma's mother's antique jewelry chest.

Hawk's arms curled around my waist, and he rested his clasped hands against my stomach. Despite the excitement pinging around with the possible discovery, I didn't want to move from that position. I felt safe and protected. He was what I wanted, and I hoped we could talk more about what the coming days would hold. We had only planned to stay at the cabin one additional day.

I want a lifetime with him.

We watched as Hannah and Liv worked the piece of glass that was fitted into the inside lid free. It took several minutes, as they were taking great pains not to damage anything.

"Got it," Liv said as she and Hannah used tools to lift it from the antique box. "Oh…" Liv held still while Hannah flashed the camera a grin. Then Liv grabbed a Kleenex and removed something from the inside lid. "I think this is a Leon Wyczlkowski painting." With great care, she lifted out the small painting so we could view it.

I pulled the phone closer to see better. The picture was of a beautiful woman.

"There's another one," Hannah said, her voice floating from behind the picture. Liv moved the one she'd held from the screen while Hannah replaced our view with a gorgeous painting of a garden. "Renoir."

My mouth fell open. My Oma had told us they'd been an aristocratic family, but I had no idea, though I should have after looking through the jewels. My heart hurt at the thought of all they must have left behind. Those two pictures were small enough to conceal. The jewelry had been hidden within my Oma's dolls to smuggle them out. *How else would they have gotten them past the guards at the train station and then the border police? And finally, through the States?*

Even with the loss of the fine art from the world, nothing compared to the tragic and heart-wrenching loss of life that had occurred.

We ended the call with Liv promising to get the paintings valued, and then we would have them insured. There had also been documents of sale tucked behind them as well. There would be no question as to who the art belonged to. In the back of my mind, an idea for designing a jewelry line reminiscent of my family heirlooms percolated.

"What do you want to do with the artwork?"

His voice pulled me from my thoughts, and a smile curved my mouth.

I knew what Hawk was asking. While my brother was in rehab and was only barely allowed contact by phone with family and no one else, he had a long way to go. If I stayed in California to live and work and he relapsed, there was every possibility that he would sell one or both of the priceless pieces of art, not to mention the jewelry. I couldn't allow that. "I want to loan them out to museums after they're insured. People should be able to see them rather than hiding them away wherever I end up living."

"You're thinking of moving?"

"Possibly. I think I need a fresh start." What I hoped was that it would be with him, but what we'd discussed wouldn't be a permanent move, at least I didn't think so.

"I'd like to continue to see you, the right way this time."

I leaned farther to the side so I could see the grin that curved his handsome face. "I'd like that, but I don't even know where you live. Not really."

He chuckled. "We didn't have a lot of time to talk about those things while we were chasing down Tridel, Rex, and your brother."

"No. But maybe we should. Rex is dead, and Tridel and all the people involved are facing trial." Mole was already in jail for the unforeseeable future. The evidence continued to mount. The start had come from the evidence Chris had compiled and the information their connections in government had gotten from the territory heads as they sold one another out. They would be going away for a very long time. The future finally looked bright again.

Hawk had insisted on helping me find the right place for

Max to get help. He and his teammates—brothers, really—Jack, Mike, and Keegan had a lot of experience with that. There was a story there about their childhood that I didn't know the details of yet.

Hawk and I were enjoying the first few days of relaxation and peace we'd had since our initial meeting in the apartment building we shared. When he cleared his throat, I stopped thinking of all that'd happened and refocused on the present.

He bent down and retrieved something from one of the totes we'd brought out by the lake. I turned my head to see what he was doing.

"No peeking." He grinned and waited until I shifted to look at the lake. My back rested against his chest once more.

He shifted my hair to a shoulder, and that's when I felt it. Heaviness settled around my neck. My fingers fluttered to the jewelry he'd put on me. The touch of it was familiar. When I looked down, tears leapt to my eyes. He'd given me back my Oma's necklace, the one I'd sold to save Max. The sun caught the green emerald and shot dazzling stars of light from it. "How?"

"I wasn't going to let you give that up."

"The money." I had to give it back to him. "Wait." I narrowed my eyes. "You've had this for a month?"

Hawk laughed. "I wanted to make sure you had a chance at your dream. If I gave this to you the same night you got the money back, you would have tried to force me to take the cash. Then you wouldn't have quit waitressing. I wanted you to give your career a shot, Red. Please consider the cash an invest-ment. A selfish one." He winked. "Besides, you helped to put a part of my past to rest."

I smiled. I knew what he was referencing. All the talks we'd had continued to help him realize that he wasn't unlovable. I would continue to despise his parents, but they'd done one thing right—the only thing. They'd given me Hawk.

"I'd like to take you out on dates, Red, so we can get to know each other more."

My heart warmed at the thought. I would have liked nothing better. "How are we going to do that? I mean, where do you live? You mentioned the apartment in California was temporary and just for business you had."

He nodded. "It is. I live in Maine, along with most of the guys you've already met. There are a few others. Since you quit working at the restaurant, would you consider staying there for a month or two, and we can see where this leads?"

"Stay with you?" *Sign me up!*

"Yes, On the same property, but you could stay in the house that Liv built when she and Liam were figuring things out. I was living there, but I could move into Liv and Liam's house. They're close." He shifted and cupped the side of my face. "You could take the time to work on your jewelry line too."

"You had me at dating." I grinned. His eyes flashed with desire, and he closed the distance between us. The first brush from his lips against mine sent a spike of need through my body. He coaxed me to open for him, and I did.

Hawk broke away from delivering a toe-curling kiss to press his forehead to mine. "It's settled then. We'll leave tomorrow."

"Yes." I couldn't wait for what the future held for us.

If you enjoyed reading VANTAGE POINT as much as I did writing it, I hope you'll consider leaving a review.

For a **FREE** novella that sets the stage for the Gray Ghost series, subscribe to Amy's newsletter.

http://eepurl.com/dEjmUD

ACKNOWLEDGMENTS

Writing a book is a pretty fantastic journey and I'm so grateful to all those who supported me on this journey.

With heartfelt thanks to my amazing critique partners and fellow authors, Emily Albright, Kristin Kisska, and Victoria Van Tiem for providing insight, candor, and camaraderie from the first draft to final edit.

A special thanks to Taylor Anhalt for helping to make this novel shine with her grammar skills, editing, and willingness to jump in despite her hectic schedule.

To Kate B. and Kristina B., two wonderful editors at Red Adept Editing, who did a fantastic job and made this story so much better. To T.E. Black for chatting at all hours and creating so many wonderful things for me, from Facebook banners, to formatting, and of course, this gorgeous cover.

To Maryellen Newton and Maria Vickers, amazing beta readers who provided incredible feedback. Maryellen, I'm so grateful for your unwavering friendship and our weekly Panera coffee chats.

Thank you Michael Pagan for letting me bounce ideas with you. Your insight and patience made this story that much richer.

Big thanks to Itsy Bitsy Book Bits Promotions for going above and beyond. To all the readers, bloggers, and reviewers who went out of their way to help and support this release—you're all so very generous and kind. Your support and encouragement continues to inspire me.

And last, but in no way least, to my husband, two daughters, and two sons, for supporting and believing in me while I follow my dreams. For their patience and understanding when the house is messy and general chaos reigns. I can't imagine life without them.

ABOUT THE AUTHOR

Amy McKinley is the romantic suspense thriller author of the Gray Ghost Novels and the Five Fates paranormal romance series. Her edges of your seat books are filled with surprising twists and just the right amount of heat and danger. She lives in Illinois with her husband, two daughters, two sons, and three mischievous cats.

You can find her at www.amymckinley.com

Subscribe to Amy's newsletter for cover reveals, book announcements, and giveaways:
http://eepurl.com/dEBqJn

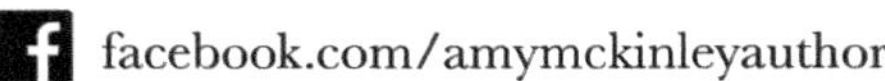 facebook.com/amymckinleyauthor

instagram.com/amymckinleyauthor

twitter.com/AmyMcKinley7

 pinterest.com/amymckinley7

Gray Ghost Novels

Moments That Define Us

Broken Circle

Eye of the Storm

Beneath the Surface

Vantage Point

The Five Fates Series

Hidden

Taken

www.ingramcontent.com/pod-product-compliance
Lightning Source LLC
Chambersburg PA
CBHW070440120726
47910CB00003B/863